MAN UP

ALEX CAY

ALISTERN PRESS
DALLAS

Library of Congress Cataloging-in-Publication Data has been applied for.
ISBN: 978-1-940221-05-2

For my Vx.
It warmed me to see you laugh along.

CHAPTER ONE

Grand Bahamas Island

WITH NINETY-EIGHT NOTCHES IN HIS BELT, Benny Lang needed just two more kills to reach Century Club status. After tomorrow morning, that number would drop to one.

Uno. Einer. Odin.

Hard to believe, after a mere three years on the job. That was an average of what, thirty-three and a third per year? Though you couldn't kill one-third of a person, really. It was all the way or the highway in this business.

In any case, Benny would soon be hanging with the big boys.

He'd heard stories of the Century Club welcoming party in Vegas. Escorts to order, poolside cabanas, and bottomless buffets. All paid for and provided by the employer. Quite a milestone and a lot of notches for one belt, sure, but built like a pregnant shrew as his mother used to say, Benny had plenty of room for them. Hell, he could fit a thousand on his belt. Then it'd be Millennium Club.

That party took place in Bangkok.

With the image of a Lady Gaga look-alike giving him a lap dance in his mind, Benny entered the Grand Lucayan Resort and Casino. He was squeezing between two potted palms at the edge of the blackjack pit when his phone buzzed. Benny had to wiggle back between the palms to escape the pinging slot machines and answer. The caller ID showed it to be Relay, the employer's operator.

"What is it?"

"The customer has requested a change," Relay said.

"First. Which customer?" Benny exited the casino through the tinted glass doors. The boardwalk was crowded with overflow from the marketplace, and the sun had begun to set.

"The senior one."

Benny stopped. "Not a cancellation, is it?"

Lowering his head, Benny shielded himself from a gaggle of co-eds entering the casino. Wearing tube dresses so tight that they looked like multi-colored sausage links, they stumbled along while surrounding the one in white. She wore a makeshift veil decorated with something he couldn't identify. Then, as they came closer, he determined the decorations were condoms, unwrapped and dangling, stapled to the lace.

Americans.

And just as Benny had resigned to a delay in his VIP status, Relay said, "Quite the opposite. He'd like to make it a double."

Smoothing his mustache, Benny said, "Double the fee, as well?"

One of the girls giggled then hurried past. He got that all the time, nobody expected the fat chink to have a British accent. Well, Benny'd been giving the world surprises for almost forty years now and he had plenty more to dole out. Starting with the task at hand.

"Triple, actually," Relay said.

"In that case, we have a deal." Benny hung up.

Taking a quick look around, he wiped the phone clean with a shirttail and dropped it in a pink and green trash bin as he re-entered the casino. Beaming now, he threaded back into the blackjack pit, walked past the five and ten dollar minimums, then sat on the first stool at an otherwise empty twenty-dollar table.

Why not? Lady luck was shining on Benny today.

And after a simple layover in Florida to notch out some goalie and a lawyer, Benny believed he would head straight to Las Vegas.

Patrick Finn deplaned into the musty West Palm Beach terminal and, no bags checked, headed straight outside. A thick, wet gust of wind hit his face like an alligator fart, and he wished he hadn't worn the suit. But he had to admit, a man of his size looked better in business attire.

Plus, the suits were left over from his prior career as a *fugitive recovery agent*—a bounty hunter focusing on high-priced, well-hidden tickets—and so he might as well use them. But this new sports agent gig was play-school compared to that circus, and the pay was about ten times better.

Finn rolled his shoulders—nice and loose—and boarded the bus to Hertz board, where he located his name and found a white Toyota Camry in his spot. Good enough. Finn would only be in Florida for a few hours, anyway. He crammed into the driver's seat and winced as he pulled over the row of iron-spiked shark teeth spanning the exit lane.

Couldn't these people devise a better way to protect their cars than self-sabotage?

An arm extended from the tinted glass exit booth, and Finn handed over the rental contract, making a bet with himself. *Female.*

When the arm reappeared, a baritone voice told him to have a nice vacation. Damn. Looked like he owed himself a beer.

Following the signs to the 1, Finn cranked the AC and checked the address on his mobile phone. Lew Kunkle, the rookie and rising star of the Texas Hammerheads, the latest expansion NHL hockey team, had decided to live at 17 Opal Bay Cove during the summer. It took Finn three conversations with Kunkle to get the kid to admit that he lived in a marina.

And yes he'd bought a boat. At least that's what he called it at the time. Said he'd rather drop anchor in West Palm for a couple of weeks and maybe head to Baja for the season. *Screw that mortgage market.*

Perhaps Finn should bring a map to Lew, show him where Baja was in relation to Florida. And had anyone informed the optimistic Canadian that they'd just kicked off hurricane season?

Goalies.

In thirty-five years of sports experience—including playing, coaching, and now agenting—Finn had never met a stranger group of human beings than the string of puck-targets in his past.

Take Lew for example. Before his first NHL game, the kid taped what he had called a *lucky paperclip* to the outside of his protective jock, claiming it radiated a safe zone in that area. Apparently it worked, as Lew avoided injury all year and then made one hell of a save to retain a shutout in his last game of the season, preserving his top spot of the league in goals against average. Too bad for the team that they had an anemic offense, one that scored fewer goals than any team had in the last three decades, ending their season anyway. On top of that, the paperclip had been knocked loose by the save and fallen to the ice, causing Lew's other skate to jerk from under him and pulling his groin.

Finn just hoped Lew was nursing the injury. Next season would mean big money for the youngster.

After crossing the Intracoastal Waterway then winding up Route 1A and through some backstreets, Finn found the Opal Bay Marina. There were only two other cars in the parking lot, one of them a glittering purple Corvette with a paper license plate.

Guess whose?

Finn parked at the edge of the pristine gangway of piers and stared up at a fat brownish pelican that sat facing away, atop the Opal Bay sign. As if offended by the opulence of the marina, he painted the sign with a thick layer of white turd.

Scanning the yachts in each slip, it would be difficult to miss which one belonged to Lew.

Because at the far end, a tall, sleek number with mirrored windows had baby blue and silver stripes denoting the Hammerheads team color and a large red maple leaf on the back, signifying its Canadian owner.

Sealing the deal, Lew had dubbed his new residence *Five Hole*.

Finn turned off the car, grabbed a folder from his bag and opened the door to an even wetter and now salty heat. Buttoning his jacket, he made his way along the dock. A few signatures and a short review of his recent *discussions* with management about the performance triggers in Lew's contract and Finn would be on his way.

As he neared the yacht, Finn tried to make out the music vibrating from the hull.

A little early in the morning for Donna Summer, don't you think, Lew? Finn took hold of the dark mahogany and metal stairs leading to the deck.

"Hey!" An older man exited a small office building at the corner of the docks. Dressed in khakis and a bright pink polo shirt, he jogged toward Finn while waving a clipboard high over his head. "Wait!"

Finn stopped at the top of the stairs and checked his appearance. Maybe the suit he'd chosen was too dark for the summer, made him look like a mobster. Holding up the folder, Finn said, "I have a meeting with Mr. Kunkle."

"Well you can't just—" The man interrupted himself and put an ear toward the yacht while making a face. He seemed to have lost all recollection of starting that sentence, as he scribbled something on the third page of the clipboard.

"You were saying?"

"You're not on the manifest." He tapped the clipboard. "Say, what kind of accent is that anyway?"

Finn shrugged. "Boston?"

"I thought I heard a touch of brogue in there. And your hair has some homeland berry in it." The man smiled. "But, you can't just come barging in here, Irish or not."

Homeland berry?

"Well, it is official business." Finn raised his eyebrows. "Did I mention that?"

"Not unless it's on this manifest, it isn't."

"I need an appointment?"

"Of course you do, this is private property. Says right there." The man pointed to the sign. Taking the cue, the pelican flapped its huge wings and floated up and away.

"And who are you?"

"I'm Walter, Opal Bay security. I keep order around here."

Finn looked around. A couple had pulled into the parking lot, but the place was otherwise deserted.

Adjusting his tie and fanning himself with the folder, Finn said, "So, let's make an appointment now."

"Well, you can't. Your friend...uh..." he peeked at the manifest, flipped a few pages.

"Mr. Kunkle."

"Right! Mr. Lewmond Kunkle." Pressing his finger to the page, he continued, "He has to make the appointment...er, add you to the manifest. For the day. We only give out day passes here."

Poor Walter was working himself right into a coronary over a checkmark. "So, let's get Mr. Kunkle and he can tell you he's expecting me."

"Oh no. We don't disturb the residents. We respect their—"

But before Walter could finish his sentence, a door popped open from the yacht's wheelhouse and a girl ran squealing across the deck. Naked from the waist up, she held her chest as she ran, half-laughing, half-squealing, "I don't want to be the filling!" Another girl came out running behind her, and they circled the deck, the first girl squealed again, "I don't even like Oreos!" They both re-entered the cabin with a slam.

"Maybe I will call first," Finn said.

"Yes, yes," Walter said, backing away as if he'd just seen an apparition. "I think that would be best." Scribbling something on the clipboard as he walked, Walter disappeared into his office.

Finn descended the stairs and headed back to the car.

So much for nursing that groin.

"Don't be an idiot," Vanessa Holmes said, snatching the camera from her partner, then tossing it to the floorboard of the vehicle. "We don't need stills."

"I'm zooming to have a better look," James Chadwick said, his face long and drawn, like an underfed camel. "What's the harm?"

"The harm, is that this Mr. Finn sees you taking his photo, raising his suspicions."

"I doubt he has any suspicions," Chadwick said as he fumbled with a map tucked under his leg. He liked to be called Sir James ever since the Queen was stupid enough to knight him for rescuing Prince Harry from some garish Welsh nightclub and then having the uncharacteristic wit to keep quiet about it.

Vanessa enjoyed the tease. "Really, JJ, I've no idea how you were hired into the service of her majesty in the first place."

Chadwick stared at her with an almost fierceness. Almost. "Don't call me that."

"Right, Chaddy."

"Not that either!" He swatted the steering wheel and sulked out the other window, muttering, "You're not exactly speaking the Queen's English yourself."

"Shush, he's coming." Vanessa shifted in her seat to face Chadwick. "Quick, open the map."

"Oh damn." Chadwick fumbled with the folds as he said, "This is ridiculous."

"What's ridiculous is that you have it upside down." Vanessa glanced at Finn. Good thing he was paying no attention to them.

"What's he doing?" Chadwick asked as he flipped the map over.

"He's taking out his willy, going to have tinkle."

"What?!" Chadwick crumpled the map down and peered past Vanessa.

"You're so gullible."

"Oh do grow up."

Vanessa pulled at her lip. "Where the hell is he going?"

"I'd say our number two is not at home."

"I'd call you Sherlock..." she pointed at the Corvette. "Except his car is here, remember?"

Chadwick had nothing to say to that.

Vanessa sighed. "We'll have to follow."

"I think we should stay put. Wait until he comes back."

"And then," she flicked the map with a finger and continued, "he'll see we've been sitting here all along. Talk about suspicious...."

Finn appeared to be laughing as he approached his car, still holding the folder he'd walked up with earlier. He hadn't even entered the boat, so he'd no doubt been asked to come back later.

"Here's your better look, get a good one."

"He's gigantic." Chadwick folded the map. "You think the goalie will be any easier?"

"Kunkle's half that size, even shorter than me," Vanessa said, then made a show of shining her nails on her shirt. "Tell you what, if you think you can't handle it, I'll kill them both myself. But then I get all the money."

"Oh do please shut up," Chadwick said as he put the car into gear and followed.

CHAPTER TWO

AFTER DRIVING THE 1 FOR A STRETCH, admiring the ridiculous homes along the water, Finn decided to grab a quick bite. He stopped at the first two joints he came across, but both turned out to be gourmet pastry shops with coffee priced at seven dollars or more. Sure, after this season and Lew's astonishing success, Finn could afford it. He got four percent of the take, including all salary, signing bonuses, performance bonuses, and endorsements. With his growing list of athletes and a few major performers, it was working out to be quite a nut this year.

But the thought of paying seven dollars for a cup of coffee made him want to stab his own eyeball with his new Mont Blanc pen.

So, Finn drove into a strip-center housing a small restaurant called Egg On Your Leg and scanned the front windows. With booths and plenty of customers, the place looked perfect. Reaching into his duffel, Finn grabbed his paperback, Crais's latest *Elvis Cole* novel—he loved mysteries and thrillers, anything with crime—and almost dropped it when he turned back around.

A wheat-thin man with skin so tanned it looked like bark was jumping rope right outside his window. With a shock of sweaty blonde-gray hair, he wore bright white high-tops, tiny gray workout shorts and no shirt. Smiling as he jumped and nodding his head, he also wore a look of delusion.

Finn eased the door open, saying excuse me before realizing the jumper also wore headphones.

The man stopped jumping and thrust his hand high in the air indicating the number one. Then he turned and walked away.

Finn locked the car and, glancing back at the jumper as he walked, entered the diner.

The smell of fried eggs and bacon hit him a fraction before the hostess's voice. "Welcometoeggonyourleg, one?" She'd already grabbed a menu and was walking away before Finn had answered.

Following her to a booth by the window, he tossed the book on the table, took off his jacket and laid it on the seat. Then he dodged a waitress carrying a full tray of dirty plates and sat on the other side.

The hostess was gone before he could thank her.

He picked up the menu and hadn't opened it before a tall red-faced waitress appeared at the edge of his table. Her rust brown outfit featured a large patch of an egg cracking over a woman's thigh. She held up a round carafe and a porcelain cup. "Coffee?"

"Sure, I'd—"

"Cream? Sugar? It's right there if you need it, hon." She pointed to the basket of condiments next to the window. "Know what you want yet?"

Finn paused, looked up at her, and said, "I'm going to need a minute."

She smiled. "Take your time, I'm Frankie when you're ready." Walking away she added, "Guy your size might like the *Toe Pointer*, though."

Right.

Like any self-respecting American establishment of the twenty-first century, the menu listed options like mini buffets, and with names like *Thigh High*, *Knees Wide* and *Ankles Up*, no meal contained fewer than six items. Finn's kind of place. And the *Toe Pointer*? It had three eggs, four slices of black forest bacon, a slice of ham, corned beef hash, potato hash browns, white or wheat toast… wheat, *seriously?*…and two buttermilk pancakes all pan fried to perfection in an oversized iron skillet.

Whoa.

Better only get one of those.

Hovering over him as he closed the menu, Frankie smiled. "Decided, hon'?"

Finn ordered the *Toe Pointer* with his eggs poached, and she gave him a look like she'd never heard of that before. Then she shrugged and walked away.

Leaning back, Finn opened his book and didn't read a single sentence before catching the activity outside the window from the corner of his eye. The jumper had returned and was hopping and nodding and smiling as he went from single foot jumps to walking to even running in circles, outside Finn's window.

"Here you go, hon." Frankie clanked his plate on the table and grabbed the back of her neck. "Need more syrup?"

Finn glanced at the dispenser by his elbow. It was so full that syrup was oozing from the top. "More?"

"That bacon goes best with syrup. May need more than that." She nodded at the dispenser.

"I'm fine, thanks," Finn said, freeing the fork and knife from its napkin cocoon.

"Suit yourself." She pointed at his coffee. "How about a warm-up?"

"Sure, but—" She began to walk away and he said, "Frankie?"

"Yeah, hon'?"

Finn pointed to the window. "Does he ever stop that?"

"Never. Here every day of the year, even Christmas." She frowned. "He's like one of them super balls, you know?" Frankie got a faraway look in her eyes and after a few seconds said, "Whew..." then walked away.

Digging into the eggs, Finn forked one onto a slice of toast and pinched it into his mouth. Perfect. Then as he was reaching for his coffee, Finn noticed a couple talking with British accents enter the diner. Nothing else remarkable about them, except the woman was much too pretty to be with the saggy-faced man. Well, that and the fact that Finn had just seen them in the parking lot of the Opal Bay Yacht Residence.

Shit.

It looked like breakfast was over.

"I told you we shouldn't come inside," Chadwick said, moving the white wrapping of cheap silverware and leaning close to Vanessa. "Look, he's leaving."

"Shush. He's no idea who we are. He never noticed us in the lot." Vanessa tried to keep cool, knowing damn well they had spooked Finn. But she wasn't about to let this clod call her out on it. "We'll have to get it over with then."

"What, you want me to pop him right here?" Chadwick reached into his jacket.

"For God's sake, no."

Chadwick patted the jacket then picked up a menu. "Don't tell me to shush."

Hiding behind her own menu, Vanessa hadn't noticed the lanky girl with a red face at her side until she spoke, "Coffee, hon'?"

"I'm not sure we'll be staying, thank you."

"Well you'll have to order something if you want to stay," the waitress said.

Chadwick leaned back. "I'm famished."

Vanessa shot him a look that said, *try me.*

"Just some eggs, Mum." He looked up at the waitress. "Won't take long, will it?"

"Nope, we're fast here at Eggonyourleg." She smiled at Vanessa.

"Fine. Order your eggs and shove them...I mean enjoy them. Please." She closed her menu.

"Right, then. I'll have the *Toe Pointer.*"

"Good God. That dish has every animal of the farm on it," Vanessa's voice cracked with disgust as the waitress hurried off.

"I told you. I'm hungry." He started fiddling with the camera.

"You're trying to prove that you can eat as much as that Finn."

"Am not."

"Are."

"Not."

She whispered, "Are," then said, "and what the hell did you bring that in here for?" pointing at the camera.

"I thought it would make us look like tourists, see?" He tightened the strap around his wrist. "Cheese," he said, snapping a photo with a flash.

Vanessa put her hand up. "You bloody fool. Erase that."

"Relax, would you? I'm only having a bit of fun." He gave her an idiotic smile.

Before she could react, the waitress returned with Chadwick's mountain of food. All piled up with the eggs split open, yolks bleeding on the rest of it, the plate looked a wreck. Holding his knife and fork wide, he said, "Fancy a taste?"

"Ugh." She turned away and watched the crazy man jumping rope outside.

The man hadn't stopped since they sat down. Must have been seven minutes straight.

Chadwick wolfed down the food like a peasant, good thing, and they left mere minutes after Finn. This would be fine. They would want him to be inside the yacht and settled before returning themselves anyway. Then they would have the two men cornered, and they could act swiftly. The problem would be daylight. She'd rather work in the safety of darkness. That said, the client had instructed them that this would be the only time the two targets would be together for the foreseeable future. And even though they would have to knock off both of them, it would still be a single job—easier than two separates in her opinion.

But as they were pulling up to the yacht club, maybe ten

minutes after Finn must have—his car was there—Chadwick announced the depth of his stupidity, "I forgot the camera."

Vanessa closed her eyes, controlling the urge to lash out. "In the restaurant?"

"No worries, we can get another."

"My face is on there," Vanessa said, holding a hand half across hers. "Like this. Any recollection?"

Chadwick stared blankly, then said, "Oh, rubles."

"What does that mean, "Rubles?"

He shrugged, "My Pappy used to say to it. I suppose he didn't like Russian money?"

Vanessa slunk deep in her seat and willed herself not to strike the man.

"Go back."

Benny Lang checked the map again. Having marked the exact location of the Opal Bay Marina, he was confident he had just a few miles to go. But now he had to piss like a drunk.

Shouldn't have had that second Snapple.

He had figured it would take an hour and a half to drive to Palm Beach from Miami International, but with the construction it had taken well over two. This placed him in danger of stopping somewhere too close and being seen someplace near the marina.

Not a wise play in this business.

And besides…he checked his watch…Finn had been due to arrive over an hour ago. He could be gone by the time Benny arrived.

He hated to do this, but he didn't have a choice.

Unbuckling his seat belt—don't try this at home, kiddies— Benny secured the steering wheel with a thigh and leaned over as he reached for the empty bottle on the passenger floorboard. His fingertips rolled the bottle forward and the car swerved into the next lane.

A Mercedes SUV honked and the woman driving gave him a dirty look. She had two kids in the car and appeared to be of the soccer mom type, sweet enough.

Benny held up a hand in apology.

The woman gave him the middle finger and as she sped off, two children—one of them in a tall booster—did the same.

Lovely, this America.

Shaking his head, Benny hit the accelerator, causing the bottle to roll back to him, and he grabbed it between two fingers. Now the hard part. Benny sat up and looked back and forth, then checked his mirrors. Nobody within a good twenty feet, he moved ahead with his plan.

He uncapped the bottle.

Then he unzipped his fly.

He shifted in his seat as he wiggled his worm out.

Steadying his arm on the wheel, he stuck it in the bottle. Or at least he thought he had.

Because the next thing he did was piss all over himself.

CHAPTER THREE

PARKED AND WAITING TO SEE IF THE couple from the restaurant showed back up at Opal Bay, Finn pulled out his cell phone. He hesitated for a second then scrolled through the phone's directory and found Colleen Coffey's number, his ex-girlfriend.

Colleen didn't answer, so he left a five-word voicemail, "It's Finn, call them off," and hung up.

Finn approached the yacht, where Lew was speaking to Walter at the top of the gangplank stairs. Walter glanced back at Finn then nodded as he passed, still holding his trusty clipboard.

"Dude!" Lew greeted Finn wearing a pink leopard-print bath towel. He held his fist forward for a bump. "Nice tie."

Finn closed his eyes for a moment, switched the folder to his other hand, then softly bumped Lew's fist with his own.

"Lucky you caught me man, I was heading out for a swim, see?" He dropped the towel, and Finn thrust a hand in front of his eyes.

"Lew, please!"

"What?"

Made of spandex and cut like a euro-bikini, Lew's swimsuit couldn't hold a taco. And though Lew looked pretty fit, his entire body was covered with a thin layer of inky black hair, like a chinchilla.

Shaking his head, Finn turned his eyes from the horror. "Wait."

He leaned back and pointed the folder toward the water. "Not in there."

"Sure, why not?" Lew followed his gaze while replacing the towel.

"Boats, jet skis, yachts...not to mention sharks?" Finn looked over the edge. "Besides, It doesn't exactly look clean."

"Well, I never said I was gonna' drink it." Lew turned around. "C'mon, I'll show you the new digs."

Finn followed Lew up onto the deck and inside the wheelhouse. A few white leather seats and a long white leather couch faced the steering station, and the walls consisted of floor to ceiling tinted windows—mirrored on the outside.

"Not much here, I'll show you the playroom."

Finn raised his brows wondering how much this little extravagance had cost, just as Lew said, "I got it dirt cheap."

"Describe dirt."

"Brother in law knows a guy who knows a guy. Grabbed it out of auction, up in Quebec."

Finn stopped. "What kind of auction, Lew?"

Reaching the bottom of the stairs, Lew shrugged. "Didn't ask."

Excellent. Finn kept quiet about that and said, "Bottom line?"

"One point three. Not bad, eh? It was appraised for over two."

"One point three million dollars?" Oh Lew.

Finn continued down the stairs and stopped at the bottom. With dark mahogany and white leather couches lining the edges of the huge space, a glossy black baby grand piano, and a Volkswagen-sized chandelier reflecting in every mirror on the walls, the *playroom* was more like a Vegas ultra-lounge. Except for the empty Cheetos bags and beer cans littering the floor.

"Snazzy, Lew."

"A steal, eh?"

"I don't know about a steal, but...what's that?" Finn pointed at some unfinished carpentry in the recessed floor centering the room. A long black marble slab sat wedged between what appeared to be an unfinished sink—an exposed pipe with handles on each side, and a circular saw.

"Putting in a wet bar. So check it, this thing has some special filter than can make salt water into drinking water, straight from the ocean. Never run out, see?"

Lew hopped down the recess and twisted a handle. Like a cannon, the water burst from the exposed pipe, pummeled the ceiling, and drenched Lew. He quickly turned it off with an *oops*.

Wiping flakes of plaster off his face with the tail of the towel, then inspecting the new dent on the ceiling, he shrugged. "They'll fix that."

"Right." Finn glanced around. "So, where are your nurses?"

"Ha! Nurses, that's funny." Lew bobbed his head up and down. "Nah, Megan delivered my chicken wings."

"You had chicken wings delivered to a yacht?"

Lew held his arms out. "Chic N' Wings."

Finn gave him an inquisitive look and Lew repeated it, this time drawing an N in the air. "You know."

"Clever."

"She's a student. College." Lew flopped onto the couch facing Finn and grabbed a goalie stick off the floor. Flat and long, the stick resembled an L-shaped cricket bat. He played the air guitar and, noticing Finn's look of suspicion, said, "What?"

Finn was wary of this territory, but he couldn't help saying, "They looked young for college, Lew."

"Well," Lew looked at the ceiling as he spoke, "She's going to be —they're going to be…next year, when—"

Finn held up a hand. "Don't say it."

"They graduate high school."

"Shit."

"Don't worry, dude, I made them show me their library cards. You know, before we did anything." Lew made a flat motion in the air with his hands. "They're definitely eighteen."

"They can vote."

"And drive. Like I said, Megan's a delivery girl. You know…"

"Lew."

"You should see the outfit she has to wear. Wings and all. She looks like some sort of…" his eyes got dreamy. "Farm angel."

"You're killing me Lew."

"And the chicken wings are solid." Lew picked up a foam container and opened it. "Want one?"

"I suppose those never hit the fridge."

"Only been out a few hours." Lew dipped one of the orange legs into a white sauce and chewed it to the bone.

"How many…hours?"

"Since midnight, so let's see…"

"Lew, you need to take better care of yourself. This contract." Finn held up the folder. "It's worth a lot of money."

"I am, dude. Look." Lew flexed his chest.

"Very impressive."

"So what's up, I'm signing something?" Lew wiped his hands and orange hot sauce all over the pink towel.

"Right." Finn placed the folder on the clean side of the coffee table and was about to open it when the boat swayed hard.

Lew looked up.

They both listened. Nothing.

Lew shrugged. "Probably a wake from Jet Skis. Hey, I should get one of those, too, eh? Or maybe a few."

Finn had a vision of Responsible Lew and Farm Angel Megan on Jet Skis. There wasn't enough insurance in the world. "Sounds brilliant."

"Yeah." Lew looked lost in thought for a moment and the yacht swayed again.

Finn sat forward and listened. He thought he heard a squeak, like a rubber shoe on the deck, and then remembered the couple at the diner.

"You hear that?" Lew leaned the stick up against the side of the sofa and stood.

Finn nodded and said, "I have a feeling this has to do with Colleen."

"You're back with her?"

"No."

"Then why—"

Finn held up a hand to quiet him. The boat swayed again, and then the distinct sound of footsteps grew louder. Someone was at the top of the stairwell.

"This is a private yacht, dude." Lew walked to the bottom of the flight, looked up, and said, "What the hell are—"

The next few seconds lasted an entire playoff series.

Lew dove left and a thick slap sounded, like a hardcover book being snapped closed. Yelling, he rolled, holding his right arm—a red ooze of blood seeping through his fingers—while Finn willed himself silent as he reached for the goalie stick, the footsteps descended, and an enormous figure appeared on the steps.

The Asian man stopped at the bottom of the stairs, Lew shouted and held a hand out, the man raised a long-nosed black pistol, pointing it at Lew, and Finn swung with all his might.

The stick collided with the wide man's head and he stumbled backwards, dropping the gun, then wind milling both arms as he tripped down the recess, slipped on the wet marble slab, and fell into a sitting position.

Right. On. The. Pipe.

The man's mouth opened in silent terror, his mustache separating in little wisps, as he reached back, fumbling to push himself off the pipe.

But his massive weight just turned the faucet's handle instead.

Finn had read somewhere that the human body is basically no more than a maze of tubes and organs layered over bones and covered by skin. Bones may break, organs can move and tear, and skin may stretch, but in the end, the body is little more than a big bag of water with one main hole for entry and one for exit. And so it was.

Because the man's eyes widened, and he convulsed. The skin stretched around his neck.

And then water shot out of his mouth.

CHAPTER FOUR

"LIKE A HOLE-IN-ONE. OR MAYBE a one-in-hole." Lew stood over the dead man, clutching his own arm, while Finn inspected the gun. It was a SIG Sauer with a silencer screwed onto the barrel. Hence the slapping sound instead of a boom. Finn turned the gun over and inspected the housing. Corning must have used some sort of acid to dissolve the serial number, as it was melted off entirely.

"Clever."

"Hey, where'd you learn to swing like that?" He glanced at the hockey stick. "Man you clobbered him."

"Did you find a wallet?" Finn asked.

"Nope. Just these." Lew held up a handful of pink and green casino chips.

No ID, as Finn figured. He glanced at the chips—they were from the Bahamas—and walked over to the body. The man's wide head had dropped back, and two streams of pinkish water dribbled from the corners of the mouth. With dark yellow skin and a feeble mustache he looked like a beached catfish.

Lew moved next to Finn and they both stood and stared for a while. Lew said, "I've never seen a dead guy before. Have you?"

"A few," Finn said. "You have enemies, Lew?"

"Aww c'mon man. You know me. I'm likeable." Lew flicked a chip in the air with a thumb and caught it.

"You said you got this boat out of auction."

"Yep."

"A Canadian Government auction by chance?"

"Exactomundo."

Finn eyed him. "And you haven't found anything out of the ordinary on board, right? A sack full of cash stuffed under a cushion? Maybe some packages of cocaine? Or weapons?"

"Nah, this baby's clean, dude. The Feds stripped it."

"Yeah, well even the Mounties miss sometimes." Finn exhaled loud. "And what about gambling? Have you been doing that again?"

"Not a once."

Finn raised a brow.

"Well, Atlantic City and Vegas a half dozen times." He paused. "Each." Pause. "Last year. But it was all legit. On credit cards."

Finn waited.

"My own," Lew nodded with a stern, serious look.

"Credit cards."

"Yep. No finance charges for a whole year. Smart, eh?"

"Shrewd," Finn agreed.

"Yeah."

"Look Lew, we should get out of here."

"No man, we should call the cops."

Finn stared at him.

"Shouldn't we?" Lew asked.

"I used to be a bounty hunter, remember?"

"Yeah, rich guys. So?"

"So. I've learned a few things over the years."

"Like what?"

"Like we're on a yacht, an extravagant setting. I hit a man in the head with a stick and he died."

"But he shot me."

Finn nodded at Lew's arm. "Yeah, about that, how is it?"

"Fine." Lew twisted his arm and showed Finn a short red stripe on his triceps. A graze.

"Nice reaction." Finn patted Lew's other shoulder.

"But he still shot at me, on my own boat. I say we come clean."

"Then they'll want to try it in front of a jury. We'll both be swallowed by the good old United States Federal Court system for years. You can kiss your hockey career goodbye. And all the money."

"Well what about...?" He looked down at the body.

"We'll need to get rid of him."

"I was afraid you'd say that."

"Got cleaning supplies here?"

"Not a one."

"And I was afraid you'd say that."

Clicking the chips and leaning closer to the body, Lew squinted. "Who was he?"

Finn rubbed the back of his neck. "I can tell you this. He wasn't a gangster or a drug lord."

"Then who?"

"I'd say a hitman, Lew. A hired professional."

"Geez, you think?"

Finn showed him the gun, where the serial number had been melted off.

"Dude." Lew stepped back and flopped onto the couch with a *thunk*. "Why would somebody want to kill me?"

"That is what we are going to find out," Finn said, as his cell phone began to ring. Colleen was returning his call. "Hold on."

He walked away and answered. She said, "I don't hear from you in, what, over a year? And you leave that cryptic message?"

"Yeah, look, sorry about that. I was just seeing things. It's nothing."

"It didn't sound like nothing, Patrick."

Right. "Thanks for calling me back."

"That's it? All I get?"

Oh boy. Finn had opened a can of Ass Pain. He knew he shouldn't have dialed. "Nothing to tell, honest."

"Uh, huh. Let me know when you want to talk."

"Soon," he said.

And she hung up.

"Who was that?" Lew asked.

"Client. Nothing."

"So, what now?" Lew glanced around.

Then Finn realized. "Damn," he said, looking back up the stairs.

"What?"

He turned to Lew. "Have you seen Walter?"

So much for the double, Vanessa thought as they parked the car in the Opal Bay lot. It had taken an eternity to return to the restaurant, and then they'd gotten stuck behind that crawling cement truck on a single-lane road leading back to the marina.

Bottom line, Finn's car was gone again.

"We can take care of Kunkle and then make a trip to Boston to finish up."

"It doesn't appear we have a choice now, does it?" Vanessa reached below her seat and peeled off the tape securing her pistol to the metal undercarriage. A P220 Compact SIG Sauer, the gun fit nicely in a specially made bra-holster. She loved the feel of the cold steel between her breasts. It gave her a rush. "Stay here."

"Your choice."

"We don't need you bungling anything else up."

"I haven't—" But she exited the car before he could finish whatever feeble retort he had managed to conceive.

Walking swiftly, Vanessa noticed the old geezer hadn't come out to bother her. Still, she kept an eye out as she walked to Kunkle's yacht. As she reached the stairs, she eased off her heels and placed them on the dock. She loved her Jimmy Choos, but they weren't the best for sneaking. The moment she started to ascend the flight, though, a fat pelican jumped off the railing from above and shat right into one of the brand new shoes.

"Bastard." Vanessa reached for the SIG, but thought better of it and continued up.

She stopped on the last step and listened. Nothing. She then continued through the wheelhouse. What a fucking setup. Joonas Saaranen couldn't have done better himself, she thought as she touched the leather sofa and eyed the custom details. Stopping at the top of another flight of stairs, this one leading to the staterooms and whatever else down below, she listened again.

Still nothing.

Vanessa descended the staircase, one slow step at a time, bent far over and reaching into her bra. Approaching the bottom of the flight, she scanned the room. A broken hockey stick, empty junk food wrappers and there, in the center of the recessed floor, an enormous body, his head and shoulders covered with a pink leopard print bath towel.

Rushing past the figure, pistol at the ready, Vanessa stormed into the first stateroom. More opulence, but empty of people. Thrusting open each door of the other rooms, then storming through the galley and back, she found no one. What the bloody hell was going on?

She returned to the body and took hold of an edge of the towel. It couldn't be. Could it?

She pulled the towel.

And she gasped.

"Who the hell is that?" Chadwick was coming down the stairs.

Vanessa put a hand to her mouth. "Don't you know?"

"Never seen the lad."

She whispered, "It's Benny."

"Benny who?" Chadwick approached, staring with wide eyes.

"He's in the network. Soon to be a member of the Century Club. Are you brain-dead?"

"Oh! That Benny!"

Vanessa rolled her eyes.

Chadwick tightened his face, staring, and said, "What in good God's name happened to him?"

Inspecting Benny, she said, "He's got water coming out of every orifice. It's like he drowned."

"Is that a sink he's sitting on?"

Vanessa stifled a laugh. "Oh shit!"

"You don't think…"

"I do." Vanessa circled Benny. "What a way to go." In midstride, she then stopped, turned to Chadwick, and said, "And I thought I told you to stay put."

"Well." Sliding his hands in his pockets, Chadwick looked away. "I wanted to be sure they weren't raping you or something."

"Raping me?" She put both hands on her hips. "What made you think that?"

"You'd been gone for a good bit. And…I didn't hear any gun pops, you know. I thought maybe you'd been captured."

"Of course not." She looked up at the ceiling. "Although, I wouldn't mind a good raping at this point."

"What. Really?"

"Well not like you think, you're a man. Forget it." Vanessa waved him off. Men think the remark refers to real rape. Violence and all that. Such idiots with their pitiful control fantasies. No. It was about giving up control, giving yourself over fully, but not being hurt, and gaining control in the act. The man loses his own and gives in to your seduction. Then he just *must* have you. Carnal and primal. She felt hot at the thought.

Of course Chadwick's voice ruined the moment. "I don't understand women."

She sighed. "Of course you don't. Anyway, I'll need your help."

"With…what, exactly?"

"Oh for God's sake, forget I ever mentioned that. Wipe your mind clean. Shouldn't be too difficult."

Chadwick gave her a blank look.

"Good." She tucked the SIG in her bra. Then she felt her face flush bright red, as she realized what had happened. "That nitwit son of bitch!"

"Who? What?"

Vanessa started pacing, hand on her forehead. "He didn't. That little, stupid, stupid, man."

"He didn't? Who didn't? What?"

"Don't you see? The client."

"What about him?" Chadwick held up both palms, like he was waiting for a gift.

Vanessa pointed at Benny with a long, stiff arm. "He hired both of us. He doubled the fucking order."

"Why would he do that?"

"Because he's a bloody damned, insect-brained fool."

"In that case." Chadwick became self-righteous, standing tall and thrusting out his chin. "We shall cancel the job."

Vanessa spun toward him. "The hell we do! That little rodent is going to pay. Double. No, triple!"

"Brilliant!"

"Of course it is. Because I said it." She started pacing again.

They would need some time, to negotiate. That meant the body had to disappear. They couldn't have the police involved right in the middle of a job. That would muck it up, make it all that more difficult to finish. She didn't think the goalie and his agent went to the police. No, if they were going to do that, they'd have called and stayed put. They were most likely scared, running.

Yes.

She stilled for a moment as a seed of a plan began to grow and solidify. Then, pacing again and scanning the room, she saw how easily it could be done, what with all the equipment and huge metal sink. She stopped pacing and said, "Did you notice the smaller boat docked behind this yacht?"

"Uhm, no, I didn't."

"Well there is one. But we'll need some fishing rods, you know, the kind for big fish. Sharks or whatever."

"Dare I ask, why we need these items?"

Vanessa locked eyes with Chadwick and drew his gaze with hers toward the machinery, then stopped on the circle saw.

"Oh no."

"Oh yes."

"You don't mean."

"I do mean."

Chadwick covered his eyes and moaned.

Vanessa walked up and slapped his shoulder. "We're going chumming."

CHAPTER FIVE

POOR WALTER.

A SINGLE BULLET BETWEEN THE eyes, so at least the old man hadn't suffered. Still, it wasn't right.

After hiding the body behind a sofa and locking the marina office, Finn had grabbed the rental contract from the glovebox of the fat man's car. The name on the contract, Elijah Corning, meant nothing to Finn. Driving now, both hands on the wheel, he glanced at Lew. "You okay?"

Lew turned to Finn and then back to the passenger side window. "Fine, why?"

"You seem deep in thought," Finn said, as he pulled behind a cement truck and leaned all the way to his left to see if anyone was coming the other way.

"Nothing. It's just..." he trailed off.

Too many cars coming, Finn eased off the accelerator and cruised behind the truck. "Yeah?"

Lew turned back to Finn and said, "Do you think I should get a new sink?"

Finn was deciding how to respond when his phone rang. Nikki O'Callahan, his assistant, was finally calling him back. He answered, "There you are."

"Three messages in a half hour? What the fuck?" With a harsh Boston accent and the language of a Longshoreman, Nikki came across much larger than her hundred pound frame, intimidating even the worst of the NHL enforcers. But to Finn, her first and only boss, she was loyal as family.

Still, he liked to push her buttons. "Hi sweetheart," Finn said, as Lew gave him a look of fear.

Nikki snapped back, "Don't fuckin' sweetheart me. We're buried here and you're off on a boondoggle."

"Buried?" Finn asked.

"You got seven messages, all of them GMs, even Sir Wayne himself."

"Gretzky?"

"No, Batman." She paused then said, "Of course, Gretzky."

"Call each of them and tell them I'm out of the office—I'll get back to them as soon as I can."

"Already did. Now what's your fire?"

"I need you to do a quiet check on someone."

"It better be an All-Star."

"Actually it's...personal."

She paused for a moment and then said in an almost-concerned voice, "You okay?"

"I'm fine. Just a bit of noise down here, and I need to know how loud it's going to get."

"So, you got a name or license plate or something? What're we talkin' about?"

"Elijah Corning," Finn spelled it out for her, then held the phone as he whispered to Lew, "Ready?"

Lew nodded.

Finn continued, "And we're going to text you a photo."

"And what am I doing with this?"

"I need to know who the guy really is. Asian mob, independent, you know. Run it through the Berans." The Berans were twin bail bondsmen in Boston who had given Finn a number of jobs back in his bounty hunter days. It would cost Finn some Bruins playoff tickets—always did—but they'd help.

"Asian mob, Patrick?"

"I don't know, just...check it out, would you?" And before she could protest, he hung up.

Lew held up his phone. "Can I keep the pic?"

"Better not."

"Aw man." Lew clicked a few buttons. "It's gone."

Driving over the waterway bridge, Finn cracked the window. The scent of saltwater filled the car and the ocean breeze felt cool on his face. He wondered if he could get used to the warmer weather but realized the dog days of summer had yet to set in. And it occurred to him. Dogs.

Lew had rescued twin mastiffs this spring and Finn had yet to see them.

Finn said,"Lew, where are your dogs?"

"Oh shit!" Lew yelled. "Dude! I forgot! I need to pick them up by eleven today!"

"From?" They crossed through the red light and Finn could see a Lowes about five lights, less than a mile, ahead.

"Dude, I wasn't going to tell you. It's embarrassing, eh?"

Finn stopped at the next light and stared at Lew. He couldn't even begin to imagine what would embarrass this person.

"We gotta' go back and get them. You have to turn around."

"Lew, we can't deal with dogs right now." Finn motioned to the backseat. "Besides, those two hair giants won't fit back there."

"I'm serious, dude, if I don't get them it'll be the third time. The doctor already thinks I've abused them or something. I need to pick them up as soon as this session is over."

"This session, Lew you're talking in code. What are you saying?"

"They're at the vet, dude."

"Are they sick?" The light turned green and Finn drove forward again.

"They just need me, okay? I can't abandon them. Not after all we've been through."

Finn pulled to the shoulder and stopped. "Been through?"

"So...it's not really the vet. They're in therapy, okay?"

"Therapy."

Lew shook his head and stared his feet. "Turn around. Please."

Against his better sense, Finn swung the car in a U-turn and headed back toward the waterway. "And then you'll tell me?"

"I won't have to." Lew looked out his window. "You'll see for yourself."

"Now roll him up." Vanessa took hold of one end of the carpet and glared along its edge toward Chadwick. Having found the old man stuffed behind a sofa, they'd dragged him onto the scrap of carpeting cut from the yacht.

"It'll be too heavy, I'm telling you." Chadwick gripped his end.

Whispering loud, she said, "Do you have a better plan? Like perhaps you can go get the saw and cut up the geezer too. Right here in the office for everyone to see." She raised her eyebrows. "Hmm?"

"Fine."

"Or perhaps we could haul him across the docks and wave at onlookers, as if it's perfectly normal to be carrying a corpse in the middle of the day."

"I said fine."

After rolling the old man into the carpet, they dragged the heap —like a boa that had swallowed a foal—right across the docks and into the long, thin speedboat. Something called a *Chris Craft Silver Bullet*, the keys to which were right on Walter's desk. Painted a muted silvery finish and lined with plenty of wood and white leather, it was luxurious for its size. They'd have to be careful with the bloody cargo and be sure to look like they knew what they were doing.

With that, Vanessa had stolen two large rods and a good bit of tackle from a charter boat docked at a deep sea fishing marina next door, while Chadwick diced Benny. The man had simply been too large to transfer in one piece...and one good hosing of the walls and the removal of the carpet had solved the cleanup. Of course, any forensic study would turn the room blue, but she was pretty well sure they'd avoided that for the time being. Now, the yacht was locked up, Benny was in eleven buckets, and they were ship-shape.

"Ready?"

Chadwick looked a bit ill. "I suppose."

Clearing the marina, Vanessa throttled the four engines.

Chadwick slumped back into his seat behind her. "Careful, you'll spill Benny!"

"No mind." She eased off as they approached the caution buoys, waving at a fellow boatsman—looked like a Congressman, maybe—along with his family in a pristine white sailboat. The lot of them dressed in colorful Izod shirts, they looked like little inbreeds pretending to be cups of sherbet.

Once clear of them and well past the buoys, she yelled, "Hold on now!" And punched it.

The boat's nose popped up in the air and an explosion of seawater blasted from the engines. Chadwick yelled out, "Slow down!" as the buckets slid into his knees. "For Christ's sake, Vanessa!"

Glancing back, Vanessa laughed. The cold wet spray felt great against her face and the air smelled divine. The fishing rods rattled between the carpet and fiberglass, Chadwick kept yelling, and Vanessa kept going.

Faster. Faster. She weaved to avoid a fishing boat.

Faster.

They hit a small wave and the boat jumped. Chadwick yelled louder, leaning over and holding the buckets now with both knees and hands. They landed with a thud and the buckets thumped to the floor. "Are you out of your fucking mind?" Chadwick yelled.

Perhaps a bit, Vanessa thought as they jumped another wave.

Landing harder this time, Chadwick cried out. His hair was wild in the wind, jumping and dancing with the gusts. "Please! I beg of you! Vanny!"

Seeing the buckets tilt to the point of tipping, Vanessa eased off the throttle. "Fine." The deep rumble of engines quieted. "Don't be such a baby."

Out of breath behind her, Chadwick mumbled to himself but loud enough for Vanessa to hear, "She's gone starkers."

She did know a thing or two about fishing, though, having grown up near a seaport in Glasgow. The simplest way to find fish was to follow the seagulls. The gulls circled the seas looking for fishbits that topped the surface when a school of tuna or whatever had a go at some baitfish. *Find the birds, find the fish.* But today was not the day for that.

Scanning the endless horizon, she saw none. Not a fishing boat in sight, either. The dark blue ocean stretched before her until it met the cloudless blueberry sky, and the scene was almost peaceful. If you could ignore the dead man wrapped in a rug and the buckets of Benny, and the imbecile behind her governing them.

"How far are we going?" Chadwick asked.

Vanessa shrugged, slowing the boat down further. "This looks good enough, start tossing. And I don't mean off."

"You're disgusting."

Vanessa smiled at her wit. As long as the chum was eaten before washing ashore, they'd be golden. And the chum may attract a fish with teeth or a bill, which could help with old man Walter. They couldn't risk him floating back to shore, and being dead he wouldn't bleed into the water to attract the big fish. They'd have to entice them with the Benny bits.

With a *swoosh*, Chadwick dumped a bucket over the side of the boat. The chunks just sank.

"Keep going, until you see anything of interest," Vanessa said, checking to see if she had a cellular signal.

"You mean like a fish?"

"No, a mermaid."

"I don't believe in those," he said as he dumped another bucket.

Vanessa shook her head and held the phone high in the air. With a beep, the phone announced a new voicemail, but when she checked it again, the signal was gone. She'd have to make the call when they returned.

Chadwick must have heard the voicemail beep, though, as he asked, "What makes you think the client will agree to it?"

She stared him down. "I'm not giving him an option."

Chadwick went back to work.

Playing the message, Vanessa listened to the pathetic little man's voice. Like a child, he stuttered and stammered his way through the indefensible lie, using code-language he may as well have picked up from a cereal box. Words like package and rush and accidental over-order. Please would she call him back to confirm the status, and the like, blah blah.

She was surrounded by nitwits in this racket.

Speaking of, Chadwick was holding his nose while dumping now.

"What's wrong, Chaddy?" Vanessa fumbled in her purse and found a cigarette. Lighting up, she asked if he'd like one, but he declined. She laid her head back on the plush leather seat and closed her eyes. The nicotine pulsed through her, evidence of the self-control she'd been exhibiting lately—she hadn't had but two cigarettes all morning. Her mind began to calm as she thought through her negotiation. The client would have little choice but to agree. He was in neck deep now and she had him by the knackers. All she would need to do was—

Her thought was interrupted by a loud spinning buzz and a plunk.

Looking up, she squinted back to the stern of the boat at Chadwick, who stood with a wide stance holding one of the large rods. The line extended out of the boat and far out into the water.

"What do you think you're doing?"

Chadwick glanced to the side but then back to the line in the water. "The chum's almost gone, I thought I'd use the last lot for a bit of sport."

"Sport!" She sat up. "We don't have time for fishing, those rods are for cover!"

"Well, I thought—"

"Listen, don't think. Put that down and help me dump the geezer." She tossed her cigarette into the water.

Chadwick's shoulders slumped at the scolding, and he jammed the rod between the back seats. "Fine."

"Grab the other end, then." Vanessa took hold of the rug and Chadwick followed. Heaving it up to the short railing, she said, "Now pull!"

The rug unfurled and Walter rolled out, plunking into the water like a thicket of sod. Minor rigor mortis having set in, the body then bobbed and ducked in the water, unable to fully sink yet. But after a few moments, some smaller fish emerged from the darkness below and began circling the body, pulling it lower.

"Will the current take him in or out?" Chadwick asked.

"Who knows," Vanessa said, pushing the rug off the boat.

A moment later, the rod that Chadwick had been using bent hard and the line began to zip from the reel, spraying their backs.

"What on earth?" Vanessa stared at the rod.

"Hey! I've got one!" Chadwick rushed to the back and grabbed the rod. "Lookit here!"

"You are not going to reel that in!"

"Why not?" He held the rod high as the line kept stripping from the reel. "It's a biggie, Mum."

"You're sick. What did you use as bait?"

With a big smile on his face, a giant idiotic schoolboy grin, he announced, "There was one bit that looked the most like a worm."

"Oh you did not."

"Well, you just watch, I bet I have a great big tuna or maybe even a swordfish on." His neck and arms straining, Chadwick fastened the rod to the metal buckle of his belt.

"A swordfish?" Vanessa took a step toward the wheel.

"Maybe even a shark!" He glanced at Vanessa and then back at the water. "Wait, what are you doing?"

"You'd better hope not." She pulsed the engines to life.

"Hold it!" Chadwick yelled, but she could barely hear it over the throttle of the engines. "WAIT!!" Chadwick braced himself, as he dropped to the floor, feet flat against the seat. "Don't do it, Vanessa. DON'T!"

And she gunned it.

With a long, high arc, Chadwick's arms popped upward first, then his torso, his feet, and the last she saw of him was a twisted look of shock.

And he was gone.

CHAPTER SIX

PARKED OUTSIDE THE *BARK TWICE IF YOU'RE Happy* clinic while waiting for Lew, Finn's phone sounded. He checked the number and answered.

Nikki said, "The Berans ran the quickie."

"And?" Finn watched outside for the couple he'd seen in the diner and then rear-view mirror for Lew.

"And nothing."

"What do you mean nothing?"

She exhaled loudly. "They said the name was not listed in any of their state or national databases, including NIBRS." The *National Incident-Based Reporting System*, NIBRS, would cover all the states that participated in entering data on their known aliases for criminals.

"Sounds like there's a *but* coming."

"But…the name was flagged in a different system."

"Which system was that?"

"They wouldn't say."

Finn said, "Shit."

"Right," Nikki said. "About the photo, Patrick."

"Yeah, that."

"I want to ask what's going on, but I know better." She paused then said, "At least not on the phone."

Finn nodded as if she could see him. If the name was flagged on a system and they couldn't talk about it, it was federal. So Finn's suspicion was correct. Elijah Corning was more than a small fry, he was a pro. Reaching into his breast pocket, Finn pulled out one of the casino chips they'd found.

Turning it over in his fingers, Finn read the Grand Lucayan inscription and said, "Another thing. Have the Berans check if Corning was on a flight to Miami recently. Maybe from Freeport."

"Got it. They said they can call in a favor if you want them to keep digging." She tapped on something in the background and said, "I'm guessing the answer is yes."

"Start lining up playoff tickets."

"Already have—I got four seats behind the Bruins bench for the first game."

"Perfect," Finn said as he watched Lew approach in the rear-view mirror, being dragged across the lot by two monster-sized Mastiffs. He told Nikki he'd check in later and hung up.

"Dudes," Lew said as he opened the back door. "Relax."

Entirely ignorant of the request, the dogs piled on each other, bumping into and licking everything in their path, including the back of Finn's head. "Hey! Lew!" Finn swatted at the dogs and caught a lick from a cow-sized tongue.

"Down!" Lew yelled as he slammed the back door and climbed into the front seat. "Sorry, dude."

"They look pretty happy to me."

The dogs panted like they'd just reached land from Cuba, hot, wet, sneaker-rot breath wafted to the front of the car. Finn waved it back, and Lew reached over and flipped on the A/C without a word. He seemed more stressed about the dipshits behind them than the guy they'd killed that morning. Finn was about to address that, but one of the dogs barked—a deep-throated bellow about one decibel below a foghorn.

Lew pointed his chin forward. "We better go, they're ready."

"Right." Finn glanced back and put the car in gear. "Nikki called."

Lew's eyes widened. "She find out who he was?"

"Not exactly, but…" Finn said as he exited the parking lot and headed back toward the Lowes, then continued, "we were right about this guy being a pro." He kept an eye on all the mirrors, watching for anyone following them.

"Dude, who would want to kill me?"

"I don't think it's only you."

"No?"

"Lew, that couple I told you about? The one I saw at the diner?"

"Yeah?" Lew asked, then said, "Stop it," as he swatted at the dogs behind him. They kept pushing and nudging each other for space and the middle of the seat. Their energy seemed unending. He turned back around with a stern look on his face. "You were saying?"

Finn glanced back and said, "I think they're involved."

"Meaning?"

"Meaning…I think I'm involved."

"How?"

"They were following me, or maybe both of us."

"Why? We're both cool dudes…"

"I have Nikki looking into—" and Finn cut himself off when he looked in the rear-view mirror. But it wasn't what he saw outside the car that alarmed him. It was in the backseat.

"Lew, what the hell are they doing back there?"

The dogs climbed all over each other, bumping into the doors and the front seats.

"Kicksave! Stop it. No!" Lew was almost in the backseat and pulling on one of the dogs' collars. "Glovesave, sit! I said NO!"

"Ugh." Lew slumped in the front seat and covered his face with a hand. "I knew therapy wouldn't work."

Finn was about to ask what the problem was, but then car began to shake left to right. Left to right.

And then the grunting started.

Finn watched in the mirror as the two dogs, locked in an

embrace, one over the back of the other, rocked back and forth together now.

"Lew? Are they doing what I think they're doing?" One of the dogs' heads' was hitting the door, and Finn punched the locks to keep it from popping open.

"Ignore them, okay?"

"It's hard to—"

"I said ignore them."

Finn tried to keep from glancing back and Lew turned to him, saying, "Look, the doctor said it is who they are, and I should let them express who they want to be. Who they need to be. And I'm fine with that, you know? Love matters more than anything. Even for dogs."

"You mean they're...?"

One dog's face driven into the door handle, he panted, tongue out and a huge smile, slobbering all over the seat as the other humped away.

Lew reached over, turned up the radio full blast, and Mariah Carey's "Make it Happen" vibrated at level ten through the dash.

"Two grand down the drain," Lew said and crossed his arms.

Finn had to almost yell over the music, it was so loud. "You're upset about the money? Or that they're, you know...homosexual?"

"Neither, dude!" Lew shook his head and stared into the rear-view mirror. Then he turned away from Finn and looked out the window.

"It's wrong because they're brothers!"

CHAPTER SEVEN

TRACY CASHMORE—TRACE TO HIS FRIENDS—PRESSED the seat adjustment button on his spanking new Bentley convertible to give Melissa more room in his lap.

"Much better," Melissa said and pushed higher on each stroke.

Feeling distracted, Trace tried to imagine his buddy Chance, Melissa's husband, watching in the passenger seat.

Fuck it, maybe he would just come and get it over with.

He imagined Chance mad now, hurrying things along. But right as he was about to let it fly, his damned phone rang and screwed it all up.

Reaching behind Melissa, he checked the caller ID. Not a number he recognized, he put a finger to his lips and answered. Melissa was quiet, but he could barely hear the voice on the other end over the sound of her knees rubbing on the custom Savannah leather. "Hold on."

Covering the phone, he said to Melissa, "Go down to finish up."

She put both hands on her hips and said in that squeaky twang, "But my juices are all over you."

"Like you've never tasted pussy before."

With a look of contempt, Melissa climbed off Trace and kneeled on the passenger seat to continue.

Trace held her hair up for her, as he returned to his conversation. "So, who is this?"

The woman sounded pissed.

Then Trace figured it out. "Oh. You. I...uh...can I call you back?"

"No, you can't call me back," she yelled into the phone so loud, Melissa heard her.

She stopped and looked up. "That better not be Kimberly." Kimberly was Chad's wife, Melissa's best friend. Although Trace would love to fuck Kimberly, she had the ass of a twelve-year-old boy, Kimberly would never do it. She was way into her lifestyle with Chad. Oh, and Chad's dad was Trace's dad's partner on the Houston Hammerheads, the NHL expansion team they'd bought.

Covering the phone again, he said, "Relax, it's the office."

She eyed him and went back to work. It felt pretty good when she swirled her tongue like that.

"So...what...I mean, is there a problem?"

"You know bloody well there's a problem, and now I'm tripling my price."

"You can't do that!" Trace sat up and yelled, pulling Melissa's hair. She chomped down and he yelled again, "OW!"

"Sorry," she whispered, smiling while holding the back of her head.

Damned women. Trace pushed her off and she sulked while staring at him from the far side of the Bent.

The woman on the phone said, "Since I'm running the show now, you don't have much choice, do you?"

"Then you're fired," Trace said, red-faced, rubbing his groin.

"The hell I am."

Not used to being talked back to, Trace was losing his temper faster than a snake in a skillet. "Look here, I don't—"

"No. You look here. I want the money—three bills now—wired to the custodian by tomorrow. If it doesn't hit the account by the end of business, I'll make one, single phone call and your daddy, your precious fortune, and all your land will be frozen by the United States IRS. Do you...understand?"

Trace swallowed hard. "Fine. You'll get it."

"The next time you screw someone in business, you indignant shit, you'd better think about who it is." She hung up.

After Kicksave had his, Glovesave went for it. Two songs later, it was over. Finn and Lew had left them in the car, sleeping, as they collected cleaning supplies at Lowes. Now, headed back to the marina, the two dogs lay crumpled into each other, awake, but eyes drooping and breathing slow.

Finn glanced to the backseat. "So, how often do they...do that?"

Lew said, "You mean are they going to do it again today?"

"Well, no, but..." Finn let his voice trail off, then said, "are they?"

Lew shrugged. "Only happens when they get really excited. Once a day at most."

"You mean twice."

"Right. Or, when you say treat or cookie. That gets them going."

"Noted." Finn raised his brow. "So, seeing you today?"

"Yeah, they were riled up."

A long period of silence stretched between them until Finn broke it with, "I don't care, you know."

"Good."

"I mean, if they're happy, to each their own. Who are we to judge?"

"Right," Lew said, "Dogs, humans, fish, whatever."

Finn gave Lew a sideways glance, but kept quiet.

Lew said, "What?"

Finn said, "Fish, Lew? I don't think that's even possible..."

"I'm just saying." Lew shrugged. "How do I know?"

"Anyway," Finn said, "it doesn't bother me. And it shouldn't bother you."

Lew nodded and held out a fist to bump, then took it back quick. "You won't tell any of the boys will you? You know how the locker-room can be."

Bumping it, Finn said, "Promise."

Finn scanned the car windows as they approached the entrance to the Opal Bay parking lot. Not sighting the Lincoln Town Car and the couple from the diner, he drove into the lot and parked. They nudged the dogs out of the car and then headed up to the yacht, large buckets and cleaning supplies in each of their hands. Finn stopped at the marina office, glanced around, and checked the door.

Still locked.

They continued up the stairs, the dogs now barking loud enough to set off two car alarms. Ushering them into the wheelhouse, they shut the door. The dogs jumped around, sniffing every single corner of the room and then bounded down the stairs.

Shit.

"Lew, can you hold them?" That's all they needed, was the dogs knocking over or making any bigger mess of the corpse.

"Dudes! Wait!" Lew dropped his bucket and ran down the stairs. Then he said, "What the…?"

Picking up both buckets, Finn followed to the bottom of the stairs and stopped as he scanned the room. Corning was gone and so was half the carpet—at least the portion that was in the recess of the room. The room smelled like bleach, too. Finn set down the buckets and scanned the place. Nothing else seemed out of order. In fact, it was in more of an order. The Cheetos bags and wing cartons were gone, along with the beer cans.

The dogs, sniffing wildly now, walked nose to the floor covering every square inch of the place. After a minute, one of them stopped right in front of the sink. Sniffing hard once, he bent over and licked the pipe.

"Glovesave, no!" Lew jumped down and pulled him out of the

bar area. "That's gross." Glovesave then jumped up and licked Lew's face. A big, long wet one.

Wiping his face with a sleeve, Lew glanced at Finn but Finn looked away quickly, pretending he didn't see the exchange.

"Maybe I should lock these guys up."

"Good idea."

Lew left the room, a collar of each of the dogs in his hands, dragging them through the hall. When he returned, he looked exhausted, announcing as he limped, "Kicksave hurt my groin."

"Shit, Lew."

"It's not bad, just tweaked."

"Maybe you should think about—"

"Don't say it. I'm not getting rid of them. They need me." He slumped onto the sofa and nodded gravely. "Now more than ever, they need love from their daddy."

Finn nodded back.

Lew looked around and held his hands out wide. "Cops came, eh?"

"Well, considering there's no police tape, crime scene investigators, or police...men here, I'd say no."

Lew frowned.

Finn walked around the room, inspecting the space. Some of the carpentry materials appeared to be missing, but he couldn't put his finger on which ones.

Lew sat forward. "Hey, where are all the paint buckets?"

"What buckets?" Finn asked.

"The big white ones, stacked behind the piano. Oh man, I liked to play bongos with those. The Bettys love it." Lew made two cups with his hands and put them on his chest. "Should've seen Maggie play those naked."

"I thought her name was Megan."

"She was like Ziggy Marley, but cuter in a way."

Finn didn't want Lew to clarify that, so he pretended to ignore it.

Glancing to the piano and back to the bar area, Finn noticed the black marble slab had been moved and all the power tools were neatly arranged behind a stack of two by fours.

"Lew," Finn said. "What do you do with your trash in this place?"

Lew shrugged and pointed at the ceiling. "Put it out on deck and it gets cleared every morning."

"Where do they take it? An incinerator or something?"

Lew shot him a *fuck you asking me for* look.

Finn knelt down and inspected where the carpet had been cut. The line was perfect and true, right along the step down into the bar area. Checking out the naked boarding underneath the bar, he looked for staining or streaking, but there was none. No evidence of the dead fat man anywhere. There was no way that this guy could be carried out of there without some sort of front loader or a crane.

And the Brits were both average size at best. They didn't look like they could lift each other, no less a man Elijah's size.

Finn glanced back at the lineup of tools. Then he heaved the marble slab over. Long, shallow cuts zig-zagged the entire length. The fat roll of plastic drop cloths was missing too. Nodding his head, he turned to Lew.

"I know what they did with the body."

"Chaddy, Chaddy, Chaddy. All dry now, warmed up?" Vanessa eyed Chadwick as he leaned away, against the passenger window. He had pointed every vent toward himself and blasted the heat. Quiet now, they sat in a tourist lot, about a mile from the Opal Bay Marina, facing the waterway. Two huge Palm trees reached high above them and shaded the entire car.

"I've told you to stop calling me that."

"Oh don't be cross. It was just a bit of fun." Beginning to sweat from the heat, she reached over and switched off the air.

"At my expense."

"You swam well." She searched her purse for the cigarettes.

"You dumped me in the water with all those body parts!"

Lighting up, she said, "They were gone, mostly."

"And what about that shark, circling me?"

"That was a dolphin."

"It was a shark."

Exhaling, she said, "No mind, you're safe now. Good as new."

Chadwick crossed his arms. "So what did the client say?"

"He'll pay," she said, smiling to herself. "I knew he would."

"And what about the other call?"

"Well, that's where things begin to get a bit tacky." Cracking the window, Vanessa tapped the fag on the glass to knock off the ash.

He looked interested now. "How so?"

"Well, it seems..." she took a long drag and exhaled as she continued, "that Patrick Finn has drug his employee into the mess. He called and told her about Benny."

"Oh good God, the bodies are starting to pile up."

"Targets you mean, they're not bodies yet."

"They will be, and I'll become a Century Club member."

"Not before me." She blew a plume of smoke at him.

Chadwick made a face, then cracked his window and waved some of the smoke out. "So do you have a plan?"

"I told home we'd take care of it ourselves. They seemed grateful, what with all the confusion caused by Benny's sudden expiration."

"I think we should split up. I'll go to Boston."

"You're trying to get rid of me." She laughed to herself. "And it won't work."

"Why not?"

"Because technically you are in employ by me. At least until this job is finished. You know how it works."

"That's rubbish and you know it. We should split up and finish the jobs out. We can meet up later."

"We'll do nothing of the sort. You'll help me finish these two, then we'll go to Boston together. We'll both get credit."

Chadwick sighed. "Maybe we should cancel the whole order. It's been error ridden from the start."

Vanessa flicked ashes at him. "You want Century Club, don't you? A holiday in Las Vegas?"

"Of course, I'm just saying—"

"Besides." She dragged and exhaled. "Finn has seen our faces."

"We don't know that."

"Plus, Benny is dead and we should avenge him. It's the right thing."

"We have to find them first."

Flicking her cigarette out the window, she said, "And lucky me, I have you to help."

CHAPTER EIGHT

IT HAD BEEN OVER A YEAR SINCE Nikki had seen the Berans.

Perfectly identical twin brothers, Bobby and Billy were five foot six and wiry thin—they dressed the same, talked the same, acted the same, and even wore their close-cropped kidney bean colored hair the same exact way. They did everything together and shared everything, including—as rumor had it—girlfriends.

And why not? There was simply no way for anyone to tell them apart.

Watching the Berans walk into the dark, humid pub now, Nikki could see that not much had changed. They both wore shiny aviator sunglasses and long leather overcoats—too long for their small frames—and strutted like a couple of IRA henchmen. Sliding into the booth across from her, Right Beran looked around and whispered, "Got those tickets?"

"Four, behind the bench." She patted her purse.

"Not even worth this," Left Beran scoffed.

"What's that supposed to mean?"

They both leaned forward and Right Beran said, "Your boss has stepped in some serious shit."

"Like an elephant-sized pile of dog...well, shit," Left Beran said.

Nikki held up a hand and then motioned for them to continue.

Right Beran looked around and sat all the way forward as he whispered, "Apparently, the only database this guy Elijah Corning comes up on is NCIC. That's FBI. We had to pull more than a few strings to even get into it."

"More than a few," Left Beran sat forward.

"I heard the first time." Nikki stared at him. She turned to Right Beran. "So, what's the bottom line?"

"Bottom line is..." Right Beran said, "*Elijah Corning* is only one of the dead guy's twenty seven known aliases."

"Twenty-seven?" Nikki sat back. "Jesus,

"Mary," Right Beran said.

"And Joseph." Left Beran finished. He looked around. "Now. You want to know why?"

Nikki gave him an *of course I want to know why, you fucking idiot* look.

He leaned back again.

Right Beran leaned all the way forward this time, gave a long, wide look around, and whispered, "You ever hear of MI6?"

Trace checked the bottoms of his black suede Gucci loafers—he always did before entering his father's office—and knocked, two hard raps. Then he fished his iPhone from his jeans and looked at another photo sent from his guy out in Long Cay. This one looked like a stingray.

Useless.

The so-called master shark exporter was supposed to be catching him hammerheads and hammerheads only. How many times did Trace need to explain it? He'd have to deal with that moron later.

Clicking the phone off, he checked himself out in the device's glass reflection. The thick blonde curls had stayed slicked back with that new hair crème and were long enough to peek out from under his ears. Chicks loved it like that.

Slipping the phone into his back pocket, he knocked again.

"Hold on!" His father, Jerry...*the* Jerry Cashmore, barked from the other side. A few moments later, the toilet flushed and the office door opened.

Zipping up, his father hadn't even looked at him before lumbering away again. "Where the hell were you last night?" he asked, settling behind his giant oak desk.

"Well...we started out at Hank's Chop House and then had some Veuve at Beau's—"

"Never mind that. I'm talking about the meeting."

"Oh that."

"If you're going to continue to draw pay from this organization as Assistant GM of The Hammerheads, I expect you to attend the meetings. All of them."

"Fine."

Reaching into a drawer, the old man pulled out a cigar box. He flipped it open and, selecting one without offering the box to Trace, he put it back in the drawer. "Have you thought any more about your little problem?"

"I assume nobody responded."

"Not a single call from any other GM all night." He stuck the fat cigar in the crook of his mouth and began to chew on it, no light.

"So, set another deadline."

"Oh what's the use. You know how ridiculous it is."

"What's ridiculous is sitting around and doing nothing." Trace stood tall at his declaration.

Jerry stopped chewing and stared at him so hard that Trace felt a warm sensation spread in the wrong place and his scalp began to sweat. "What? That's what you told me."

Jerry breathed in slow and loud through his nostrils then fast out, like a rodeo bull strapped for bucking. "What I told you was... your idiotic deal would come back and bite us square in the behind."

"Jesus, Dad, are we still on that?" Tracy pushed the chair,

almost knocking it over.

"Do not take the Lord's name in vain in my office, son!"

"Oh for fucks sake, Dad." Tracy kicked at the carpet.

"Sit. Down."

Tracy turned back and stared at the man, wondering why they ever got into this stupid racket of owning a professional hockey team in the first place. They could make more money selling goddamned cupcakes in this city. You know, the ones with fancy sprinkles and icing in the middle. Those places were a mint these days.

"I said. Sit."

And Tracy did...with a crunch. *Shit*. Looks like another trip to the Apple store. Oh well, now he could get the newest model. He wanted that one anyway. "So. What are you going to do?"

"Nothing." Jerry sat back and folded his hands over his midsection.

"Then...what, we eat it?"

"Not we." Jerry swung his thick head back and forth, the bull now flaunting his horns.

The air began to suck from the room as Tracy processed the possibilities, knowing there was really only one with this man. It felt like that ride at the state fair, where they spin you fast and drop the floor out from under you. He wobbled in his seat. "H-How?"

"Consider it your first lesson in big business, but, as with everything, you tend to learn the hard way."

"Dad." A bead of sweat had trickled between his legs and down his pecker, then Trace realized it wasn't sweat. "That's twelve million dollars."

"And that's why you have a trust fund, boy. For little fuck ups like this." Jerry slapped a hand on the desk and laughed, giving Tracy momentary hope that it was all a joke. This was nothing more than a little lesson for him and half his future hadn't really evaporated. All a show, a big production for the benefit of Trace.

But then Jerry stood and said, "I'm finished with your

cleanups."

A deep pit settled into Trace's stomach as the horror reached volcanic level. Before he could respond, Jerry handed him a sheet of paper with four crude drawings, like a comic strip, showing a stick figure in action. The figure, with its short curly hair, was bent over and pulling toilet paper off a roll then using it.

Trace looked up at the old man, standing above him. "Is this a joke?"

Jerry poked the paper with his cigar and said, "That there, boy, is a manual." He pointed the cigar about an inch from Trace's nose. "I suggest you start usin' it."

It had taken Finn almost an hour to walk Lew through the logic of waiting to hear back from Nikki before sailing away in the yacht to *let things cool off*. Once convinced that their little problem was not going to disappear along with the bodies, and that they most likely had two more professional killers after them, Lew instead suggested they go for ice cream.

So now, Finn and Lew sat on a bench in the top row of temporary bleachers at a public pool, shaded by tall palm trees, watching a game called Octopush. Much like hockey played underwater, Lew explained, it involved four players aside, each wearing snorkel equipment and holding mini hockey sticks while trying to push a metal puck along the bottom of the pool into the other team's net. "No goalie, though," Lew said, sounding disappointed.

Watching the players bump into each other while swimming for long stretches underwater, Finn found himself holding his own breath until the players came up for air.

"She's the best one, eh?" Lew pointed at a girl wearing a blue-striped one-piece. After getting halfway down the pool, she emerged, spitting water from the tube of the snorkel. "See her here every day."

"You come here every day?"

"Pretty much." Lew puckered the top of his cone. "You know, to escape all the stress."

Guy just bought a yacht, parked it in Palm Beach for the summer. How stressed could he be?

The blue-striped girl stole the puck from the other team and Lew yelled for her. Pretty sure she couldn't hear them, Finn used his inner-voice to cheer her on instead.

"What about you?" Lew asked. "What're you doing this summer?"

"Working, Lew."

Lew looked confused. "Yeah? Doing what?"

Finn raised his brow. "I'm a sports agent, Lew. Yours."

"Oh right." Lew stared at the blue-striped girl who was now climbing out of the pool. "She's a stud, eh?"

"Pretty special," Finn said.

"No doubt," Lew said as the girl glanced up at them, then smiled and bent over to get a water bottle from under her bench. "I think she did that on purpose."

"Nothing gets past you," Finn said.

"That's why I'm a 'tender," Lew said, then, "I'm gonna' get a number—text her later." And before Finn could advise against it, Lew was halfway down the stands.

Good thing, because Finn's phone began to ring, and it was Nikki.

"We gotta' talk," she said, sounding harried.

"Tell me about it." Finn leaned over and dropped the rest of his cone into an open trashcan below the stands.

"Your ass is in some serious shit, boss."

"How could it be any more serious?" Finn said.

"I'm freaking out here, Patrick."

Finn turned his head and talked low, "Calm down. Start at the beginning."

"Not on this line."

"Give me a hint."

She exhaled loud. "I'm dying my hair, and I'm the fuck out of here."

"Nikki—" but before he could talk sense into her, she yelled, "Holy fuck!"

Finn heard something drop in the background. "Nikki? What?"

The phone bounced around a bit and she called out, "I left the damned dye in too long!"

CHAPTER NINE

"W<small>HAT DO YOU MEAN YOU'VE LOST THE</small> signal?" Vanessa said into her cell. She'd never met the man known as Relay and had just spoken to him a handful of times, as he'd only been in the Network for a few months. She already hated him.

"Finn must have turned his phone off," the dolt next to her said.

Turning to Chadwick, she responded with a smile, "Do you think?"

With barely enough wit, he sensed her sarcasm and shut up.

"When you do know something, let's do us all a great big favor and try to call back, hmm?" She hung up.

"Have you decided?" She asked Chadwick.

Standing in the small shop open to the street, five blocks from the Opal Bay Marina, and sorting through the array of baseball-style hats, he picked each up with a frown and placed it back down again. "Not yet."

"What seems to be the problem?"

"I don't like the colors. Or if I do like the color, I don't like the stitch."

"Does it really matter?" She folded her arms across her chest. "It's merely a temporary change of appearance."

"Look." He held up a dark blue hat with an NY on it. It said New York on the back. "This is a good color but the NY stands for Yankees, and I don't want to be one of those."

"Really, Chadwick." She rolled her eyes.

"And here," he said, holding a green one with a cloverleaf on it, *Celtics* was written on the back. "I like clovers, but I don't like green. Besides, it's too obvious, Finn being Irish and all."

"You truly are an inbred, aren't you?" She sifted the pile and held one up. Dark blue and black, it had a large musical note on the front of it. "How's this? It's blue."

"Oh I rather fancy that. I love jazz." He took it from her and held it up. "The brim doesn't bend either, it stays nice and flat. And it's a long brim, too." He tried it on.

"What do you think?"

His ears sticking straight out, the brim half black, half blue, and with the words Utah and Jazz written in huge graffiti style along the sides, he looked like an absolute fucking imbecile.

"Perfect," she said.

"It's not as good a disguise as yours." He ogled himself in the small mirror on the hat stand as he spoke.

She had to agree, peeking at herself. With a wide-brimmed, pink-striped sun hat, something that could be worn at a polo match, and huge round sunglasses, a la Jacqueline Kennedy—what a magnificent creature she was—Vanessa felt like royalty.

"What do we do now?" he asked.

"We watch for them. We're not making another move until the money hits the account."

Boarding her flight, Nikki scanned every row she passed, scouring for anything out of the ordinary. Each accent was exaggerated: English, New York, even Southern. Outfits seemed contrived. Everyone appeared to be acting, pretending to be someone else.

Yep. Nikki's state was on DEFCON 4.

Feeling a tap on her shoulder, she nearly jumped from her seat.

She spun around. The man behind her leaned forward with shit-ass breath and asked if she knew what time they would land in Miami. He had a normal Boston accent, as far as she could tell. She told him the exact time, down to the minute, and he thanked her. Then he complemented her on her hair color. Said it looked *peachy*.

Yeah, well this peach spit lava and would singe his beard off if he said another fucking word about it, she informed him.

He didn't bother her again.

Two minutes later, a man took the seat next to her and offered her a piece of gum. He could take his gum, chew it himself and then shove it up his own ass, she told him. Nobody was going to poison her, dammit.

He too, kept to himself.

Settling deep into her own seat, Nikki spent the entire flight concentrating on every word, syllable, and inflection uttered by passengers within earshot. Two distinct English accents and one soft English accent were audible in separate areas of the plane behind her. The distinct accents were from two college-aged guys. They talked football the entire flight, arguing about Manchester United this and Chelsea that. They were nothing but a couple of morons, with their obsession of Wayne Rooney and arguments that no footballer on their respective team would leave their country or their English teams for money.

Can you say Beckham, you dopes?

But the soft English accent was a woman's and she sounded older, perhaps in her late fifties or maybe even sixties. She was traveling alone, though, and Nikki only heard her speak to the flight attendants, nobody else. Nikki had glanced back and seen that the woman did in fact have grey hair and was reading a magazine. Oprah? Really? Still, she kept to herself the entire flight.

Everyone around Nikki kept to themselves.

Everyone except that woman. The one with the soft accent and grey hair, reading Oprah.

That one ended up following her.

Ignoring Faith's incessant blabbering, Trace pulled the Bentley into the Ellington Field private entrance. The entry gate keypad stuck and he had to enter the number twice.

Nothing was going right today.

Screw it, he thought. He was on vacation and shouldn't be thinking of stressful things anymore.

But right as he was beginning to think of the Bahamas and all the hot MILFs he'd see out there, Faith started talking again—about purses this time. Then, on top of it, the lot attendant made him park on the far side of the plane.

"What the hell?" he said, getting out, having walk all the way back around the tail end just to reach the steps. What a hassle.

Faith, of course, bitched about it, as did both the kids.

Looking down at them from the top of the stairs, Trace half-wondered if they were his. Not even teenagers yet and with their Texas summer tans they looked like fat little Mexicans. It was embarrassing. The whole lot of them were.

"Good morning, Mr. Cashmore," The new flight attendant said.

"Yeah, hi," Trace managed to smile. With bushy blonde eyebrows and too much lipstick, she was grody compared to the last attendant they'd had.

Selecting a seat near the front of the plane, he placed his briefcase bag on the one next to it. That would keep Faith from getting any ideas about talking all the way to Freeport. She could sit in back with the kids and their nannies. Besides, he had brought the latest Sports Illustrated and ESPN magazines to catch up on all the NHL trades and chatter from last month. The assistant GM job was more demanding than he realized when he agreed to take the position. And expansion teams were way harder to manage than his dad made them out to be.

The kids wobbled past him and his daughter said, "Dad, did you bring my iPad?"

"Listen, it's not my responsibility to bring your things, when are you going to learn this? Ask the Marias what they did with it." He hated to be so hard on her, but the little shit needed to learn that it was her nannies' responsibility to look after her belongings. Not his.

Speaking of, he turned on his new model iPhone. Pressing a few buttons, he got to the email thread he was looking for, the one with the photos. At least Manny had found more than just that stingray this week. He'd caught a bunch of hammerheads along with the useless bull sharks and whatever else. Anyway, he was up to like five now. Trace was pumped to see them and his dad would be so surprised when he showed him. Of course, there were a few loose ends to tie up before then.

Yeah, all he needed to do was meet with the banker and transfer some cash. Then his trust fund issue would go away, and he could resume a normal life.

CHAPTER TEN

"So, how do you know she'll be here?" Lew asked Finn, as they entered the baggage claim area of Terminal D at Miami International. They both wore black Wayfarer sunglasses, courtesy of a recent sponsorship gig Lew had signed with Ray Ban. Finn still had his suit on, no tie, and Lew had covered up the spandex bodysuit with a bright blue velour sweatsuit. He looked like a Serbian hit man.

"I bought the ticket," Finn said, scanning the crowd.

"Oh, I thought you were psychic," Lew said, punching Finn's arm. "You know, my aunt reads palms and stuff."

"Stuff?" Finn said, half-ignoring Lew.

"Yeah, she told me I was going to be drafted by an NHL team a whole week before it happened."

"She did, huh?" Finn switched on his cell phone, in case Nikki had tried to call when she landed.

"Amazing, right?" Lew said as he tapped the linoleum flooring with a foot.

"She must be tapped into the Universe," Finn said, then, "Although, Lew, there were articles in the paper every day about that. Everyone knew you'd be drafted." No messages, Finn slipped the phone back into his pocket.

"Yeah, but she said I would be playing for San Jose. Got that all wrong."

Finn turned to Lew. "She did?"

"Yep." Lew stopped tapping his foot. "Why?"

"They're both…sharks, Lew."

"Wow. She must be psychic."

A few seconds later, the walk of a short woman caught Finn's eye. He couldn't see her face, but she appeared to have Nikki's *fuck with me only if you don't value both testicles* strut. She turned, and Finn could make her out clearly. It was Nikki, no doubt, except her hair was a strange color. Not red, not rust.

But bright, almost florescent orange.

The color of icy sherbet.

Wondering how the hell she managed to screw it up that bad, but smart enough to keep the comments to himself, he just nodded to Lew. "There she is."

Lew turned and yelled, "She looks like a Nerf ball!"

The glare from Nikki sliced through the crowd, across Lew's mouth and right into Finn's face. The two of them stood as still as geckos as she approached.

Dropping her bag at Finn's foot, Nikki said, "Well, well, if it ain't the Blues Brothers."

"You look…chipper," Finn said.

"Shut it."

"I'll get your bag," Lew said.

"You'll get a whole lot more than my bag, bug-nuts." Nikki tilted her chin up to both of them. "First, can we get out of plain view?" She led them to a vending machine behind a long row of luggage carriers, while muttering about all the trouble Finn and Lew had suddenly caused her.

She had a point.

"First, watch," Nikki said.

"What're we looking for?" Finn asked.

Lew leaned out to buy a candy bar from the machine and Nikki jerked him back. She whispered, "There, the one with gray hair in a bun and carrying a black purse, no luggage."

"Who?" Lew asked.

And as Finn turned his attention to the woman Nikki was pointing to, he caught a glimpse of a person that stopped him cold. With the presence of a panther, sleek and smooth in her movements and with long, glossy black hair, she would have stood out to Finn over a mile away.

Before he could ease back behind the vending machine, she turned her head, and her gaze landed right on Finn's. She held it.

"Damn," he said.

"What?" Nikki asked, still looking further ahead, toward the other woman.

"My fault." Finn stared straight ahead, as Colleen Coffey walked straight toward them. Like a Scud missile, she had them locked in her sites, no way for them to escape now. "I'll take care of it."

"Fault?" Lew asked, and then noticed her too. "Who's that?"

"That's Colleen," Finn said. "My ex."

"Shit." Nikki said. "Where?"

"You were married?" Lew asked.

"Girlfriend," Finn and Nikki said at the same time.

"Oh, that Colleen!" Lew tilted his head. "She's hot. Why'd you break up?"

"Did you leave that part out, too?" Nikki asked Finn.

"Never came up." Finn shrugged.

"Now may be appropriate," Nikki said.

"What're you guys talking about?" Lew said, head tilted up and peering under his sunglasses.

"So..." Finn said. "I didn't leave her because she was boring."

"Then why?" Lew said.

"I left her because she kind of works for..." Finn paused and then finished, "Because she's CIA."

The sun was down now and with a good breeze, Freeport was way less humid than Trace had feared. Still, he'd used about double the amount of product as usual in his hair, as he was meeting with Tabia DeRoux tonight and the last thing he wanted was to show up with a big blond frizzy Afro. And he couldn't just re-shower, that would set off alarm bells in Faith's head. Too obvious, even for her.

They deplaned on the private airstrip, and Trace pretended to smile at the welcoming committee, four native Bahamians, who took their bags straight to customs for them. At Island-time pace.

Faith said, "This is going to be a great vacation, Trace." She even hugged him.

She was sticky.

"Look, I need to work tonight, I told you. So don't get any ideas about romantic shit or garden bathtubs."

"That's fine." She beamed. "Maybe we can get room service and order a movie."

"Don't order anything for me. My meeting is over dinner." Trace said, setting the tone with Faith right away.

She made a face but then smiled as she pointed out two dying palm trees to the kids.

Following the welcoming committee to customs, Trace nudged the nannies to take care of the kids. Otherwise, they'd end up at the wrong building, or worse, playing on the runway.

It took almost a full half-hour getting through the dark, crusted customs area of the building—damned uniforms wanted to look through every bag. The floor was dirty, and the people wore old clothes—sure they were colorful and all, but color doesn't hide dirt. At least give the front-line soap, people.

Faith even noticed, saying, "It's so sad how a whole country could be so poor."

"It's not a country," Trace corrected her, "It's a Commonwealth."

"Well I don't see any wealth," she said.

The customs agent waved them through.

A black Lincoln Town Car, probably the only one on the island, picked them up right in front of the airport. Trace directed the nannies and kids around the front of the taxicab line and into the first one. Some Europeans in line made a comment, but what could he do? His Town Car was waiting and it was obvious they couldn't all fit in that. And what, should he make the nannies stand in line? Ridiculous. Besides, the kids were giving him a headache and he needed get away from them for a while.

As he leaned up front to check his hair in the mirror, he said to Faith, "Tomorrow I'm going out to see the sharks, you can take the kids to the pool or something."

"That sounds exciting," she droned.

Trace played it down. "I have to go all the way to the other side of the island."

"Trace, how did you get that approved by the Agriculture Department or whatever? I mean, bringing sharks to America, isn't that illegal?"

He patted her thigh, which felt larger than he remembered. Or maybe he was just getting used to Melissa's tight little ass. So fine.

He said, "It's all in who you know, I've told you that."

"Just what my daddy used to say."

The cars pulled into the Parrot Beak Resort, a six-story island building with white wood slats and a bright pink porte-cochere. So gay.

The kids—all sweaty from the nasty looking cab ride—bolted for the lobby.

Trace signed the car voucher and gave the guy an extra dollar, since he had stayed quiet the whole ride and didn't try to pump Trace with any voodoo religion crap like the last guy.

Entering the lobby, he tried to imagine it was a Four Seasons or Ritz, or some other low-five star resort. That said, he'd be happy if the shower wasn't stained. But with the dull marble black and white checkered floor, ceiling fans—thank God for those, really—

and that bongo-island music piping at him from above, he had a hard time picturing anything but a glorified thatch hut. The kids were dancing to the shit, wiggling their fat asses around like those two characters from the Lion King, that muskrat and the pig.

Bypassing the front desk, the porter took them straight upstairs, saving Trace from the music. Until it started up again in the elevator. Faith straightened her sundress and smiled at Trace, and he rolled his eyes then patted Trace Jr.'s head.

This made his hand sweaty, though, so he wiped it on the kid's shirt.

The room smelled good, like coconut milk, and was larger than Trace had hoped. Though it was dominated by the steel-canopy bed with faux mosquito nettings and the wood flooring wasn't antique or anything, the place did have a nice-sized balcony with an ocean view. But the television was one of those old LCD models, and not very big, maybe fifty inches. No way was it 3D. Still, Trace gave the porter an extra dollar—these guys loved American dollars —and requested a wake-up call for nine am.

"When will you be home...er, back to the room?" Faith asked Trace as he hung his clothes and changed into standard island-wear, linen pants and a blue silk shirt.

"No idea," he said, which was partly true. He knew Tabia's husband would expect her to be home by midnight. Being a banker, she never worked later than five, and dinners should only last a few hours at most, even business dinners. Island people never worked more than that, ever. And how long could they fuck for anyway? He hoped she didn't expect too long. He just needed to get off.

"Any idea where you'll eat?"

"Nope." Fiddling with the buttons on his shirt—real pearl, they were thicker than usual and didn't fit in the little slits too well— Trace hoped Faith would get the hint, maybe go next door and hang out with the nannies and kids.

But she didn't.

Trace's phone buzzed and he got excited. He loved that this thing worked in almost every country...Commonwealth, whatever. Tactfully turning his body to read the screen, Trace's heart sank. A simple text from Tabia said, *change of plans, my husband Mickel is coming, can you bring yours?*

I don't have a husband, genius.

Closing his eyes for a second, he weathered the blow. He wondered why she hadn't mentioned this stiff Mickel before. Fuck it, I'll bring Faith and show you I have a hot—he looked at her checking out her growing ass in the mirror—well, pretty hot wife. Then Tabia would be jealous when stacking Trace up against her own husband.

Good plan.

He turned to Faith. "How would you like to come with me tonight?"

"Really?" she asked.

Yes moron, what do you think I'm joking? I'm not cruel like that. He said, "Just this once, though, don't get used to it."

And she actually squealed.

"So she's CIA, too?" Nikki asked Colleen, and Finn knew she was referring to the gray haired woman that had followed her.

"Actually, an independent contractor. But yes, she was working for me." Colleen, who sat up front, hadn't stopped staring at Finn who was driving.

"Where is she now?" Nikki said. She sat in the seat behind Finn, and Lew kept quiet while tucked deep into the other seat.

"Headed back to Boston, she was a chaperone...to make sure you got here safely. I was already in the area for unrelated work."

"And how'd you know I was coming to Miami?"

"We picked up your last phone call." Colleen glanced at Finn.

She sat cool and collected, with her hands folded in her lap.

"This all just happened this morning, are you kidding?" Nikki asked.

"The wonder of surveillance," Colleen said. "See, Patrick, here, sent a text message containing an alias we've been tracking. Two hours later, we had your cell phones in our loop."

"But Patrick never said where I was going."

Colleen sighed as if bored by the whole thing. "Please, I could find you any time of any day."

Finn could feel the nuclear radiation of resentment emanating from the backseat.

But then Nikki spoke in a calm, even voice, saying, "As opposed to this place you have us going in circles to find."

That Nikki. She did have a way with subtlety.

Colleen laughed. "I need to get you to the facility securely. That takes patience." She smiled at Nikki and then turned to Finn. "Take a right here."

Finn noted the road was marked *Maintenance Personnel Only.*

"That'll take us back onto the airport grounds," Finn said.

"Exactly."

Then, after staying completely silent for the twenty minutes since meeting Colleen, Lew announced, "I gotta pee."

Finn glanced in the rear-view at Lew. "Is there a place at this… facility?" He asked Colleen.

She shook her head. "I don't think so."

"I can't wait." Lew began to squirm.

"For the love of Jesus," Nikki said. "Pull over before he bursts."

Finn pulled the car to the shoulder, and Lew was out the door and behind a beaten palm tree before Finn had even put the car in park.

"Is he retarded?" Colleen asked.

"A goalie." Finn shrugged.

"And makes more money in a year than you can in a decade," Nikki said.

Colleen turned to Nikki. "Doubtful."

"Think you'll pull in twelve mil by then?"

"Twelve million dollars?"

"Well, pre-tax," Finn said.

Colleen looked dumbfounded. "Is he that...good?"

"He was last season," Finn said. "And that's all that matters."

Lew climbed back into the car, all smiles, zipper wide open.

By the time they reached the so-called facility, Finn realized that whatever Colleen was up to, she was doing it without explicit authorization. The chaperone—an independent contractor—plus illegal domestic cell phone wiretaps, and the fact that she showed up less than four hours after Finn's first call to her all added up to a special project.

One that Colleen seemed to be running herself.

On that, the facility was nothing more than an abandoned airplane hangar at the end of a winding dirt road. Dank, humid and with strips of evening sunlight beaming through broken glass high above, the place had the ideal environment for a pot-farm.

Colleen led them to the wall on the right. Pulling a rusty fuse-box open, she flipped a switch. A moment later, a huge metal fan embedded in the ceiling rumbled to life, loud enough to vibrate the aluminum walls. The dust stirred up, Nikki coughed then waved a hand in front of his face.

Colleen said, "Precautions for possible listeners."

"As in MI6?" Nikki asked,

Finn squinted through the dusty sunlight. "Did you say MI6?"

Colleen gave him a deadpanned look.

Lew gave him a blank look and a shoulder shrug and Nikki held her orange hair with both hands.

Colleen nodded once. "As in British intelligence."

Finn said, "Why exactly would they be listening?"

"Somebody's listening to us?" Lew looked around.

Finn glanced at him, and Nikki let go of her hair and leaned over to whisper an explanation.

Colleen leaned against the aluminum wall. "Let's start with what happened today, okay? I need to know everything you did."

"How do we know you have our best interest?" Nikki asked

Colleen crossed her arms. "Don't you think I'd have already have you arrested or whatever, if that were the plan? I know you've killed a man...or at least caused his death."

Finn stayed silent for a moment.

Tough spot they were in. They'd killed a man, and perhaps there were hired killers still after them. The CIA was now involved, official or not, and Colleen, Finn's ex-girlfriend, seemed hell-bent on controlling the situation.

He said, "And if we give you details?"

"I'll reciprocate."

Finn said, "Why would you do that?"

"Simple. I can help protect you with my information and resources, and with your information, you can help me complete my case."

"Quid pro quo."

Lew clapped. "Dude, I didn't know you knew Spanish!"

Colleen suppressed obvious amusement and said, "Tell me everything you can, from the moment you stepped off the airplane in Palm Beach to the moment you saw me at Miami International."

Finn hesitated, reluctant to tell her much, but decided that they needed help, and CIA or not, he could use some answers from Colleen.

So he recounted the day, start to finish, including Flash with his jump rope—you never know who could be eyes for intelligence. He told her about Elijah, who Colleen called Benny, and his casino chips, then about the couple from the diner, and Walter. He told her about the circular saw and his theory on body disposal. Lew added a few thoughts of his own, including Chick N' Wing Meghan and the Octopush girl, and between them they hit just about every minute of the day to that point.

"I didn't realize a man could die like that," Colleen said.

"Probably could happen to a chick, too. If she was fat enough," Lew added.

"That's helpful Lew, thank you," Nikki said.

Finn said, "He's been hit by a lot of pucks."

Colleen stared at Lew for a moment. Then she said, "So, we know two major things about the killer...or killers as it may be, in the case."

The three of them waited for her to continue.

"First, we know they have an established network. In fact, one of the first contractors for this network was this Benny, who..." she glanced at Lew, then continued, "died this morning."

"Hell of a way to die." Lew shook his head. "Hell of a way to die."

Colleen continued, "Second, we know the network is made up of former British and American Intelligence agents. MI6 and CIA, mainly. But there could be Army Intelligence too."

"That's great." Nikki rolled her eyes.

"It gets worse. These agents have all been expelled, fired, or decommissioned by their various agencies. Caught stealing from missions, killing to cover up mistakes, bribing and being bribed alike, they were crooks. And for the most part, they were stupid enough to get caught."

"And what exactly is their purpose now?" Finn asked.

"They are all available for hire. To kill."

"The rejects?" Nikki said.

"Wow," Lew seemed to be in a trance.

Finn asked, "And how exactly does someone hire one of these guys?"

"It could be a girl you hire," Lew said. "I mean, not for sex, but you know..." he whispered, "to kill someone."

Colleen pushed off the wall. "The Network has selected an elite group of clientele. The rich—no, ultra-rich—the most powerful, the uber-connected. It's a closed club."

"They're using MI6 and CIA as a selling point," Finn said.

"Precisely," Colleen said.

Nikki said, "And their pay is…"

"Astronomical. Even for assassins," Colleen said.

"Ballpark it," Finn said.

Colleen glanced at Lew, who was picking at something on his shirt, maybe dried chicken wing dip this time, while humming a Ricky Martin song.

"Enough to give this guy a run for his money."

Smoking her seventh cigarette of the day, while staring at the Atlantic Ocean from a wood-slatted bench, Vanessa regarded the full moon and wondered if it had caused their miserable failures of the day.

"Where on earth could they all be?" She said to Chadwick, exhaling smoke on the last word.

"Maybe they stayed in Miami."

"Now why would they do that?"

Chadwick shrugged, making the bench, uneven on the concrete, wobble. "It is late, maybe they became weary, rented a room for the night."

"Weary."

"Yes."

"They've killed a man and met with a CIA agent. Do you think they're just going to bed down then?"

"I don't see why not."

"Maybe they've gone on holiday at Disney, then. Catch a few rides, some fireworks, perhaps?"

"I've heard those are magnificent."

"You bloody idiot." Vanessa flicked her cigarette and it hit Chadwick in the arm. "They didn't go to Disney. And take off that ridiculous hat, you don't need it anymore, it's pitch black out here."

"I thought you said it looked good." Chadwick said, rubbing his arm.

"I lied."

With a pained look, Chadwick removed the hat. Then he stood up, walked to the trash bin and shoved it through the swinging door. "I don't know why I listen to you."

"Because I'm smarter? And I'm your boss? And I'll cut off your baubles and feed them to you if you cross me? Maybe those reasons?"

"They are good ones." He walked back over and sat.

"The network isn't helping a single bit, either. I don't know why we work for them anymore. They aren't getting us the same information they used to. A single phone signal is all they picked up in the last four hours. Miami International Airport, no less. It's as large as all of Yorkshire. Finding two people there would be like searching for a thought in your skull."

"I don't think I understand."

"See?"

"So what shall we do?"

"I'll tell you what we're going to do. We're taking matters into our own hands." Vanessa stood up. "We're going back to the yacht and wait for them to return. I don't care if that CIA agent is with them, we'll kill her too. The network can figure out how to clean that up. We'll still get paid."

"But I thought HO said this Kunkle man has guard dogs."

"HO? What's that?"

"Home Office. It's what everyone's calling it now."

"Sounds idiotic."

"Not to me."

"Precisely."

Glaring at her, Chadwick said, "But what if they're there?"

"Who?"

"The guard dogs."

"In that case…" Pacing, Vanessa said, "We'll need to stop at the grocer."

"I'm not following again."

"Come on then, I'll drive." Vanessa headed for the car.

After a quick trip to a marketplace called Amici, damned expensive that place was, Vanessa and Chadwick drove straight to the Opal Bay Marina. Getting out, Vanessa held still for a moment. Another yacht had been tied into the slip across from Kunkle's, making three yachts now. She wondered if the newest arrival had looked for the security man. None of the lights were on in either of the other two boats, and Finn's car was still missing, so she whispered to Chadwick to come along.

"I'm not scared of dogs, you know." Chadwick hurried to catch up to Vanessa, carrying the grocery bag.

"That's good."

"I've even been bitten by one before. In the back."

"Lovely," she said.

"It hurt."

"Splendid."

"Are you listening?"

"No."

"Well you must be or you wouldn't have answered that."

"Answered what?" She said as she climbed the steps of Kunkle's yacht.

She kicked off her shoes and marched through the wheelhouse, then began descending the stairs inside. Pausing to listen, she reached back and whispered, "Hold here," while putting a hand on Chadwick's stomach. But she'd missed and touched his groin instead.

"Mum!"

Blushing, Vanessa held her hand there for a moment. Chadwick had a small hog hidden in his pants. "My, Chaddy. Are you excited?"

He pushed away. "Not in the least. I'm flaccid."

"I wonder." And she shook her head to expel the image of what she'd touched becoming hard.

"Can we please move on?"

"Yes." Vanessa escaped the trance and continued down the stairs. "Do you have those goods ready?"

"I do."

The moment they reached the bottom of the stairs, the barking commenced. Deep, booming woofs echoed down the halls and through the great room.

"Hurry! Open them! Before someone hears!"

"We forgot a tin opener." Chadwick held the dog food in both hands now, having dropped the bag. "Where's the kitchen?"

"You mean galley. And it's down the hall."

The barking continued, louder now, and scratching had commenced on the doors.

"Towards the dogs? What if they're in the kitchen?"

"Galley. And if so, we'll have to hurry then won't we?"

"Good God, Vanessa, listen to that, they'll tear us to shreds."

"Don't be a wanker. Come on!" She hurried down the hall.

Chadwick followed behind her, a good five steps back.

Listening at each door, Vanessa opened them one by one. On the third try, she'd found the galley, empty of dogs, thank God. With glossy red teak wood, glass-door cabinets, and black granite counters, the place looked nicer than the finest of London flats. Chadwick stood in awe.

"Do start looking!" Vanessa waved a hand before his face.

"Right."

They pulled open all the drawers but all they found was a churchkey.

"We'll have to make do," Vanessa said, taking a can of food from Chadwick and working it with the key. It took about thirty triangular holes to wrest the top of the can off.

"Here, pop it into this." Chadwick placed a cereal bowl on the counter and Vanessa shook the food into the bowl.

"Ewww, that stinks," Chadwick said, holding a hand to his face.

"Awful," Vanessa agreed, placing the bowl on the floor. "Do the other." She handed him the can and opener.

Chadwick worked on the can while Vanessa headed down the hall. The barking hadn't ceased for a single moment, and she was worried they would soon have visitors if they didn't shut the animals up. Approaching the door, Vanessa braced herself. Then she flattened against the wall and flung the door open. The dogs, enormous, gigantic, beasts as they were, burst through the doorway, knocked Vanessa clear off her feet, and bounded down the hall into the galley. Their grapefruit-sized testis slapped the insides of their legs as they ran.

Chadwick yelled first, then came the sound of the bowl skittering across the floor, and then ceramic breaking.

Vanessa drew her gun and ran to the galley.

Chadwick was up on the counter, flinging the food from the can onto the dogs and the floor.

"What are you—"

But before she could finish, the two dogs bumped her to the wall as they raced to the counter and lapped the food from wherever it had landed.

"Shoot them, Vanny," he said, "Shoot them!"

The rabid beasts growled and chomped on each other's coats where food had stuck to their fur, then bit at the floor for scraps and chunks, smearing the brownish slop all over the place. They were famished, downright starving, ready to eat anything. Vanessa could have served them the inside of an elephant's ass and they would've eaten it.

"We're trapped! What do we do?" Perched up on the counter Chadwick looked like an injured vulture.

Pistol at the ready, and feet secured between the door and the counter, Vanessa stared them down. One of the beasts turned to her, barked, then burped.

A foul cloud of dog breath wafted into the air.

"Oh dear," Vanessa said.

Chadwick pressed himself all the way to the cabinets and waved frantically to dispel the odor.

The dog then took a step toward Vanessa, its mouth hanging wide open, saliva oozing out and onto the floor. The other dog followed right behind it.

Chadwick said, "Eat the treat, you beasts!"

Steadying her aim, Vanessa switched back and forth between the two, unable to decide which to shoot first.

But before the first dog reached her, the second one became so excited that it tried to climb over the other's back. The space too small, it couldn't get past. Still it kept trying, thrusting its hind legs and pawing the first dog's shoulders.

Vanessa aimed at his skull.

The first dog dropped its front paws under the weight and then grunted.

And Vanessa realized what was happening. She lowered her arms.

Chadwick leaned forward. "Are they?"

The second dog was now moving rhythmically, pumping away, while the first smiled and panted, drool slinging from its mouth. He seemed to be enjoying it.

It was a he, wasn't it?

Vanessa dropped to her knees and checked.

They were both hes.

"But, how could they?" Chadwick tilted his head and stared.

"I don't know if they're actually — "

"It damn well looks like it."

"Yes. Yes it does."

"Should we leave them…alone?"

"I think we'd better had." Vanessa eased around the back of the dogs and into the doorway as Chadwick followed.

"So much for the guard dogs," he said.

Placing the cold pistol back between her breasts, and in a complete daze as she backed out, Vanessa said, "So much."

CHAPTER ELEVEN

As THEY WALKED BACK TO THE CAR, Finn humored Colleen who grilled him about his history with Lew. Quite thorough, she asked them about anything that could cause them to be targets, like seeing something they shouldn't have, or maybe racking up black market gambling or drug debts…she nodded toward Lew at that one…and finally relented, realizing that they needed more information about the killers themselves to figure it out. The logical place to start was the payments. Follow the money, find the source, she said.

Agreeing with the logic, Finn watched Colleen inspect Lew's arm.

"You're quite lucky."

"Not luck, eh?" Lew pulled away and made a goalie move. "I was fast."

"Blazing," Colleen said, then, "Here we are."

As they rounded the corner, Finn realized the rental was gone. In its place, a shiny black Chevy Tahoe. Government issue, by the looks of it.

"What the?" Nikki said.

"I took the liberty of having the rental replaced with one of mine."

"Magic," Lew said.

"Great," Nikki said. "Where are we taking it?"

Everyone stayed silent again for a while, until Colleen said, "Patrick, you said you found some casino chips on Benny."

"Grand Lucayan Resort."

"As in the Bahamas?"

Finn said, "You thinking offshore?"

"Could be the source." Colleen asked.

"Good a plan as any," Finn said.

"What plan? Where's the source?" Lew asked.

Finn said, "We need to figure out who is after us, right?"

"Sure." Lew shrugged.

"So, whoever hired the hitmen would have to pay them somehow."

"And you think they live in the Bahamas?"

"Not exactly," Colleen said. "But, the Bahamas is a pretty good place for...hiding banking activity."

"But, if it's secret, how can we find out where the money came from?" Lew asked.

Colleen caught Finn's eye and looked away. Finn said, "That... may take some work."

"Why don't we just tell the police or FBI or whatever?" Lew said.

Finn groaned and Colleen said, "I could hand this off to the Feds, but like Patrick said earlier, that would tie all of you up for months, maybe even years. And me too, of course. This is a highly sensitive case."

"No way," Nikki said. "I don't trust the Feds."

"So then what's the plan?" Lew said, as he picked at a mustard stain on his shirt.

"Well. It's only about 80 or 90 miles from Palm Beach, through the channel, right?" Colleen asked.

"Whoa whoa whoa. No way," Nikki said.

"Got a better plan?" Finn asked Nikki.

"Private jet," Nikki said. "That's better."

"Safer, but...manifest is still traceable," Colleen said.

"What channel?" Lew asked.

"The Atlantic," Finn said.

"Patrick, all the way to the Bahamas in a yacht? Who the fuck is gonna' drive?" Nikki held both palms up.

Simultaneously, Finn and Colleen turned to look at Lew.

Lew said with a clap of the hands, "Sweet. It'll be my second time!"

Tabia and her so-called husband were late.

Trace survived the purgatory alone with Faith by guzzling two Banana Daiquiris and an Apricot Daiquiri, while she'd sipped on a Piña Colada or Yellowbird or some shit like that and commented on the beautiful ocean and breeze from the patio table.

Barf.

He'd eaten at Luciano's last time he'd been to Freeport—really the only restaurant with edible food. Well, other than that street vendor who sold deep-fried conch across from the bank. Couldn't let Faith know about that guy though, she and the kids would park their asses on that corner every day and eat enough conch that they'd have to retro-fit the plane with bigger engines to get them all home. Trace had no problem burning off the extra meals though. A few extra bench presses would do the trick, maybe some curls. Shit, if Tabia had kept their original plan, Trace would've fuck-burned another thousand calories that night. He downed the rest of the Daiquiri and ordered another.

"Trace? Hello?" Faith waved her hand in his face. "Why don't you ever get me another drink, too?"

"That's her job." Trace pushed Faith's hand away and nodded at the waitress' back. "Besides, I'm trying to take in the sunset you're blabbing about."

Faith held her hand up in the dying light. "Do you think my

ring is big enough? Melissa just upgraded to four and a half carats and Kimberly started with over five." She scrunched up her face like a pug.

"So?" Trace burped banana and blew it toward the ocean. He hadn't noticed Melissa's ring being any bigger than Faith's that morning, though it was hard to see it when Melissa had her hand in his pants.

"So..." she dragged out the one syllable, then said, "I need an upgrade."

"That's a four point three carat diamond on your finger, Faith. I bet people in Africa were killed for it."

"It's their job to find the diamonds, so we can buy them."

He nodded at her hand. "Have one of the Marias clean it. Make it look bigger."

"I don't want it cleaned. I want a bigger one." She gave a pouty face, now. Lip out and everything.

Trace sighed. "Faith, this isn't the best time for me to go blowing a few hundred thousand dollars on a rock, okay?" He was about to bullshit her about needing money for taxes or something —he couldn't let on about the trust fund issue, she'd freak out—but Tabia showed up with her husband.

The guy was way bigger than Trace hoped. And muscular. Probably a plantain farmer.

Trace stood, bumping into Faith who had decided to stand at the exact same moment. She gave him a look and he gave her one right back.

"Nice to know you." Trace held out his hand to Mickel.

"Likewise." Mickel gripped Trace's palm like he was trying to fuse the fingers together. Asshole. What happened to island-tude? Laid-back-ed-ness and all that, mon? Jesus.

The girls introduced themselves and then Tabia finally came over and gave Trace a feeble half-hug, the kind where she turned her body so no more than their shoulders touched. Ridiculous.

The four of them sat and ordered another round of drinks. Tabia got her signature Mai Tai and Mickel got a club soda. What a bore. Trace stepped it up and got a Rum Colada. Faith ordered some pineapple shit he'd never hear of off the drink menu.

"So, what do you do?" Trace went right for the jugular with Mickel, to make him see he wasn't even in Trace's league.

Mickel glanced at Tabia and back to Trace. "What do you mean, do?" His accent was nowhere near as smooth and sensual as Tabia's. It sounded like a rock bouncing along the bottom of a toilet.

"Work." Trace leaned all the way back in his chair, totally casual and in control. "What kind of job…assuming you have one." He looked around and laughed.

Faith kicked him under the table.

"Ouch!" Trace yelled loud enough that a few people from other tables turned. "What did you kick me for?"

Faith turned bright red and said, "Maybe we could talk about something else." She blinked about a hundred times as she said it.

"I'm making conversation."

"It's okay," Tabia said then sipped her water—fucking waitress still hadn't brought the next round—and winked at Faith. "Mickel comes to a lot of business dinners. He's used to getting the questions."

Mickel said, "I'm a trainer for the resorts on the island."

Ha. Worse than farming. Guy was pretty much a chick trainer. Probably dressed like Olivia Newton John in that video. *Physical*.

Not like Trace. He'd been on the football team both in high school and in college, not many people could say that. Sure he didn't dress for any of the college games, but the team was like one of the best in the whole conference. And besides, he practiced for an entire year before his career-ending finger injury. The thing was still a little crooked. Plus, he now owned a whole professional hockey team. Well, part of it, but still…he knew sports better than this clown. Trace leaned forward and said, "So, what exactly makes you qualified…" he laughed a bit, couldn't help it, and continued, "to be a trainer?"

"Well," he said. "I represented my home country Trinidad and Tobago as a marathon swimmer in the Olympics."

Trace snarfed the Daiquiri and it went up his nose, burning so badly that he coughed and his eyes began to flood.

"Oh my," Faith said. Then leaned to Tabia and whispered loud enough for them all to hear, "He must have great endurance."

Jesus, Faith, get any wetter and you'll slide off your seat. Trace wiped the apricot oozing from his nose with the napkin.

"He does," Tabia said as she took hold of Mickel's hand, her own swallowed by it.

A pretty lame country for swimming, Trace thought. He probably didn't even finish the race.

"How did you do?" Faith asked.

"Silver."

Trace slumped back into his seat. Guy was a showoff.

"Wow! That's incredible," Faith said, leaning over and patting his arm. "Congratulations."

Groan. It's not like it was a Gold Medal.

The waitress approached, thank God, and broke the precious moment with the round of drinks. But then she screwed up and reversed Trace's and Faith's order, and his dumbass wife took a sip of the Daiquiri before Trace could grab it from her. So, he took a healthy gulp of hers before handing it over. Scrunching up his face, he was sorry he had. The thing tasted like tequila and cherry, nothing island about it.

Faith appeared to be idiotically pleased with it, though. Taking a drink, she said to Tabia and Trace, "So...you two are doing business?"

Duh. Why do you think we're here, Faith?

"If you could call it that," Tabia said. "It's mostly paperwork and contracts."

"Sounds important," Faith said.

Trace said, loud enough for the people at the bar to hear, "I just need to move some of my money around. A few million, give or take." He looked around and laughed.

Nobody else did.

Not able to figure out what everyone's problem was, Trace announced, "Since we are doing business..." he winked at Tabia, then continued, "I'll buy dinner. Everyone order whatever you like." And before he could even take another drink of his Daiquiri, Faith declared that she was ordering the seven-pound lobster special and Caviar Malossol for the table.

Trace quickly flipped open the menu. Who knows what the fucking lobster would cost. Seven pounds? And the Malossol was listed at a hundred and thirty bucks a pop. Dammit. He looked around. Maybe the others didn't like caviar.

"We love caviar," Tabia said.

Fuck.

Oh well, he would write it off anyway—charge it to the Hammerheads. But, Trace would definitely be the one to order the wine. Faith wouldn't know Rothschild from Ripple. She'd just point at the most expensive thing on the menu, like always.

After an endless dinner and excruciating conversation about everything Mickel, where both women fawned all over Mr. Olympia, Trace felt like he was going to puke.

Tabia announced that she had to use the restroom, and Trace jumped out of his seat. "Me too!"

He stumbled into the person seated behind him, they'd put the tables so damned close together, and Tabia made it across the restaurant too fast for him.

Pushing the door open to the men's room, he fumbled into the corner and leaned on the wall in front of the urinal. Pissing never felt so good. Except he squirted so hard that it sprayed all over his khakis and hands. Zipping up, he stumbled back to the sink and patted his pants dry with a paper towel. He had to hurry to catch Tabia before she headed back to the table. Pushing open the door, he almost ran her over. She had been waiting for him by a phone booth.

Fucking third world country...Commonwealth, whatever...still used phone booths?

"Tracy." She smiled at him.

"Call me Trace, you know that." He reached up to touch her face but missed and fell forward, his hand landing on her tit.

He gave it a little squeeze.

She pushed the hand away and propped him against the booth. "You have had a bit too much banana, no?"

"Apricot."

"Whatever. Look, we cannot do this here. And..." she glanced around, then said, "I think we should not be doing it any longer anyhow."

"What do you mean?" Trace burped and tried to blow it the other way.

She made a face. "You know exactly what I mean."

"Can we talk about this tomorrow?" Trace needed to get her alone, remind her how hot it was to fuck the rich guy.

"I'd prefer that, yes." She drew a fold of papers from her purse. "You still need to sign the documents that open your new account."

"Fine."

Handing them over, she said, "Are you worried at all about the IRS or anyone else who could be watching you?"

"Why should I be worried?"

"You need to be aware is all I am saying, mon."

"Look." He swayed and steadied himself as he signed. "My people are the kind that the IRS can't even touch."

She pocketed the papers. "It must be nice."

Remember that, he thought as he followed her back to the table. When they arrived, Faith had both hands under her breasts, pushing them up and making a V with her cleavage.

"Don't you think?" she said to Mickel. "They're almost four years old. These things need to be replaced peridontally."

Dinner was obviously over.

CHAPTER TWELVE

Sitting with Chadwick in something of an all-night coffee shop a few miles from the yacht club, she scoured the Internet for more information about Kunkle. In mere minutes, she found a wealth of information about the rookie NHL sensation.

Playing for a brand new team called The Houston Hammerheads, Kunkle had completed what ESPN writers said was an outstanding year for any goalie, rookie or not. He had let in fewer goals than any other starting rookie goalie in over twenty years. Because his contract was not disclosed at the time of signing, the writers couldn't be sure, but they were quite certain he would reap the benefits of this season for years to come in the form of performance bonuses and such, *blah blah*.

Terribly boring stuff, but it gave Vanessa an idea. A rather bright one, too.

It seemed that her client, the young heir, had no idea what was really going on and what had happened this morning. He was a pompous little shit and she was sure he'd never had to do anything he didn't like before. That would change starting now.

In fact, Vanessa mused, it already had.

Most of the patrons had left, although one couple was still there, tucked onto a wide lounge seat together and sharing a bowl-shaped cup of coffee or cappuccino or something. She asked Chadwick, who had done little more than sip tea and stare into space for the last hour, "What time is it?"

"Quarter to midnight. Why?"

Vanessa flipped her laptop closed. "Let's go."

"Where to?" Chadwick followed right behind her, close enough that she could feel his breath on her head. She thought of the billy-club he had hidden in his trousers and shook her head to erase the image from her mind.

Exiting the shop, Vanessa said, "We should be hearing a report from The Network any moment now, and I want to be ready."

"Aren't we going to wait for the money?"

"That may not happen for another..." she calculated in her mind and said, "seventeen hours."

"What if it doesn't?"

"It will." She stopped at the car. The heat had not disappeared with the sun, and the humidity hung in the air like sweaty pantyhose. "The client has clear instructions."

Chadwick got in the passenger side. "Did you specify a time zone?"

"What do mean, time zone?"

"Well." Chadwick touched the flat portion of the dash in front of him. "We're in Florida—"

"Yes, I know we're in Florida."

"And the client is in Texas, correct?" He slid his finger down the dash and to the left.

She bowed her head toward the wheel in exhaustion. "Correct."

"And the bank. Well. It's in the Bahamas." He slid his finger all the way past where he'd pointed first and stopped to the right of that spot. So, that's three separate time zones. How does he know which one is the one that matters?"

Vanessa stared at Chadwick with her mouth half open. She tilted her head and leaned toward him, saying, "You know. You're right."

With a huge smile of satisfaction he leaned back against the window.

She waved him toward her, as if she would kiss him for his unending brilliance.

He cocked his head, hesitated and leaned forward.

She bent to him, opened her lips slightly, and when he closed his eyes, she bit his nose.

Hard.

"*Ouch!*" He yelled and pushed away. "What did you do that for?" He asked, rubbing his nose franticly.

"Because you're a dolt."

"What do you mean?" He kept rubbing.

"It doesn't matter what time zone we're in, all that matters is that he wires the money before the bank closes. Tomorrow. Do you understand?"

"And, I thought you said we only get half the money anyway. We won't get the rest until the job is done."

"Yes, we get half up front. But that half is now triple the first half we received. Get it?"

"I think so."

"Take your time."

After a full minute he said, "I get it."

"Splendid, I'll alert Mensa." Watching him rub his nose, she took notice that he did have large hands. No, they were gigantic. She leaned back and looked at the floorboard. His shoes were huge too.

"What are you looking at?"

She glanced at his crotch and then away. "Nothing."

"Perhaps we should rent some rooms. Get some proper rest. It has been a long day, fishing and all."

He said something else, but the mention of hotels sent her mind spinning again and she wondered what was wrong with her, thinking about sex at a time like this. Maybe it was those shagging dogs that had gotten her all riled up. Did that make her twisted? Thinking of sex with Chadwick? I mean, really, Vanessa.

She said, "Not a chance."

"Why not?"

"We're already exposed having rented this vehicle. I don't want my...sorry, our...names on anything else. Even if we use new aliases."

"Then what, we sleep here? In the car?"

"Haven't you ever?"

"Of course, but...alone."

"You don't snore, do you?" She crossed her arms.

"No." He glanced at her. "Do you?"

"Only after sex." There it was again. Dammit.

"Pardon?"

"Nothing," she said.

He glanced around, as if he hadn't heard it. "Well, it won't work here. Too many lights."

"What about there?" She pointed to the opposite edge of the parking lot where the spaces were lined by a row of tall hedges and a lamp had burned itself out, leaving the corner quite dark. She wondered if he knew what she was thinking. She wondered herself just what on earth she was thinking. Perhaps the stress had finally toppled her. Made her stark mad.

And she realized she was...wet.

"As good a spot as any, I suppose."

Exhaling, Vanessa said, "Good, then." She started the car and backed out. As she was driving across the lot, she couldn't stop her mind from snapping right back to it. The next thing she knew she said, "Chaddy, tell me something?"

"What?" He sounded cross.

She blurted out. "Your...thingy."

He eyed her. "What about it?"

"Well..." she said, as she drove straight across the empty spaces, happy there weren't any parking bumpers in the lot. "It's just that it seems...quite large."

"What would you know about it?"

"I've touched it."

"Not really."

"And I've seen your hands." She circled the car to fit into the corner spot, the darkest one with the most cover. "And, I did notice, your feet are quite large too."

"Vanessa!" He squirmed in his seat.

"Go on, tell me."

"Tell you what?"

Vanessa parked the car and pushed the emergency brake down with her foot, then cut the engine. "How big is it? Exactly."

He turned away. "Big enough."

"Can I see it?"

"Good God no! We're working here."

"We're not working now, we're waiting."

"No!"

"Why not? I won't bite it, I promise." She giggled.

"I said no!" He stared at her, and even in the dark she could see that his face had flushed bright red.

"I just don't..." she leaned to him and peered over the center glovebox and at his crotch, then continued, "think I've seen one quite that large before."

"I'm sure you haven't."

"C'mon then." She raised her chin. "Give us a look."

"Absolutely not." He had his arms crossed now, his back pasted to the door.

She needed to ease his anxiety about the nakedness of it, perhaps. Make him feel safe? She said, "Look, I'm sorry about your nose."

"Never mind." He reached up and rubbed the red spot, then eyed her.

"Also..."

He squinted now, but said nothing.

She continued, "I promise to not say a thing about it to anyone. Ever." She shook her head and frowned.

He stayed silent.

"And…" she continued, "I promise not to do anything but sit back and…watch."

"Watch what?"

"You take it out. Maybe, you know…play with it a bit."

"Oh for God's sake, you must be joking."

"I assure you," she said wide-eyed. "I'm not joking."

"Well I am not going to play with it."

"Can I, then?"

"God, no!"

"Why not? I said I wouldn't bite."

"I am not an amusement ride!"

"Oh, but you could be." She nodded high and hard.

"Vanessa, what has gotten into you?"

"Let me see it."

"No!"

"But a peek."

"No!"

"A hint?" She reached over and put her hand in the spot between his legs. He jumped back, but it was too late, she'd had a good feel. It was half-hard now, perhaps from all the talk. "Oh my!"

"Wait!"

"For what?" She rubbed harder and it got…harder. Focused on nothing but the size of this monstrous thing, she couldn't stop.

Chadwick tried to grab the door handle, but hit the lever instead, sending his seat all the way back to become a lounger.

"Good idea," Vanessa said, and before he could respond, she had his zipper down, the knight out of its castle, and both her hands on it. "Oh dear Lord!"

And with a simple loud groan, Chadwick had lost the fight.

The next thing she knew, Vanessa had her panties off, her dress up over her head, and her feet planted flat against the windshield, Sir James between her thighs and her hands bracing herself against the thrust. The wonderful, amazing, entrancing and all-encompassing…

Thrust.

One orgasm. A second.

Another.

Then a mind-blowing, record-breaking fourth.

All but screaming into her own forearm, Vanessa drenched in sweat now, had her fifth and largest, most exquisite and final orgasm at the same time that Sir James came.

And as she fell back into the seat, one foot stuck in the steering wheel, the windshield wipers going, the music bumped to loud, she heard herself say the oddest words of, "Vivat Rex! Vivat Rex!"

Long Live the King.

And she collapsed.

When they arrived at the marina, Lew quietly begged Finn to keep a lid on the whole guard dog thing, and Finn assured him that he would handle it. Then, after a mildly pained look, Lew locked the dogs in the master stateroom, marched back up to the wheelhouse and navigated the yacht out of the marina. A few minutes later, they were in deep water and heading due East to the North of Bimini, toward Freeport.

Nikki agreed to stay with Lew and keep him awake for the trip, though she conceded that this was probably unnecessary, as Lew chomped his second bowl of cocoa puffs with Red Bull.

"No milk?" Colleen had asked. When Lew shrugged, mouth too full to respond, she nodded and faded to a stateroom for rest.

Finn snuck off to his own stateroom to crash too. He was thankful Lew had kept the dogs from barking, but wondered what he had done to quiet them. He didn't wonder too hard though, and with the hum of the motors and gentle rocking of the yacht in the current he drifted into a solid state of sleep. But not for long.

Nikki visited first.

Sitting on the edge of the bed and glancing around, she asked, "So, what did the Starship Enterprise cost, anyway?"

Finn eased an eye open. "Lew said it's worth over two million."

"I believe it," she said, looking around.

A long span of silence hung between them until Finn asked, "What's on your mind, Nikki?"

She sighed long and hard and said, "You gonna' tell me what the kid did?"

Finn squeezed his eyes shut and blinked them open to wake up. "I have no idea."

"And are you sure they're after him and not you?"

"Why do you ask that?"

"Just saying."

He nodded. Fair enough. "Nikki, I haven't chased fugitives in almost a decade now. Anyone I helped put away is ancient history."

"Maybe, but prison is nothing but time, and there's plenty of it —especially for plotting revenge."

Finn shook his head. "You heard what Colleen said about this group. They're high flyers, only work for the ones who make royalty look poor. All my guys lost their money before prison."

She sighed. "If that is true...and assuming..."

"Assuming what?"

"Assuming she's not lying." She twisted her lips. "I mean, really Patrick. She knows about this MI6 guy but not who hired him? She's CIA, if anyone would know, she would."

"Maybe."

"Well I think she's full of shit."

He pushed up onto an elbow. "Got a theory?"

"No, but." She eyed him. "Is Lew fucking someone he shouldn't be? Owner's wife or maybe an owner?"

Finn gave Nikki an *are you serious* look and said, "An owner?"

"Hey, no judgment here."

Finn sighed and started to rebut the remark but decided against it. He said, "And how would that involve me?"

"You know about it and maybe you've been hiding it? I don't know…"

"Look, nothing like that has happened or is happening, okay?" Finn lay back down. "Why don't you go get some rest, it sounds like you need it too."

"Yeah, yeah." She stood up. "One more thing."

"Yes?" His eyes were closed as he answered.

"Why did you call Colleen?"

Finn opened one eye again and said, "That was a mistake."

"A big one," Nikki said.

Then she left.

Finn fell asleep a few minutes later, but soon woke to another figure entering the room.

Colleen.

Squinting his eyes open, Finn peered through the darkness as she got closer. He listened while keeping his breathing rhythmic, pretending he was still asleep.

She leaned close enough that he could smell her perfume.

She stood over him, still and quiet, and Finn waited to see if she did what he thought she would do. His mind flashed to a moment much like this, two years back.

They had been living in Boston, separate apartments, but staying with each other almost every night since their engagement. He had been on the road agenting for a full week and gone straight home to wait for her. Of course, she'd been working on a criminal case and never arrived before midnight that month. That didn't bother Finn, though. He expected it from the moment they first got involved.

But when she had entered his bedroom that night, Finn had been asleep for a solid two, maybe three hours. She'd undressed without word. Then she'd slipped into the bed. She'd touched him awake. And they'd made love without ever saying hello.

Twice.

He'd fallen back asleep and then woken to an empty apartment. She'd gone back to work. When he wandered into the kitchen for coffee, he noticed she'd been snooping around again.

She'd done it twice before, but he'd chalked it up to new-relationship curiosity.

Now it seemed habitual.

And she'd gotten sloppy, leaving two clues. One, his laptop had been closed abruptly causing it to go to sleep rather than shut down. She had logged in as Finn, not herself. And two, his phone was in his front right jeans pocket. He always carried his phone in the left pocket. Never the right.

After that, it took Finn three days and about seventy phone calls to figure out the truth about Colleen Coffey.

She wasn't born in Albany, New York.

She had lived in Boston for over a decade, not one year.

She was not an only child whose parents had died when she was five. In fact, she had two brothers and a sister, and her parents were very much alive—all of whom she was apparently estranged from, or maybe just hiding from.

Because she didn't work at the EPA in Cambridge.

She worked for the CIA.

In the Clandestine Division.

And that's all Finn needed to know. Because in the end, you can't trust the girl with trust issues.

Now, with her standing still above him, Finn thought he heard her say, "You don't know the mistake you're making." And she left.

When he woke the next morning, he wondered if she'd been there at all.

The buzzing, incessant buzzing was what woke Vanessa from the deepest, most satisfying sleep she'd had in over a decade. She'd left her vibrator on and it was tickling her foot. Prying her eyes open to the sunlight, she began to re-orient herself to her surroundings. Was she in her flat in London? No, too bright. In her new apartment in LA? Too hot and stuffy. A steam room? Blinking to consciousness, Vanessa realized she was in a car. A passenger seat. Why was her *jimmy* at her feet?

She tilted her head to see that Sir James Chadwick was driving. Wait, no, he had fallen asleep too.

She jolted awake and sucked in a fast breath. The car. It wasn't moving.

With her heart still racing, she glanced at the floor. The vibration was no *jimmy* at all, it was her phone. It had buzzed her awake. A quick look at the dash told her it was after ten am.

They'd overslept.

"Bloody Hell!" She yelled and Chadwick woke so hard that his head popped up and hit the roof.

"Ouch!" He bent forward to rub it and hit his forehead on the steering wheel. "Bugger!"

"Oh." Vanessa frowned, watching the spectacle. Then she bent to pick up her phone. A *617* area code indicated that it was from Boston. She knew better, though. It was actually a sophisticated satellite and cellular loop that Stanley—their operator who had been nicknamed Relay—had programmed to hide their Headquarters' true whereabouts, The Bahamas.

She answered it quick.

"We've had a change of plans," Relay said.

"What sort of change?" She rubbed the sleep from her eyes.

"Your party. It's departed. We believe it's en-route to The Bahamas."

"Don't tell me. Freeport."

"That's our guess."

"Guess, is it?" Vanessa took a long deep breath in and exhaled so loudly that it came out like a raspy shriek and Chadwick jumped in his seat again. He didn't hit his head, though. Too bad.

"When?"

"They should be reaching shore in approximately three hours, according to our sources."

They were headed where the money was and would soon pick up the trail leading to the Home Office. Then her.

"Perfect." She hung up.

And that's when she noticed her panties were in a ball on the floor of the vehicle. Oh dear. Chadwick's zipper was undone. And she recalled the interlude. All of it. Or them. A shiver crawled across her thighs and then up her neck.

But glancing at Chadwick, she caught the pulp-eating grin spanning from eyebrow to eyebrow on his camel-shaped face. Her stomach turned, then it flipped. Ignoring his request for an update, she fumbled in her purse for her cigarettes and lit one fast with shaky hands. She calmed her mind, told herself it was a one-off. It would never, ever happen again.

Ever.

Taking a long, deep inhale of the cigarette, she vowed it.

CHAPTER THIRTEEN

TRACE PRIED HIS EYES OPEN AND GLANCED at the clock by the bedside. The damned front desk forgot his wakeup call. Sitting up, his head began to pound and he realized he was naked as a newborn colt. He glanced back at the other side of the bed, empty, then to the floor.

Her arms and legs spread wide like a giant starfish, Faith was naked too. A ray of sunlight cut through the slats of wooden blinds and streaked across her white ass. Her arm, having knocked the phone off the hook, sat tangled in the cord.

Hence the missed wake-up call.

Trace stood up and the world spun hard, sending him back to the bed.

Twenty minutes and a can of mini-bar Coke later, Trace headed to the lobby. He'd left Faith comatose on the bedroom floor, hoping her ass got sunburned. They were still playing bongo music throughout the lobby, and he went straight outside. The air was a little cooler coming in from the Atlantic, as opposed to back home, where the Gulf turned Houston into an oily steam bath. At least the air here was breathable.

Donning his island daywear—Polo Purple Label shorts, green suede Gucci loafers, and a silky burnt orange Tommy Bahama shirt—Trace slipped on his new bright red custom Tom Ford sunglasses. He didn't wear any Ray Ban or Oakley garbage. These cost him over a thousand bucks and looked like it.

The concierge followed him outside and waved a cab over from the far side of the porte-cochere. Trace waited for him to open the door and then gave the guy an American dollar for the effort.

More bongo music in the cab, but Trace had his phone out and told the guy he needed to make some calls, could he please turn it down. The cabbie nodded his Rastafarian beaded braids and said *whatever you want Mon* and turned it off.

Silence.

Checking his missed calls, he saw that he had three messages from Melissa. What the hell was she thinking calling him while he was with Faith? And then he had the grave feeling that something was wrong. Maybe she was pregnant. Or worse, she'd gotten caught by her husband Chance. Oh that would suck. At least the pregnancy could be undone.

Trace stared at the phone. One message was thirty-four seconds. The second was over a minute long and the third was almost two! Thinking long and hard about it, Trace decided to do the single thing that made the most sense and protected him in every way.

Erase all three.

That way, whatever it was, Trace could claim he never knew. How could he have helped? The messages never came to him in the Third World known as the Bahamas. And three quick touches later, the messages were gone.

Trace immediately felt better.

Putting his head back against the grimy seat, Trace closed his eyes. Nothing but a boring road from the hotel to the end of the island with a bunch of woods in-between. A minute later, he drifted deep into a hangover nap.

When Trace opened his eyes again, the cabbie was bent over him, shaking his shoulder.

Trace wiped the drool from his chin and blinked hard a few times. His sunglasses had fallen to the floor. Picking them up, he said, "Okay, okay, Relax Ziggy."

The guy stepped back and gave Trace an offended look.

Trace gave him an extra dollar for his pain and suffering of being likened to someone with musical riches, then got out.

The cab spun off, kicking rocks and dirt all over Trace's legs, and he swatted the dust off then looked around. Manny had a nice little setup out here. The drive-up value was shit, just a pastel green, maybe light blue—hard to tell with the shades—wooden house with a pea-gravel path to the entrance. But it did have a pond. Though it was crowded by a bunch a crap brush and looked more like a hole than anything.

Trace strode to the front door and, unable to find a doorbell, he settled for a traditional knocking of three times with his knuckles. Then, flipping up his sunglasses to the top of his head—it was rude to greet someone with them over the eyes in America, so he assumed it would be here too—he waited.

The house was more of a purple, actually.

Trace hoped this yahoo island-ite was easier to work with in person than through text messages. Their exchanges had been frustrating for Trace, as he had no idea if Manny understood the urgency of the situation. He needed fifteen sharks by summer's end, and Manny had only caught five so far. In fact, he'd caught more stingrays than hammerheads.

Ridiculous.

Maybe it was because Manny was a hoppy Rastafarian like the cab driver and most of the other people on these islands. Next time he'd be more careful about his hires. Or at least meet them, be sure they were responsible before starting anything. In any case, he'd have to have a little talk with Tabia about this, she was the one who'd recommended the loser.

Rocking back and forth on his heels, Trace checked his watch. He was barely an hour late, not so bad. Manny should respect that a busy man like Trace would be a little late anyway. He had real work to do, he wasn't fishing all day.

He knocked again, three quick taps.

Five minutes later, Trace was still standing at the front door, waiting.

He knocked once more. This time he rapped five full loud times, an obvious show of irritation.

Still nothing.

Sighing, Trace walked down the path to the driveway and around toward the back of the house. Here, as he made his way over the crest, the dark blue ocean came into view. The purple house opened up to a wall of glass in the back with a long white balcony looking out to the ocean. A wooden bridge-like walkway zig-zagged down the rocky cliff and ended at some docks below, where a small boat sat— a dinghy, really, 30-feet-long at most. It looked like some sort of fishing boat, what with all the wires, rod-holders and the steering wheel way up on top of a deck.

Pulling his sunglasses back down to cut the glare from the ocean, Trace tromped down the bridge toward the dock. Before he got there, though, a nice little number emerged from the boat.

With long, tan legs, a firm little ass and yes, blonde—almost bleached—hair, the chick was smoking hot...in an athletic, x-games kind of way, anyway. No makeup, though. And no jewelry. Still, Trace would definitely fuck her.

After the job was finished, of course. Manny being a client and all, Trace couldn't go fucking the guy's wife. Yet.

"Well, well. He arrives." She said, wiping her hands on her cut-off jeans. Her voice was higher than he expected and kind of sensual. Smart move for Manny to have the hot chick meet the clients.

A bit out of breath from the steep decline, and unable to stop staring at her legs, Trace said, "The cab driver got lost."

"Nice sunglasses," she said.

Trace smiled. The smartest babes could always tell which guys had the cash. "They're Tom Fords." He pulled them off and inspected them.

"Fords." She stepped up onto the dock and walked over, barefoot, then stared at the shades.

"You know, the fashion designer." Trace said. Might as well lay the roadwork for future piping, right?

She said, "They look like women's glasses."

Trace's face flushed red and he put the glasses in his pocket. "I have an appointment with Manny. Where is he?"

Trace spun around, searching, but all he saw was the chick holding her hand out. "No way. You're the shark-guy?"

"Way." No fingernail polish. Not even a bra.

Great, a lesbian.

Trace stared at the hand for a moment then shook it fast and wiped his own hand on his pants. "Trace Cashmore, as in The Cashmores." He paused for a moment and waited for it to sink in.

She raised her brows in a questioning sort of way. As if she didn't know.

"Of Texas."

"Oh..." she winked. "Sounds like you have a rich daddy."

Trace's face flushed again and before he could think of a comeback, she said, "I do too." Then turned and walked away. "Let's go then, we're late."

Staring as Manny walked away—what a waste of a great little ass—then climbed into a boat even smaller than the fishing rig, so small he hadn't even noticed it before, he said, "What do you mean, go?"

He hoped she didn't think he was getting in that thing with her. It was a goddamned skiff, not even a real boat. Like a long rowboat, except white and with a tall platform for poling in shallow water. He'd seen duck blinds bigger than that thing.

She tilted her head. "You do want to see the sharks, yes?"

Trace glanced back up the cliff at the house. "Of course, but..."

"Well, Tracy...excuse me, Trace." She smiled. "They're not up there."

Trace's face flushed yet again. "I know that."

Why was he self-conscious all of a sudden? She was nothing more than a Bahamas beach bum fishing guide. A chick, no less. Trace was the heir to a billion dollar fortune. He had power and money *and* looks. He was like a triple threat.

"Is there a problem?" She pulled her hair back into a ponytail with a black rubber band.

"We're not going in that..." he laughed at her, regaining authority.

"Unless you want to swim." She shrugged. "Up to you."

He glanced at Manny and then back at the boat. "Swim?"

"I'm afraid that exhausts your choices in this case."

What was exhausting him was Manny. Tabia was definitely going to hear it from Trace now. He deserved better treatment and she knew it. He was the goddamned client. A client who could buy her whole bank and fire her if he wanted to.

Well, his dad could. Trace would just have to convince him.

Besides, who said this wasn't all part of a ploy to get Trace alone...and maybe kidnap him. For ransom. He'd heard of crazier plots. He'd never met this Manny before. What if she had some guys waiting somewhere to jump him? Tie him up. They were all the way out here at the end of the island. In the goddamned Bahamas. Did they even have police in this dump?

Trace was too smart to risk putting himself in such a precarious position. No way, no how. He folded his arms across his chest, not budging.

Manny sighed. "There's a topless beach on the way."

"Really?" Trace hurried to the boat and climbed in. "How... how far, along...the way?"

Finn stood alone at the stern of the yacht, staring out at the blue expanse before him. The damp ocean breeze cut through his wool pants and white t-shirt, remnants of his suit from the prior day, and the sun radiated behind a thin morning haze. It felt good on his bare feet for now, but in one hour the effect would be scorching.

He'd woken with a slight headache that became full-fledged with Nikki's voice.

"One fucking mile away, and we're out of gas. You believe that shit?" Nikki said, rounding the deck to join him.

"Good morning," Finn said.

"Yeah, lovely."

A black and white bird circled above them and then dove near the railing, screeching as it passed.

"The hell is that?" Nikki asked, ducking.

"Laughing gull, I think," Finn said, watching the bird glide off. "Native to the islands."

"Ugly little shits," she said.

"So...no cell signal." Finn held up his phone and checked for the seventh time. "How about radio?" He asked.

She twisted her mouth and shook her head. "He said the carpenter must have screwed with it—half of it's missing."

"Any other ideas?"

"Unless there's a service station out here."

Finn made a show of looking around.

"Then I'm fresh out of brilliance," she said.

They stood there, listening to the easy sounds of the ocean for a few moments. Then Finn nodded toward the water and said, "There's a gulf stream between Florida and the islands."

"He still fucked up."

"Plus the wind." He held up a hand. "Probably caused us to use twice as much gas."

Nikki raised both eyebrows as far as she could. With the orange bob on her head, she looked —and spoke, for that matter—like a character from South Park. "Yeah, well, I didn't plan on this trip." She pointed to her head. "I didn't plan on this."

"Hope not."

"Watch it," she said, pulling a strand to look at. "And I certainly didn't plan on getting stuck in the middle of the ocean with that retard at the helm."

He watched her for a moment and said, "Let me ask you something. The calls yesterday? From the GM's?"

"What about them?" She dropped the orange strand and looked up.

"Did any of them say why they were calling?"

"Nope. I assumed it was all congrats this and that."

"Not during playoffs, they wouldn't."

She tilted her head. "Good point."

"And you said Cashmore called. Was it senior or junior?"

"Senior. Why?"

"Curious." Finn scrolled through the oddities of the last two days. The phone calls, the hitman named Benny, the British couple, Colleen. A thread of connection was in there somewhere.

"I'll tell you what's curious." She raised her open palms in the air. "Colleen showing up last night, out of the blue."

"I told you, I called her."

"And she just happened to be coming to Miami? Please, Patrick."

Finn exhaled. Nikki was right and he knew it. Colleen had something up her sleeve, no doubt, but what it was and how she could be involved, he hadn't figured out yet. Still, he couldn't get Nikki too riled up about it. She was like a compressed shock spring, and he didn't want her coming uncoiled.

Not yet, at least.

Finn leaned onto the railing and motioned for Nikki to come closer.

She turned and propping her elbows up on the railing.

He whispered, "Look. The way I see it, we need to play her game for as long as it doesn't hurt us. If Colleen wants to make her career on this case, so be it. As long as Lew is protected and we're in the clear, I don't care."

"You know she reminds me of Catherine Tramell."

"That's a character from a movie. Not real."

"I think the icepick is missing from the kitchen."

"Relax, Nikki."

"Not yet. Here comes Ms. Tramell now."

Finn turned to see Colleen walking toward them. Barefoot too, she had pulled her hair back and wore large black sunglasses. Her blouse was unbuttoned one notch below acceptable.

Not helping his case with Nikki.

"Call that Company chopper to rescue us yet?" Nikki asked.

Colleen glanced behind her and said, "This thing can't land a helicopter, can it?"

Nikki rolled her eyes and pushed off the railing. "I'm going to kitchen. You know, count the utensils."

"Good luck," Finn said.

Nikki walked about six inches too close to Colleen, forcing her to lean back a bit to let Nikki pass.

When Nikki disappeared behind the glass, Colleen said, "I get the feeling she doesn't like me very much."

"Your intuition is uncanny."

"Are you the reason?"

"Me, how?"

"You know." She traced a finger to the top of her blouse.

Finn shook his head. "She's like a baby sister."

"More like a baby viper." Colleen took a step closer and leaned on the railing, appearing quite at ease all of a sudden. "Nice out here."

"For the moment," he said, as a laughing gull, maybe the same one from before, circled above them. Finn turned to Colleen. "Sleep okay?"

"Best sleep I've had in months."

Finn eyed her. Was this more bullshit? Or was she really better? Either way, they had to press on, so he was fine with it. He said, "What else do you know about this so-called network?"

"Already told you all I know, all we know."

"Did you locate the bank account?"

"There's the rub."

"Rub?"

She smiled. "I got a voicemail sometime last night—before we got out of range I guess. Anyway, we know Benny opened an account at First Bahamian Trust."

"But?'

"But...the bank is denying it."

"So...we go visit them."

"Agree." She squinted in the direction of Freeport. "Assuming we can get there."

"Lew said he has a raft here somewhere. We just need to find it and hook up the small outboard."

"How big?" She asked.

"It can fit four."

"Patrick, I'm not great at math, but..." she looked back to the wheelhouse.

Finn said, "Think about it, Lew won't leave his dogs. And I don't think we should leave him all alone on this yacht."

"Dogs?" She glanced around, looking panicked.

"Relax, they've been...asleep." Finn wondered what would happen after whatever medication Lew had given them for the trip wore off.

She said, "Lew can stay. He is an adult."

Finn eyed her.

"I'll go."

Figuring she would volunteer herself, he said, "And I'll join you."

"Why?"

"In case."

"You mean, in case I need a big, strong man around?" She turned and leaned closer to him.

"Don't you?"

Her skin was smooth and the sun shined on her high cheekbones as she said, "I'm pretty good at avoiding trouble." She leaned even closer—so close that he could feel her warm breath on his cheek—as she continued, "at least the wrong kind."

"Like being overpowered?" He smelled her skin as he took in a breath.

"Is that what you'd like to do?" She turned ever so slightly, so that her thigh brushed against his groin. "Overpower me?"

Finn glanced down and regretted it the moment he looked. Colleen was wearing a white lace bra underneath the blouse and it was cut in a way that showed the fullness of her breasts and pushed them inward, creating a deep crease of cleavage. The memory of being with her made his mouth water.

"Patrick," she whispered.

He let his gaze meet hers. "Colleen."

She reached out and took his hand, saying, "Would you consider—"

But before she could finish, a loud bang sounded and both Glovesave and Kicksave bounded across the deck, Lew behind them, yelling, "No! Sit. I said SIT!"

Slipping and hopping along the deck, the two dogs barked at each other as they ran toward Finn and Colleen

Colleen pulled away and shielded her body with her arms stretched straight out.

Both dogs bounded toward the railing.

"SIT!" Lew yelled again.

Too late, though, one of the dogs jumped. Good thing the railing was too high. His front paws reached over, but his gigantic body held him back, and he fell onto the deck with a loud thump. The other dog tried the exact same trick and ended up on top of the first.

By then Lew had them both by the collars and was dragging them backward toward the door leading inside. "Sorry dudes, they love water. Can't keep them out of it, eh?"

Finn turned back around and stared at Colleen, who had drawn her pistol. She stood with it pointed straight at the dogs being dragged away.

"A bit excessive, don't you think?" Finn said.

She eased the pistol into a holster at her lower back as she continued, "You know how I feel about dogs."

"Right, but shooting them seems…unreasonable."

"Big dogs, too," she said, smoothing her clothes. "Who knows what they would do to a stranger."

"I don't think these dogs…" but he let his voice trail off before finishing, respecting Lew's request—albeit futile—to keep the sensitive issue under wraps.

"You don't think, what?"

And before Finn had to say anything else, Lew yelled from the wheelhouse, "No! Kicksave, down! Stop it. Oh man, not again!"

And Colleen saw the beautiful glory for herself.

"I lied," Manny said. She was at the top of the platform, above him now, poling the skiff through shallow water.

Bitch, Trace thought, leaning forward with both elbows on his knees. They'd driven for almost twenty minutes straight out into the ocean, and were now in the middle of nowhere.

No land visible. No other boats.

And no topless chicks.

Just a blazing sun, the occasional gray-black sea bird, and a circle of mangroves up ahead. It was bullshit.

Trace sat back and eyed her from below as she poled. "So how did you make your money?"

"What do you mean?

"You said you were rich."

"No. I said my dad was."

Semantics. "Then how did *he* make it?"

"Beer."

Of course. Her family was a distributor. That made sense. Trashy money, they were a dime a dozen in Texas. "Miller?"

"That's one of them."

One of them? That made no sense. You only distributed for one company, you couldn't have two. Then he realized it. Even worse than a distributor, she really was a bottom feeder.

"A bottler."

"Something like that."

"Right." Her granddaddy probably made glass for beer and coca cola. No rocket-science there. She was embarrassed by it, as she should be, and with almost no effort he'd put her in her place.

They reached the edge of the mangroves and Manny stopped poling. Climbing back down to the deck, she pulled her shirt out of her cutoffs and tied it in a knot at her ribs. Then she grabbed a bag full of dead fish from a cooler hidden under the floor and—without warning, just a *swoosh*—she was over the side and diving in.

"What the hell are you doing?" He yelled.

Swimming on her back and dragging the bag, her dark nipples showing through the knotted shirt, she said, "Shark time, big boy."

Trace muttered, "I'm not getting in the water with these shoes."

"I'd advise you wear something. Coral can slice your feet open, like a razor knife."

"You're not wearing any."

"I'm experienced."

He stared at his Guccis. Whatever. There was no way was he going to ruin a thousand dollar pair of shoes with salt water. That would be idiotic. His feet could heal, but these were not a typical pair of Guccis. They'd been the last lime green suede pair at Nieman's and he was damned lucky to have gotten them the day before the trip. If he ruined them, he'd have to wait like four to six weeks to get another pair.

Plus, he'd have nothing to wear to the casino that night. Totally not worth it.

Besides. *If a skinny chick could do it.* He slipped the loafers off.

Climbing up on the lip of the boat, he considered the shirt next. He wanted to take it off, but the sun was baking hot and he had no sunscreen.

Judging the depth, Trace stood up on his toes, prepared to launch, and then stopped. What about sharks? The ones they hadn't caught yet...

Scanning the water fast, all he could see was the bright glimmer of the surface.

He hoped there weren't any trolling around the flats for food.

But if they were, their fins would show, right?

Of course.

He settled his mind and bounced back up on his toes and sprung from the boat and into the water. A smooth, easy dive took him underwater and he glided for about ten feet until he felt a jab and scrape across his ribcage.

Something was attacking him! It had his shirt!

He flailed and kicked, swinging his arms and swatting at whatever it was...then planted his feet and jumped from the ocean floor, screaming as he exited the water.

"Shark! Shark!"

He ran in the water, backwards and then turned, running and swimming and falling and crawling to get away, but it had him, it was pulling his ribs and arm. All he could see was its long, white, twisted belly.

"Help! *Help!*"

He fell under and it bit his arm. Then his foot and his knee.

Gulping water and feeling like he was going to drown, the beast pulling him under, Trace saw in a flash of what it must have been like for all those wealthy people to suffer death in the deep ocean because a lesser, greedy man had built a ship called the Titanic.

He was just like them.

And then he felt his arm jerk from his body and something soft and strong was pulling him up off the floor of the ocean. His head burst from the water and he sucked in air and coughed and almost fell again, but he didn't.

Manny was holding him upright and...

Laughing.

Gasping for air and angry, but too tired from the fight to care, Trace was barely able to articulate, "Why are you laughing? The shark, where is it?"

Shaking her head, she looked him up and down. He followed her gaze.

His shirt was torn from collar to ribcage, blood seeping from a gash in his chest. His arms and both knees were bitten up and bleeding. And his feet had glass in them, or was it the shark's teeth? Did their teeth come out when they bit? They had so many of them...

He spun in a circle, looking for the beast.

Still laughing, Manny said, "Tracy—"

"Where is it? Where?"

He spun again, and searched, and then...he stopped. Glancing back to where he had swum from, a thin trail of blood dissipated in the water, momentarily coloring the drift. The water was calm. There were no fins anywhere. There was nothing at all, but the quiet breeze and blazing sun. And then he saw it.

A thin, twisted piece of white coral—about four feet long—with a swatch of his orange shirt hanging from it, swaying in the easy current.

Manny leaned over and reached into the water. When she came back up, she handed him his Persols. They had a scratch across one lens. Dammit.

She said, "Ready to see some real sharks?"

Grabbing the sunglasses, Trace hobbled through the water as he followed Manny into the tangle of trees. Rooted in the ocean floor, they were about six to eight feet tall and bushed with little green leaves.

After a few minutes, and between winces, Trace said, "So, what? Is there some sort of tank in here?"

"Not a tank, but..."

"How do you get the sharks out here?"

Tranquilizer," she said, matter of fact.

"Really?"

She gave him a look that made him feel stupid again, then said, "No."

He supposed they would drown if asleep in the water, but didn't know, so he said, "Of course not, I knew that. But then how?"

"I have my ways."

Trace rolled his eyes. This chick was a piece of work. He was glad he wasn't married to her. Though he wished he wasn't married at all. Actually, that wasn't true. He got the kids as deductions on his taxes, that was nice.

"Right there." She pointed between the branches. A black and gray hammerhead cut through the glassy water, about ten yards away. The shark was about three feet long.

Trace stumbled backwards and Manny grabbed his wrist. "Relax, big guy, they're fenced in."

He bent lower to look. A dark gray metal structure spanned between the branches, forming a long fence in front of them. "Is it closed?"

Manny gave him an *are you serious?* look.

"Right," Trace said.

"C'mon, let's see if we can find the big one."

"Big one?" Trace asked as he stepped gingerly and bent to get through the branches. His face dipped below the water and he caught a silvery flash as he blinked to the surface. The saltwater stung his eyes and he squeezed them with his fingers, wiping the water away.

"I call him Elvis."

"Elvis."

"Yep." She led Trace to the edge of the fence. "He has a way of disappearing."

Trace inspected the fence, wondering if there was some sort of regulation to ensure it maintained structural integrity, especially in this saltwater. He glanced around. It was containing sharks, for God's sake.

"What?" She said.

Trace took a step back. "How did...who...I hope you have a permit for this."

"A permit?" She raised her brow. "Sure, Trace." She waded back to the fence and climbed up and motioned for him to join her.

Trace hesitated. This crazy bitch had serious mental issues. No way was he getting up there.

She leaned back. "You need to see from up here."

"I don't like...sharks," he said. "It's a phobia. I was... diagnosed."

"I see." She gave him a puzzled look and continued, "then... why would you buy them?"

"Never mind." Trace waded forward and grabbed the fence, then hefted himself up. The fence leaned back a few inches with his weight.

Manny gave him a sideways glance. "Time to cut down on the red meat, maybe?"

Too engrossed with the scene before him, Trace didn't respond.

In a makeshift circle and partially shaded by the mangroves, the fence must have extended a good thirty yards across. The water was a bit deeper in the center, as if it had been dredged. On the far edge, the unmistakable glide of three hammerhead sharks cut the clear water.

"They're small," he said, in full disappointment. "That's all you've gotten?"

"Elvis is bigger...if we can find him." She hefted the bag from the water and hung it on a post of the fence. Loosening the string, she pulled a few dead fish out and flung them into the pool. Within a few seconds, the three sharks raced across the pool and into a bloody battle for food. Two sharks tore at the same fish, sending a fog of blood and remnants to the surface and around them.

"Good news is," she continued, "I've found a great spot to catch them. These guys seem to be congregating every morning at a place called The Cathedral."

"So why don't we have more?"

She gave Trace a glance, "The fishing there is a bit dangerous. It's a blue hole. Ever heard of one?"

"Oh yeah! I saw that on National Geographic. An underground tunnel sucks water in with the tides or something."

"Sort of." She tossed another fish out. "But this one has a vortex that could swallow that skiff whole," she nodded to the edge of the trees, "and me, if I'm not careful."

"So what do you do?"

She shrugged, "I'm careful."

What a weirdo, Trace thought, watching the sharks roam the edges for food.

Manny threw a few more fish. "Now. If we could just find that sneaky little Elvis." She searched the water. "He's here somewhere, maybe right next to us." She peered over the edge and looked down.

Trace squeezed his toes tight and leaned away from the edge. Then, realizing he was holding his breath, he inhaled deep a few times to catch up on oxygen.

"There."

"Where?" Trace's heart began to pound in his chest and he wanted to let go, run away from this crazy person. But he couldn't do that without looking wimpy and he couldn't look wimpy to a chick. Especially not this crazy-ass bitch. He needed to show control and physical strength, especially after the coral incident.

"Straight ahead." She reached for the bag of fish, but it came untied and dropped into the water behind Trace. "Damn," she said, then hopped off the fence and into the water.

And Trace saw the shark. The enormous, hulking, massive, largest hammerhead he had ever seen in his entire life. The head itself was about the width of a Land Rover. And it was swimming. Straight. Toward.

Him.

But Trace had become paralyzed. He couldn't let go of the fence. He couldn't run. Instead, he watched, mesmerized by the casual, graceful glide of the monster. Trace felt strong, staring down the beast. He would show Manny how to deal with a creature like this. Careful, ha! He'd give her a little lesson on braveness.

He'd show her how to man up.

"Help with these fish, would you Trace?" Manny called behind him. "We need to get Elvis some food before he gets mad, trust me."

Swinging his huge head back and forth, the shark gained speed. Faster. Faster.

Faster.

Until he was racing toward the fence. Right at Trace. He barreled toward him.

Faster.

Twenty feet.

"Trace?"

Ten.

"Oh shit," Manny said and stepped back.

Faster.

Five.

She slipped and fell into the mangroves.

Faster. Two.

Trace held tight, his knuckles as white as the shark's belly.

One.

Elvis rammed the fence, throwing Trace back into the trees, where he hit his head on the knot of a branch. And as he sunk into the water, eyes still open, he felt a warm pop and then saw the brown bulb of his own turd float to the surface.

Right above his own face.

CHAPTER FOURTEEN

AFTER THEY'D DONE IT TWO MORE TIMES in the Town Car passenger seat, Vanessa had renewed her vow to abstain. She then let Chadwick drive to Opal Bay while she smoked the last of her cigarettes. No longer disgusted with herself, she felt satisfied by the interludes—certain that the reason for her sudden obsession with sex had more to do with stress than anything else. It was most certainly not due to physical attraction to Chadwick.

Though, he did have that wonderful pleasure-zucchini didn't he?

Back in Walter's speedboat now, she shook her head to clear her thoughts and concentrate on the white-capped water ahead. Almost at full-throttle, she had them racing across the ocean toward Bimini. On her figure, they would arrive in Freeport in less than two hours, a mere one hour after the targets would have arrived. Not too bad, though she may have to do some damage control if the targets beat her to the bank.

She glanced behind her at the black, threatening sky hovering above Florida.

They had maybe four or five hours before the storm caught up.

Chadwick dozed in the cushions at the back of the boat, wearing a puffy red flotation device. Perhaps he didn't trust her after their last outing. Though, each time she hit a wave, the boat skipped, Chadwick popped up a few inches, and she gripped the wheel tighter. So she couldn't blame him.

But who he shouldn't be trusting were those slippery bankers. They hadn't returned either of her calls before launch this morning, and the one named Tabia had all but ignored Vanessa's requests for immediate notification that the client's new funds had arrived. Tabia had explained that their system was not set up for that type of urgency.

Bullocks.

An international institution—offshore bank, no less—like First Bahamian Trust would not only have the capability, they would boast the system to potential clients, as Vanessa was certain they had to The Network when they'd set the accounts up in the first place. Still, she hadn't met Tabia and she couldn't be sure what this low-level banker would know anyway. Perhaps the higher-ups kept the ones like Tabia in the dark for security purposes. That would make sense.

Glancing around at the empty horizon, Vanessa started to feel better about the whole situation. Now that they had all three targets headed to a single, secluded, self-contained setting, the job had become quite a measure easier.

Not to mention, the law enforcement in the Bahamas was even less attentive and threatening than that of Florida.

Yes, the plan was coming together well enough. Soon they would knock off the main subjects, no worry on the Nikki girl, they'd leave her to the Home Office. She was, after all, not Vanessa's problem. Then, after this job, Vanessa would take the money and disappear for a time. She was not in a rush to hit Century Club, like old Chaddy. She'd rather have her own holiday.

Taking long, deep breaths and feeling the pending success with each bump and spray of saltwater, Vanessa exhaled the stress and worry away. She had to admit, after all the orgasms of the last twelve hours, she felt quite liquid.

Chadwick had served his purpose and he had his merits, so she believed she was beginning to fancy the man. She peeked back at him drooling on himself.

Well. Let's not go that far.

"I thought you said it was a life raft," Colleen said, staring at the bright pink camouflaged rubber float.

All four of them stood around the boat as it finished inflating. The sun, rising fast, blistered down on them, along with a threat of humidity. If it weren't for the ocean breeze, the heat would be unbearable. Finn wondered if a storm was coming.

"It has a motor," Lew said, pointing to the device clipped to the back, about the size of an electric toothbrush.

"Can this thing even go a mile?" Colleen asked. "It looks like a toy from Sharper Image."

"I wouldn't ride in it," Nikki said, shaking her orange bob. "Shark out here could swallow that whole."

"It'll be fine," Finn said.

"Not with you in it." Nikki pointed up at him. "Thing's gonna sink."

Finn shrugged. "Maybe."

"Look, it even has its own cup holders." Lew pointed at the molded plastic cups in the sides. "See?" He twisted a can of half-empty diet coke into one of them. "Now you won't be thirsty. And it's carbonated. Lighter than air." Lew nodded hard.

Nobody responded for a minute and Nikki said, "I'm amazed you can figure out which net to stand in each game."

Lew shrugged. "I just wait until the other goalie is in his, then I know which one to skate to."

Nikki said, "Lew, your own team skates around one end for warm-ups, did you know that?"

Lew looked deep in thought for a moment, then said, "But what if they're all wrong?"

That shut everyone up, and Finn said, "The raft is perfect, Lew. Thanks."

Lew nodded and said, "Hey you look good in those clothes."

"They're a bit small." Finn checked out the black stretchy shorts and baggy yellow t-shirt.

"You look like a yoga instructor. A really big one who may have eaten a student."

"Thanks, Nikki," Finn said.

"Who's also allergic to sun," she continued, then turned to Colleen. "What's that called?"

"Photosensitivity?" Colleen said.

"Yeah that's it," Nikki said.

"Very helpful," Finn said.

"I'm not allergic to the sun," Lew said, checking out his skin. "I can get a killer tan."

"Okay, everyone. Thank you. I'm not allergic," Finn said.

"But you look like you are." Nikki said.

"Or part al-rhino."

Everyone looked at Lew, who wandered off, maybe for another coke.

Colleen said, "He seems to be all tangled up in his mental underwear."

Nikki snorted. "More like his mind's gone commando."

Ten minutes and a less than coordinated exit later, Finn and Colleen were cruising in the raft toward shore—Colleen drenched head to toe. Good thing she'd asked him to hold her cell phone for her descent down the ladder and into the raft. Though she hadn't asked him to hold her firearm, and he caught a glimpse of the SIG —a compact P229—tucked into a hip holster at her lower back. These spooks loved their SIGs, didn't they?

The raft seemed sturdy, though it would take them a good hour to get to shore at this rate. Still, the yacht was diminishing in the distance and they were moving along better than he'd expected. Fast enough that the salt water sprayed them once every few waves.

Colleen said, shielding her face with a plastic pink oar, and loud enough to overcome the high-pitched whine of the motor, "Is he really worth twelve million a year?"

"Well," Finn said, one hand on the motor's steering paddle, the other on the rubber hull. "It's what his contract pays him."

"Spoken as a true agent." Colleen raised her brow. "Now tell me the truth."

"Here's the thing," Finn said. "He was originally signed for far less."

"He's a rookie, right?"

"He was. This past season."

"But now?"

"He had a very good start."

"And?"

"And…" Finn smiled, "A very good agent."

"Brilliant, I'm sure." She gave him a patronizing smile. "So, what did this brilliant agent do to make such a young man so rich?"

And Finn sensed Colleen was wondering about the same things Finn had been mulling over the last number of hours. He wasn't about to share any theories with her, though. And he wasn't going to give her enough information to come up with the same theory on her own. So, he answered, "Contracts are confidential, but let's just say that Lew performed well enough to get a few bonuses."

"And you? Do you get a set amount, or a percentage?"

Finn eyed her. "Why?"

"Curious, that's all." She looked away.

Now he considered the possibility that Colleen was regaining interest in, not him, but his recent level of compensation. He kept it cryptic, saying, "I am rewarded for the work I do."

Colleen said, "A percentage, I see."

They continued on for a while, in silence, Finn wondering what was going through the woman's mind. She still looked fantastic.

And now, with her shirt drenched through, he had to concentrate to keep from being piggy and staring at her breasts.

She, on the other hand, had all but abandoned subtlety and stared straight at him. "Do you have a girlfriend?"

"No."

"Then, are you seeing someone?"

"Not, exactly, no."

She sat back. "You aren't married, are you?"

Finn glanced at her. If she'd been checking up on him she'd know all these answers. So she was either playing stupid or she really didn't know. He said, "I haven't been serious with anyone since you, Colleen."

She looked away. "We weren't that serious, were we?"

Well played.

But before he could answer that, Finn saw a small boat speeding toward them from a distance, its bright silver nose and sides flashing in the sun. The trajectory looked to put the boat in line with their little raft, and it was going fast enough to create a wake that would tip them right over.

"Shit," he said.

"What?"

"Could be Bahamas Coast Guard, or maybe Customs." He turned the motor to change direction, get out of the other boat's way. "Though it looks like a speedboat."

Colleen turned and settled her gaze on the boat.

"Then again, maybe they're pirates," Finn said.

"We're not in Yemen," Colleen said, then, "Well son of a bitch."

Surprised at her rare use of profanity, Finn looked back to her. "What?"

"Nothing, just..." and with the hint of cynicism, she said, "I think they're headed straight for us."

Vanessa leaned back and slowed the boat a bit. "Chaddy," she said, then, "Chadwick!"

He stirred, looking confused and rubbing his eyes. A bright red stripe had formed across his cheek, where it had been exposed to the sun. "What mum? What is it?"

"There." She pointed ahead and to the right. "See it?"

"It looks like a boat." He squinted, then said, "Or maybe a yacht."

"Not a yacht. *The* yacht, you fool."

"How can you be sure?"

"The flag. It looks like that ridiculous maple leaf."

Leaning forward and squinting harder, he said, "I don't see a leaf."

"Oh for God's sake." She jerked the wheel to the right and Chadwick fell back into the cushions and almost off the seat. She said, "You'll see I'm right."

Scrambling to sit upright, Chadwick felt his face. "I think I've become sunburned."

"I told you to use the lotion."

"I will after we have a look at that boat."

"Hand me your gun."

"Why mine?"

"Because," she said as she cut the wheel harder. "I can't get to mine while I navigate. It's…" she glanced between her breasts and said, "tucked away."

"I'll fetch it." He gave her a sordid smile.

"You wish." She couldn't help but smile back. Thoughts of another orgasm rushed through her mind and she headed them off with, "Yours, Chaddy, hurry."

"Don't call me that." He fiddled with his floatation vest and unsnapped the holster, then drew out his SIG. "And I want it back."

Vanessa took the gun. "Now get ready."

"Ready for what?"

"In case they see us, they're likely a bit jumpy after yesterday."

"But you have my weapon now."

"Oh, right." She glanced down, then back at him. "Then pay attention. You might duck if they start shooting at us."

"Well then don't get too close." He slumped back and sulked at her.

"Oh Chaddy." Vanessa slowed the boat again and said, "See?"

As they approached the rear of the yacht, the name, Five Hole, came into view, as did the large red Canadian maple leaf. But the boat sat quiet in the water and not moving, as if anchored. Two birds circled high above with no other sign of life.

"What are they doing so far out?"

Peering at the deck and the windows, Vanessa searched for any movement within but saw nothing. Not even the dogs. "Perhaps they've moored here to avoid customs."

"That wasn't very bright." Chadwick made a moronic face.

"It was if they don't want their firearms taken from them." She jerked the boat to the left and Chadwick fell again.

"What are you doing?" He pushed to sit upright.

"They're not out here, that's obvious." She throttled hard ahead, cutting a spray of saltwater in two huge streams behind them. "They've gone inland."

"How can you be so sure?" Chadwick had turned around and, kneeling on the seat, looked straight back at the yacht disappearing behind them.

"Because I do this for a living, that's how."

"And so do I," he called over his shoulder. "Go back, let's board and be sure."

"We don't have time. We have to beat them to the bank."

Chadwick shut up on that and sat back down, as Vanessa throttled even harder. "Hold on now, we're going to speed things up a bit."

"Vanessa! Wait!" Chadwick lowered himself and widened his arms to grip the seat backs.

And she gunned it.

The nose of the speedboat popped up as the motors ate then spit out the ocean behind them.

"Slow down!"

Going so fast now, with the wind gusting into her eyes, she could hardly make out the horizon before her. A daring sea gull followed from above, swooping down and squawking at her. She waved her gun at the bastard and he screeched. Then, up ahead, she saw it. A small boat of sorts with people in it. But she was going too fast to make out how many people or what type of boat. Still, she couldn't slow now.

The speedboat cut the waves then hopped high on one, sending Chadwick up in the air grasping two pillows. He thumped back down and screamed, "Vanny! I swear you'll kill us both!"

She leaned lower and squinted to see through the glass windshield.

Two figures, a man and a woman sat in a pink boat, no it appeared to be dinky little raft, and with an amazing stroke of fortune, it was Patrick Finn with a woman. She couldn't tell from there, but figured it wasn't that Nikki character—she had supposedly painted her head orange. Either way, Vanessa still held the element of surprise and was not going to waste it.

But she realized that she was going too fast.

"We're going to hit them!" Chadwick called out.

"Shush it!" Vanessa cut the wheel hard and aimed her pistol as they barreled down on the man named Finn. And as she zeroed in on the target, one hand on the wheel, her attention moved to the woman behind him. Vanessa blinked and stared, not believing her own eyes. Not only did she know this woman, she knew her well. It was Colleen. Colleen Coffey.

Her boss.

Drawing out her SIG, Colleen glanced back at the fast-approaching boat and said, "You may want to lean down a bit. You're a big target."

"It's hard to hide in the middle of the ocean, Colleen. In a raft the size of a bagel, no less."

"Right. Just keep the bagel steady then."

"Working on it."

"Is it your tail?" She asked, squinting past Finn.

Hard to tell with a quick glance back, he said, "I'd bet on it."

"Persistent."

Finn tapped the motor with a finger. "These guys really MI6?"

"Former. But yes."

"They're a bit obvious."

They hit a wave and the motor whined, coming up out of the water.

"They have other skills...apparently."

"Limited to killing?"

"Mostly."

"How many are there? In the network?"

"We don't know."

"That's reassuring," he swiveled a bit to get a better look.

The speedboat skipped then whined with each wave and Finn could make out the boat's red clay interior with the British woman from the diner at the steering wheel. A laughing gull swooped low and she swiveled toward him. He couldn't tell, but it looked like she was holding a pistol.

Was it dumb luck or had these two been following them all along?

The speedboat, clearly going way too fast to stop now, wasn't slowing or even steering. It was barreling straight toward them.

Finn said, "You may want to use that gun."

Colleen looked a mix of angry and perplexed, but she didn't shoot. She just froze, staring.

The speedboat screamed loudly as it spit and sprayed water out the back. Pummeling the water and coming at them like a missile.

Thirty feet. Twenty.

"As in now!" Finn yelled.

Colleen watched as the speedboat pounded toward them, she looked pissed.

Finn jerked the motor. The raft skipped three feet to the right, and the speedboat hit a wave and popped high, right over them—the motors screaming and saltwater spraying and drenching them both as they dove to the bottom of the raft.

Finn was up first, steadying the raft in the now-choppy water, then Colleen was up on both knees in the firing position.

A little late, Colleen.

The speedboat cut hard to the left and spun back around, creating a momentary wall of water. Then it gunned right back toward them, the laughing gull making the same turn with the boat. With one hand on the controls and the other pointing a gun at Finn, the woman stood no more than ten yards from them and had a clear shot.

"You have to pull the trigger!" Finn yelled at Colleen.

But she waited, just a half-second longer, and the British woman hesitated too. They stared each other down.

Then they both shot.

Finn felt the buzz of a bullet directly below his armpit, then he heard a thump. Not a plunk or a dink, as one would hear when a bullet hits water, but more of a hollow sound. And in that millisecond, he knew.

Before he could yell again, though, Colleen took her shot. Right as the gull swooped again.

The bullet hit the bird. The bird hit the woman's face. And the woman hit the throttle.

And the next thing that Finn knew, the boat shot forward, past them again, and skipped high, then turned, and Finn could hear the scream of the British woman, "Bloody bird!" and the yell of the man, "I told you, Vanny!" as the boat, seemingly suspended high in the air, twisted over itself like a corkscrew, once, then twice, and a final half twist flung the two Brits into the water and the boat on its head.

Then a hissing sound began—a loud, whining, *pffft* of air—and the back of the raft created bubbles as it sunk into the water.

CHAPTER FIFTEEN

MICKEL DEROUX SAT IN A WOODEN ROCKING chair, staring out to the ocean from the back porch of the small Bahamian safe house, while drinking a tall glass of ice water. The screened windows behind him vibrated with the warm ocean breeze, and a storm lamp swung from the corner of the deck. He had been going by the name Mickel for almost a month now and was getting used to it. He almost wished he could keep this one. Though he wasn't sure what his wife thought of it, he liked her cover name too. Tabia.

He glanced at his phone, standard Company issue, and then his watch. She was three minutes late, so far.

A scratching noise caught his attention, and he noticed two land crabs on the short strip of craggy lawn before him. Their blue bulbous backs glittering in the sun, they were fighting over what appeared to be an old chicken leg. The larger crab was trying to steal it from the smaller one. In a tug of war, they backed up onto the deck and across the ledge. The larger crab grabbed the leg and flung it behind himself. Then, taking hold of the smaller crab with one claw, he pinched its face with the other. The smaller crab did not give up, though, as he swung his free claw and smacked the larger in the head.

Mickel, taking a sip of water, laughed at the smaller crab's will.

The larger crab pinched harder and the smaller emitted a squeal-like sound, then jumped backwards, almost off the edge.

Still not done, though, he charged the larger crab and, crawling over him, reclaimed the chicken leg, turned and then, hefting the leg like a club, whacked the larger crab so hard that he sent it right off the deck.

Well done.

Rocking and glancing at his watch again, Mickel heard the crunching of a truck pulling into the neighbor's gravel drive. He leaned over and watched around the corner of the house as the tall, arched blue and green recycling truck came to a halt at the edge of the backyard grass. The neighbor, a man of about fifty, climbed from the cab, unzipped his dark blue jumpsuit and threw it in a ball back onto the seat. Then, closing the driver door, he hopped down and climbed into his Jetta. About two decades old, the Volkswagen had seen better days. Though it served its purpose, as the man worked maybe two hours each day, three on longer routes, returned home, hid the truck in the drive, and shot off to the pub for the rest of the day. He did this, as far as Mickel could tell, every single day, save for Sunday.

Quite a routine.

As the Jetta pulled out, Tabia drove past him and up her own driveway. The black Lexus SUV stood out in the neighborhood—it would anywhere on this island—but they would need it for the image today.

Mickel watched in the reflection of the lamp as Tabia, wearing high heels and a yellow sundress, tiptoed across the stones lodged in the grass and up onto the back porch.

"You are late." He sipped the water.

"And you aren't dressed."

He glanced down at the khaki shorts and flip-flops. "I'm not naked."

"I'm not joking, mon. We will have but one shot at this."

"Stop with the accent, we're alone here."

"Then get your ass dressed."

He stopped rocking and turned to see her standing as tall as she could, arms crossed. Her face softened when he caught her gaze.

She said, "Please."

"Don't forget who's orchestrating this."

"How could I?"

He waved a hand. "Give me the update first."

Tabia walked to the railing and leaned back with her arms crossed. "Vanessa Holmes called twice. Once last evening and once again this morning."

"And you have not returned the calls?"

"Correct. Both messages ask about the receipt of new funds."

"Have you moved the money?"

"Done."

"Good. And what about Agent Coffee?"

"She called too, asking about Benny Lang's account."

Mickel rocked back and forth, nodding while looking away from Tabia. He held up his phone. "She's on the way here now."

"How do we know?"

Mickel smiled. "Stanley, of course."

"What did that cost?"

Mickel laughed a deep, throaty laugh and said, "He thinks he's getting twenty large."

A strong breeze swept across the patio and Tabia had to hold down her dress. "I must admit, you were right about that boy."

"Everyone has a price. His is just pitifully low."

"Right." She glanced at her watch impatiently. "So are you, or are you not changing clothes? We may have to meet Colleen now."

"I've decided we won't try to win her over." He stood, towering over Tabia by a full foot, which was quite a bit considering she was over five and a half feet tall herself.

Looking up at him, she said, "Tell me."

"We already have Lang's account." He stretched his legs. "I say we take the rest of it for ourselves."

"Mickel, is that wise?"

"Why not?"

"When she discovers—"

"She won't discover."

"How can you be sure?"

"Tabia. We have the entirety of the CIA at our disposal. Don't you think we can hide this? Hide ourselves?"

"And she has the same."

"Had. She had the same. Not anymore."

"So we're not bothering with her at all then?"

Mickel placed the water on the edge of the railing and inspected his hands as he made them into fists. "We won't, no." Emphasis on *we*.

"Mickel."

"Do you see another choice?"

"You said no killing."

"No." He reached up and touched her face with the back of his hand, then stroked it. "I said…that it won't be us."

Wading through a stretch of glittering greenish-blue, flat water, Finn glanced back at Colleen. With her shirt untucked and pants' legs rolled up to the knees, she looked like a drenched Shakespearean peasant. He said, "Where'd you learn to swim like that?"

She answered, a little out of breath, "I elected to take water training, you know, at Langley."

"They have a pool at Langley?"

"On the training ground, Patrick."

He stepped up over a tangle of coral. "The Farm."

"Not that place, but yes…" catching up to him, she stepped over the same coral and said, "something like that."

It occurred to him that there were a lot of things he didn't know about this woman. Strange, because he had dated her, pretty seriously, for almost a year.

No reason to pull punches now, he said, "So tell me, yesterday?"

"What about it?"

They reached the white-sand shore and she flopped onto her back.

He stood over her. "Were you arriving in Miami or leaving it?"

"Arriving." She squinted up at him. "Why?"

"Just wondering." He sat down next to her. Pulling his cell phone out of his mesh back pocket, he said, "This is fried."

"Mine too." She pulled her phone out, opened and closed it, then dropped it in the sand by her head. She lifted her hips and pulled out the pistol. Then, releasing the clip, she said, "And this. Wet is one thing. Waterlogged, well…I'll have to oil it."

Finn said, "Why'd you hesitate back there?"

Colleen turned to face him, shielding her eyes with a hand. With no makeup now, her face showed smooth skin and a smattering of light freckles, making her look young. Au natural. Better than ever, to be honest. She said, "In the boat?"

Finn refocused. "You could have shot first."

She shrugged. "I was determining whether the man behind her was the real threat. If she was distracting me for him to act."

"Tell me," he pressed on, "How many hours did you spend target shooting during training?"

"A few hundred, maybe."

That was along the lines of a Navy SEAL. And still, she hit the bird. Finn was reminded why it hadn't worked out between them. Two years, and she was never straight with him.

After a good five minutes of silence, she finally said, "We'll go to the bank first."

Finn didn't respond.

"Then we'll hit Customs, see what they have on incoming manifests for the last few weeks. Maybe the one who hired Benny came here to meet him in person. That's a requirement of this

Network, as far as we know — meeting face to face.

"And then we'll hit hotels, high-class establishments, and maybe the casinos."

Finn waited until he was sure she had finished and said, "I'm glad you have our itinerary worked out. How about food? I'm hungry."

"After the bank."

"And clothes?" Sitting forward into a crouch then standing, he said, "I need a change."

"Right." She sat up. "Maybe something local. You know, to blend in a bit."

He laughed. "I couldn't blend in here if I grew dreadlocks and wore a rainbow knit hat."

"You'd be surprised what you can get away with if you act like you belong," she said, standing.

Reverting back to small talk, they walked about half a mile along the beach until they came to the private access area of a boutique shop named Boney's. Finn opened the wood-framed glass door and a small ring of bells at the top of the door joint jingled. He pulled Colleen close as they greeted the shopkeeper. Tall and emaciated, the older black man eyed Finn with more than a hint of suspicion. Boney. The man said, "Hello there, mon. How can we help you?"

Finn smiled, glancing around. We? There was nobody else in the shop. He took Colleen's hand and glanced around at the half dozen circular racks of shorts and island shirts. "My wife and I are just looking for some clothes."

"I see that." Boney gave them both a full up and down, staring at the clumps of sand they'd dragged into the shop.

Colleen picked out a sky blue golf shirt with the name Boney's stitched on the chest, an ankle-length wispy multi-colored skirt, and a pair of plastic flip-flops. As Boney showed her a few other choice island items, Finn selected some clothes for himself.

What Finn really needed was to ditch Colleen.

Because the six GMs who called yesterday morning were all in serious need of a goalie and were previously interested in Lew Kunkle. Coincidence? Finn's bet was that the Cashmores had been shopping Lew. Perhaps in a panic. Perhaps because they'd tripped the salary cap. Or maybe they'd sunk their own budget and rumors of the team going under were true. And with the terms of Lew's contract, no other team would be insane enough to trade for him.

If so, that left the Cashmores in a panic. They needed to get rid of Lew at any cost.

So, Finn was banking that they would find Tracy Cashmore on this island, at the bank or with a banker...or at least find evidence that he'd been there recently. But he couldn't go searching for him with Colleen. No, her opinion on how to handle this situation would interfere with Finn's.

It already had.

For instance, she planned the itinerary perfectly backwards. So, he grabbed a few items and followed as Boney walked them around the corner and showed them two dressing curtains. Then Finn bumped into Colleen.

Hard.

"Ow!"

"Sorry, I'll take this curtain." He turned around, tucking her pistol under the pile of clothes in his hands. Couldn't leave her running around with that now, could we?

Thirty seconds and a change of clothes later, Finn was gone.

With no real structural damage, the speedboat bobbed upside-down in the water with the current, and so Vanessa and Chadwick bobbed along with it. Vanessa had swum to a floating seat cushion that had been flung from the wreck, and then paddled with it back to the boat, almost wiping herself out from the exertion. Or perhaps it was from her recent resumption of smoking, and so she vowed to quit that too. Chadwick, already wearing a preserver, had sought refuge from the sun by diving under and then floating in the hollow of the boat.

She knocked on the hull and Chadwick yelled, "Stop that, it echoes under here!" Loud but muffled, she could barely make him out.

She yelled, "Are you all comfy in there? In the shade?"

"*What of it?*" His yelling echoed under the shell of the boat.

"Because I'm out here, in the sun, alone."

"*Well you should be!*"

"Why's that?"

No answer.

She knocked on the hull. "I said—"

"*Because this is all your fault!*"

"My fault! How do you reckon?"

"*I told you to slow down!*"

"It was that bloody bird's fault! Hit me right on the nose!"

"*And you took my gun!*"

She stayed silent and he continued, "*And lost it!*"

"Right. Sorry about that," she muttered, rubbing her nose.

"*What?*"

She banged the hull hard. "I said sorry!"

"*I want yours.*"

"The hell you do!"

"*Then Sir James is officially off-limits!*"

"Oh don't be like that, Chaddy, er...James."

He stayed silent.

She said, "I can be nice."

"*No you can't!*"

She waited, but he said nothing more. So she sighed to herself and then rolled her eyes. She'd have to do some damage control if they were to orchestrate a proper rescue. That is, if they were even lucky enough for someone to boat within a mile of them out here.

They could be stuck for days.

Closing her eyes and feeling the water lap at her shoulders and neck, Vanessa gathered her resolve then took a deep breath and plunged into the water. Swimming a few feet while dragging the cushion with her, she reached up and felt the wooden stern and then air above. She was inside.

Surfacing, she gasped and said, "It's pitch black in here."

"Like your heart," Chadwick said. The words echoed in a way that sounded like he had turned his back to her.

"Chaddy." Vanessa said. "Don't be cross." Holding the cushion, she kicked over and bumped into him. "Is that you?"

"Who else would it be?"

Bobbing together now, back to back, she said, "We are in a bit of a mess, I admit it."

"And?"

"And..." she swallowed, rolling her eyes to herself, and said, "much of it is my fault."

"Much? How about all?"

"Well, I wouldn't say—" she cut herself off and said, "Okay, fine. It's all my fault."

"I don't feel that was sincere."

"Well then, how about this?" She turned around and let go of the cushion, wrapping one arm around him and keeping her other free.

"What about it?" Chadwick continued displaying his affront.

"I'm not quite there..." and she reached with the other hand to find Sir James.

Chadwick popped up in the water and she held on. "Don't get jumpy on me."

"I didn't..." he said loudly and then softer as she massaged him, "expect...that."

And Vanessa wondered if there was even a way to do it out here, under here, whatever. But with Sir James growing at her touch, she would figure something out. Maybe she should get him off, make him happy. That would be fun enough.

And as she kneaded *not-so-little-James* into the size and shape of a small cricket bat, she let her mind wander. Chadwick began to breathe louder and then he moaned a bit.

Pulling harder, she wrapped her legs around him for leverage.

Chadwick leaned all the way back and started whispering something. She leaned closer and asked what he was saying, but he ignored her. She kept going and he started whispering louder and faster. And right as it sounded like he was beginning to chant, Vanessa heard a noise.

A low, throttling grumble, and a vibration in the water.

She stopped and listened.

"What are you—"

"*Shhh!*"

Sitting as still as she could, listening, she was sure of it. It was a boat. And it was approaching.

Diving under the water and emerging in the sunlight, she began waving her arms frantically, yelling, "Here! Over here!"

A tall white boat with all kinds of pulleys and cables, a fishing vessel of sorts, buzzed in the water toward them.

Banging on the hull, she yelled, "Chaddy, it's our lucky day! A boat! Come see!"

He ignored her, though, and stayed inside.

Waving, an arm high in the air, she yelled again, "We're shipwrecked!"

The white boat, a good hundred yards from her, turned slightly and headed straight her way. She sighed in relief. Then she pounded the hull. "We're saved Chaddy!"

He didn't respond.

The boat, a small deep-sea fishing outfit, cruised up to the overturned speedboat, circled it, and then stopped about fifteen feet away. Vanessa was about to swim to the ladder, but then the boat began to back up. And when it appeared the two large engines would eat her, the boat abruptly stopped.

The engines shut off.

An older blond man, with a bit of a pooch, emerged from the top of the wheel deck and descended the ladder. Then Chadwick popped up beside her.

"Ladies first," she said, almost having to push him aside, and grabbed the bottom wrung.

"Ahoy," The man said in a raspy voice. "What in Job's name did you do to that boat?"

"He crashed it," Vanessa said, pointing at Chadwick.

"I did not," Chadwick said.

"Nice vessel, too," The man, wearing what amounted to an American tennis or golf outfit said, as he peered over Vanessa. "Looks like a Chris Craft. Silver Bullet."

"It was," Chadwick said.

"Here, let me give you a hand, young lady." The man reached out and helped Vanessa up the last rung and into the boat.

"Thank God you came along. I thought I'd be stuck with him forever." She thumbed at Chadwick.

Chadwick didn't hear her as he cleared the last step and stumbled onboard, making the boat rock back and forth. The open area of the boat's stern had nothing but a tall rail and a single white leather seat positioned in the middle of the white flooring. A haul of rods and reels were stacked on one side and buckets and other fishing tools sat on the other. Everything appeared to be organized and in order, each item strapped or secured in some way to rings bolted into the boat.

"Name's Darwin, David for short." He held out his hand.

Vanessa shook it, saying, "I'm Colleen, and this is Patrick. We were headed here from…Miami…where we…live. But not together, separately. We're friends, that's all." She made a face of disgust.

"Can't have too many of those, can you? I'm pleased to meet you both." Putting his hands on his hips he said, "Now what in Jimminy Cricket happened to your beautiful boat?"

"We hit something."

"A bird," Chadwick added.

"Right," she said.

"A bird," David said.

"She was going too fast, you see," Chadwick said.

"And it hit me in the face."

"Well, those Silver Bullets can hop along, can't they?" David inspected the upside down boat, bobbing lifeless in the water like a giant dead crane. "So it hit you…"

"I lost control," Vanessa said. "And fell. On the throttle."

"I see…"

"Do you have some water?" Chadwick asked.

"Yes, please, water, we're dying of thirst."

"Absolutely. Two waters." David disappeared into the room under the steering platform.

"What should we do?" Chadwick whispered. With a glance, Vanessa realized he was no longer excited. A shame, she liked it big.

"Do?" She said. "Nothing. What do you mean?"

He leaned forward and tilted his head toward David. "He's seen our faces."

"But he thinks our names are Colleen and Patrick."

"So we let him live?" Chadwick asked, eyes wide as two Frisbees.

"Of course we let him live. We need him to take us ashore."

And before Chadwick could answer, David returned, holding two bottles of water and two towels. He handed them each a set.

"Thanks so much," Vanessa said, draping the towel around her shoulders.

"Yes thanks," Chadwick said, as he used his towel like a hood.

"So." Taking a swig, she asked, "What are you doing all the way out here? You don't look native."

"Native? No." David laughed and then said, "I'm coming from the Keys. Florida."

"I know where they are," Vanessa said and then reminded herself to be nice.

"See." He looked at his shoes and said, "My beloved wife just died after a long illness—"

"Cancer?" Chadwick blurted.

Both Vanessa and David looked at him, Vanessa with a tight brow.

David said, "Renal failure."

"Oh," Chadwick said, sipping his water. "Sounds messy."

Vanessa slapped his arm and they all stood there, silent for a few seconds, Chadwick watching one of those blasted gulls land on the upper tier of the boat.

David continued, "Anyway, she and I always had this dream. We'd come out of retirement and become fishing guides. She would come with me and we would be the best guides in all the Keys."

"Sounds absolutely…" *Dreadful.* Vanessa gave him a fake smile, and continued, "Lovely."

"Yes, we thought so as well." David looked pensive for a moment and then he said, "But there's nothing left for me there. Kids are grown, all our friends have moved inland, and, well, Muffalee is gone."

"Muffalee?" Vanessa asked, spilling water as she interrupted her drink.

"That was a nickname," David said.

"We have nicknames too," Chadwick said.

"Do you?" David asked.

Vanessa jabbed Chadwick, saying, "I'm exhausted. Do you mind if I sit?"

"Well of course, of course." David ushered her over to a short white bench. Turning to Chadwick, he nodded toward the speedboat and said, "We'll leave that there. I've already alerted the Bahamian Coast Guard."

"Have you?" Vanessa asked. "That was kind."

"Nothing at all. Ready for shore?"

"Indeed," Chadwick said, gulping the rest of his water and twisting the cap back on.

"Would you like to come up top with me? See the view? It's tremendous."

"Absolutely." Chadwick smiled wide, like a twelve-year old retarded boy, and followed David up the ladder to the wheel.

"Be careful," David said, "It's a bit steep."

"I have it," Chadwick said, his cheeriness grating on Vanessa.

Wondering if he was ever going to remove that idiotic life preserver, she sat back and listened to the fools preparing to steer her back to land. Then she heard, "Bullocks." And saw a bottle fumble off the rail and bounce right into the water.

"Oh well," Chadwick said, as the bottle floated away.

"We can't litter," David said. "Don't you worry, though, you've been in the water enough. I'll get it."

And then, descending the ladder, David smiled as he passed Vanessa, kicked off his boat shoes, and climbed onto the ladder at the back of the stern.

Vanessa heard Chadwick fumbling around with things up top and she wondered what he was doing. David must have heard it too, as he said, "I don't mind you looking at the controls, but don't press the big black button." He laughed and then climbed over the edge and plunked into the water.

"What one?" Chadwick yelled down.

Paddling about in the water, David called up, "Doggone it. It's floated under the outboard."

And before the vision could even enter Vanessa's mind, she heard Chadwick fumbling more and then she heard a kick. Then another. Then a loud buzz. A scream.

And she saw an arm, just the limb and nothing else, flung up over the silver bottom of the speedboat. And then another.

And then she heard an, *Oh Rubles.*

Jumping up, she yelled over the grind of the motors, "Chadwick!" Then she hurried up the ladder, steadying her rise as the boat vibrated against itself.

"What did you—?" Immediately out of breath, she continued, "What did you do?"

And Chadwick, standing with his back to the controls, sporting the frown of a schoolboy who forgot his homework said, "I may have pressed the black one."

Mickel straightened his jacket and tie as he sat in the small waiting area of First Bahamian Trust. Facing the street, so as to keep his profile off of the camera in the upper-back corner of the bank lobby, he watched the sleepy activity of the Royal Bahamas Police Force. Weather stains and stress cracks bled down the corners of the rectangular bluish green three-story police station, making it look about a hundred years old.

Mickel guessed it was more like twenty.

In contrast, the First Bahamian Trust building, also rectangular, had a newly painted stucco exterior and tall dark glass windows. No stains and no cracks, the Trust looked regal in comparison. Evidence that the business of offshore banking was thriving in the Commonwealth. On that, two officers of the Royal Force stood at each side of the entry, guardians of the local economy.

Mickel checked his watch.

As it was, he'd been in Freeport for almost a month and had successfully avoided being introduced to anyone from the bank. Thus far, he'd only met a few of the islanders, and the reason he'd joined Tabia to dinner last night was to see the client himself. Photos were good, but nothing could replace a face-to-face meeting.

He'd learned that the hard way over the years.

Uncomfortable in the regular-sized waiting chair, he repositioned himself while pulling the wide Zero Halliburton metal attaché case to rest between his legs. Turning back, he noticed Tabia approaching from the other side carrying a gray folder. Meeting her gaze, he waited until she reached him to rise.

"Good afternoon, Mr. Lang, it's been a while."

Body shielded from the palm tree camera angle, he rose and turned at the same time, keeping back to the camera. "Too long," Mickel said, tapping his watch in annoyance.

"Yes, well, let's get started right away then." And with deft accuracy, Tabia negotiated her way through the bank floor in a circuitous route, pretending to give Mr. Lang a tour of the bank, but actually avoiding the surveillance equipment.

Good girl.

She stopped at a tall, narrow, black door and picked up a wall phone. "Mr. Lang has arrived."

Less than a minute later, a man almost as tall as Mickel approached them. He wore a custom suit with prominent stitching —quite a statement all the way out here—but the statement was ruined with a flashy gold nameplate on his lapel. *Antoine.* "It is a pleasure to finally meet you, Mr. Lang. We appreciate your business here at First Trust."

Opening the door, Antoine showed them inside and then motioned for each of them to sit at a small table with four chairs.

Choosing a spot that faced the door, Mickel sat first, placing the case on the floor.

Antoine and Tabia sat on the other side, facing him.

"So, is all of the necessary paperwork in order, then?" Antoine said to Tabia.

Tabia nodded and opened the folder she had been carrying. Flipping through the papers that Tracy Cashmore had signed the previous evening, she found the instruction page and showed it to Antoine.

"Very good," Antoine said, putting his entire hand over Tabia's and rubbing it.

Mickel, not surprised but also not pleased by the act, kept his gaze stoic.

Antoine turned to Mickel. "Now, may I see your passport, please? I will need it for proper documentation, of course."

"Of course." Mickel reached into his jacket pocket and presented the passport. Black with gold imprint, the Hong Kong Passport had become difficult to attain ever since the territory's reunification with the Chinese Republic. That said, if done right, it opened many doors.

Antoine inspected the photo then smiled at Mickel, no doubt studying Mickel while maintaining the facade of ceremony. The bank was about to hand over more money, in cash, than anyone on that island would have seen in their lives.

Except bankers.

Antoine handed the passport to Tabia and said, "We'll need a copy of this."

"Of course," she said, then stood and left the room.

Antoine, still studying Mickel, said, "To be sure we have honored your request, I must ask if there is anything else we can help you with."

"I believe this is all, thank you."

"We very much appreciate your business and hope to see you again in the future, Mr. Lang."

"I'm certain you will," Mickel smiled. Not a chance in holy hell.

Mickel then let his mind wander while answering idiotic questions about the weather and tourist attractions and whatever other mindless droll Antoine could touch on. After almost five minutes, Tabia returned.

Standing behind two men dressed in black business suits, she watched as they rolled in a metal cart with a gray cloth draped over the top.

Without a word, they tucked the cart to the edge of the table and left.

Handing his passport back to Mickel, Tabia sat back down while Antoine stood and removed the cloth.

Mickel then stared at the sleeves of euro bills stacked before him.

He'd seen plenty of money in his career, but most often it was in the form of petty payoffs, bribes, or consulting fees...money paid to informants. None of those could even touch this.

Five million euros. The equivalent of over seven million dollars. The Network's nest egg.

"We strongly encourage you to count the withdrawal. We will need you to sign a release once you have agreed that it is accurate."

Not answering, Mickel stood, then counted them up. One hundred thick stacks of pristine euro bills denominated in 500s. Hefting one of them, he then placed it back on the cart, turned to Antoine, and gazed directly into his eyes. "I trust it is correct."

"No need to be polite, Mr. Lang. This is a substantial amount of money."

"Not for me." Mickel smiled.

That stopped the show for a moment, until Antoine, in bad bank etiquette couldn't help himself, asking, "If you don't mind me asking, Mr. Lang, what sort of business are you in?"

Mickel regarded him for a moment, sending the signal not to pry further, and said, "Consulting."

Antoine swallowed. "Very well." He turned to Tabia and said, "I'll let you handle it from here. Good afternoon, Mr. Lang."

When Antoine left the room, Mickel turned to Tabia and said, "Is this all of it?"

"What do you think?" Tabia raised her brows.

He put his hands on his hips. "I think I'll need a bigger case."

"I told you that."

He gave her a look of annoyance and then hefted the Zero Halliburton onto the table. Unlocking the latches and spreading the metal case open, he began to place the stacks inside, counting as he packed them. Tabia stood behind him, watching in silence.

When he reached three million, he stopped. Then he rearranged the bills longwise and added another twenty stacks. Four million.

And the case was full.

He stared at the remaining ten stacks.

Over a million euros still unpacked. Stuffing the four stacks in each of his suit breast pockets and then four more in each of the hip pockets, he tried to stuff the last two in his pants pockets but they wouldn't fit.

He considered breaking the bands and stuffing the bills here and there, but decided that would be too messy.

"I'll take it," Tabia said.

He ignored her and unzipped his fly.

"What are you doing?"

Stuffing the last stacks into his crotch, he re-arranged his knocker and then hopped up and down twice as he zipped back up.

"You can't travel like that."

"Of course I can, we'll be on Jet Skis."

Looking him over, she said, "You just gained forty pounds."

Rearranging his groin, he said, "and a few inches, too."

CHAPTER SIXTEEN

IT HAD TAKEN FINN FEWER THAN TWENTY minutes to find new clothes and a disposable mobile phone—one of those island models that had about seventeen stickers to choose from inside the package. He picked Andros Island, stuck it on the front, and activated the device. He paid for everything in wet US dollars; the merchants seeming happy enough to get the American currency didn't say anything.

Finn approached the lobby of the Parrot Bay Resort sporting a replica Manchester United jersey and faded khaki cargo shorts. Stopping right outside, Finn dialed the Berans' number from memory.

One of them answered—to this day he still couldn't tell them apart—saying, *Berans, your bailout specialists, how can I help you?*

Finn smiled at the familiar greeting. "It's Finn."

"Patrick! Where the hell are you?" Then another voice, on speakerphone now, "Feds and Nikki and a body, what the fuck?"

"Easy, fellas. I'm fine."

"Tell you what, you're missing one hell of a playoffs. Bruins are on fire."

"Yeah, hotter than Nikki. So where's she? With you?"

Finn waited for a pause and said, "We're both fine."

"Good, 'cause if something happens to her, I'm holding you personally accountable, got it?"

"That goes for me too."

"She's fine," Finn said.

"Keep it that way."

"Yeah."

Finn couldn't help but laugh at these two, as he glanced around and then nodded at a bellhop walking past him. Turning his body to shield the conversation, Finn said, "So, guys. I need a favor."

"Gonna' cost you."

"Big time."

"Right, I understand." Finn said.

"What you need to understand is tickets. Next round."

"They're going to the finals, I'm telling you, Patrick."

"That's great guys, I—"

"You should've signed that Chara. He's smoking hot."

"Yeah, and that Kredji too. Why didn't you sign him?"

"I tried to sign them."

"Yeah, well, you should've tried harder, could've made a mint with those two."

"A mint, yeah."

"Right guys, like I said, I need—"

"Or even that Frenchie, Bergeron. Fuckin' Frog is hopping around the ice like a cougar."

A pause, then one of them said, "Well, not a cougar like Nikki, but—"

And the other cut him off, saying, "She's not a cougar, she's like, what, thirty-two? You gotta' be over forty to be a cougar."

"I'm just saying.'"

"Well you don't know what you're talking about—"

"You're telling me that Courtney Cox is hotter than Nikki? No way."

"I'm not saying that, I'm saying that she's not old enough. Courtney Cox is like fifty or something."

"She's not fifty you hockey puck. She's like forty something. Cougar-aged."

"Puck. You're the—"

"Guys. I only have a couple of minutes. Can we focus here?" Finn said.

"Right. Focus. Like the Bruins."

"Yeah, They're focused. Focused on Lord Stanley's Cup."

"They should go ahead and engrave it now."

"Don't be stupid, they gotta' win first. You'll jinx 'em."

"They're gonna' win."

"If you don't jinx 'em."

"Whatever."

When there was a moment of silence, Finn said, "I need you to go to my office."

"That where you keep the tickets?"

"Not tickets, no. I need you to find something in my files, then fax me a copy of it."

"What's so important that you need a fax of it now?"

"Level with us, Patrick."

After Finn was sure they'd shut up long enough for him to speak, he said, "I need a copy of Lew Kunkle's contract."

"Shit, shit, bullocks. Bloody hell." Vanessa kicked the sand and stared out at the fishing boat motoring into the ocean. It had bounced around a bit, went in a full circle, but then straightened itself out. Now it was a good half-mile from shore. The sky loomed black beyond, accentuating her idiocy.

"What?" Chadwick asked, looking like an overgrown toddler with his shoulders back and belly pushed out.

"My gun. My bloody fucking gun!" Patting her chest, she said, "I put it in the sun to dry and left it on the blasted boat!"

"Did you?" Chadwick asked. He still hadn't moved. Standing there like an imbecile, he stared at the boat drifting off and said,

"Well, it's gone too far now. We can't very well swim to it."

Swatting his shoulder, she said, "I know we can't swim to it. That's why I'm vexed!"

"Oh."

Sighing loudly, she threw up her hands. She deserved to be stuck with him. The two of them were ninny-peas in a dingbat boat. They couldn't find a pint in a pub for God's sake.

Scrolling through their options, Vanessa searched her mind for an idea of how to get another gun. It would prove difficult all the way out here in the mango-land. She knew exactly nobody. She had zero connections. And the last thing she wanted to do was report the gaff to Home Office. This operation had already caused them to be the laughing stock of all professional killers.

Brooding over this, she squatted and held her head with a hand.

And she thought they'd done so well, avoiding customs and all. They'd cruised right onto shore, no Coast Guard, no reception, not even a dock. Just a short retaining wall near an abandoned house. She glanced back, or maybe the house was unoccupied for the season. Do they even have seasons out here? Then she noticed that most of the windows were missing. It was abandoned.

Sighing out loud again, to herself this time, she closed her eyes.

Then, as she ruminated on the possibility of going around the Network and directly to old contacts at MI6...ones who could get her a gun in a matter of hours, Chadwick broke her thought.

He said, "Well, it's a good thing you have me then."

"You?" She looked up with disgust. He wore a grin, like he'd just eaten a whole stockpile of donkey doo. She wanted to shove her fist straight through the grin and out the rear of his skull. "How exactly does that help?"

"Well for one, I saw the gun sitting there on the bench."

"So?" She gave him the *I don't understand how a person can be such a lame-brained chowderhead and still be alive* look.

"So." He reached behind his back, fumbled a bit, then brought out a dull-black metal piece. It looked like a pistol. A SIG Sauer.

Her SIG Sauer.

"You didn't!"

"I did." He gave her a long camel-nod.

"Chaddy! You're brilliant!" Popping up, she leapt into his arms, wrapped her legs around his middle and rubbed his tallywacker hair.

Laughing now, he said, "I've been telling you that, all along."

"Well, it's not that I didn't believe it." Swinging back and forth, she said, "I just hadn't seen it for myself is all."

He smiled back, a child who'd scored an A.

She hopped down, reached out, and said, "Give it here then."

He stared at her.

"Chaddy." She smiled again.

Then he slowly moved his hand and the gun away from her and behind his back. Tucking his arm tight against his side, he said, "It's mine now."

Tilting her head, she said, "As I recall, you lost yours at the bottom of the ocean."

His face twitched and he said, "You! You lost it. After you made me give it to you!"

"You didn't have to hand it over."

"With you yelling at me like that? What was I to do?"

"Well." She darted to grab the gun, but he was too quick, moving back himself.

"Give it." She darted again.

He stepped back. "No."

"Stop playing. I'm being serious." She reached.

He turned. "As am I."

She stood still, then straightened her shirt. "Fine. You can hold it."

"I can?"

Rolling her tongue inside her cheek, she said, "On one condition."

He eyed her. "What's that?"

"You never. Ever. Ever ever ever ever tell anyone about our little...agreement."

He looked confused. "Agreement?"

She blushed. What was she was blushing for? Crossing her arms and raising her brow, she said, "*Sir James*?" She glanced at his pecker and back to him.

Now *he* blushed, glancing at his crotch and back to her. "Why would—"

She held up a hand. After spending half the day thinking about the embarrassment she'd endure if the Home Office ever discovered them, she'd devised a reason for Chadwick to keep quiet. After all, she'd been ridiculing the man for weeks now. He was a total dimwit and they all knew it.

But they didn't know he had a lamppost hidden in his shorts.

"Let's just say...it wouldn't be good for business. You know, since we work together and all."

"I see." He stood as if pondering this, and then the thought broke, as he said, "Hey. Look. A carriage."

And behind the old house, a dark green van with the word *Taxi* painted in yellow on the door drove past at about five kilometers per hour. When it reached the other side of the house, it made a full U-turn and stopped. The driver appeared to be on the phone and the backseats were empty. Perhaps he was lost.

Vanessa glanced at Chadwick, saying, "Good eye!" Then she ran for it.

Chadwick, with his long strides, caught up in a few steps and right as they reached the grass drive at the side of the house, grabbed her shoulder, stopping her dead.

"What're you?"

"*Shhh*," he said.

"We need to get to the bank." She brushed his arm off her shoulder and, pointing, said, "We need that taxi."

"Yes, but." He looked around with a conspicuous stare.

"But what?"

"We should wait until he's off the phone."

"Why?"

And before Chadwick could give any of his dunderhead reasons, the driver snapped the phone shut. As he was about to put the vehicle in gear, Vanessa yelled, "Wait!"

The driver turned his head and gave her a look of shock.

She wondered if it was her clothing, all wet and wrinkled, or the fact that there were actually two people all the way out here, nowhere near any actual residences or establishments, and without a vehicle. Or perhaps it was the sight of Chadwick—the upright simpleton—that had startled the man.

"Do you need a ride, mon?"

"I'll handle this." Chadwick started forward, glancing about. He walked toward the vehicle, took a good look back and forth, up and down the road, drew his hand out from behind his back and… the gun.

He pointed it.

And then, Chadwick tripped over a stone, and the gun went off.

Dumbfounded, Vanessa stood still for a moment, mouth agape.

Gathering himself off the ground, Chadwick looked up and said, "Oh rubles."

The driver had been replaced by a splattering of red.

Shoulders slumping, Chadwick approached the car and opened the door.

The man fell out of the seat and onto the ground. A soft-shell taco rolled from his hands and into the grass.

She watched as Chadwick then dragged the man and his torn yellow shirt and placed him under the broken stoop. He folded the legs under the bottom step to hide them.

Then, wiping his hands on his pants, he turned to her. "Well at least we have a vehicle now."

Mouth still open, she said, "A vehicle."

"Perfect, if you ask me." He held his hand out. "A carriage."

"It's a van." Staring at Chadwick, she lowered her head. "And what were you doing, pointing the gun at him like that?"

"I was going to steal it, of course."

She said, "And...why would we have to steal it?"

"How else would we get to the bank?"

She straightened her arm and then slapped Chadwick across the head.

"What'd you do that for?" He said, shying back.

"Chadwick."

"Yes."

"It's a taxi. A car for hire."

"And?"

"And so we approach the vehicle. We get in the back. We tell him where to go. That is how it works."

"I suppose...we could have done that."

"But instead." She glanced at the pair of spongy-soled shoes sticking out from under the stoop. "We've killed him."

Chadwick stood there, dolting. "Stealing it seemed like the best idea at the time."

"And now." She held out a palm and presented the front seat. "We have blood and body all over the place."

He peeked in the car. "It's not that bad."

"Not that bad?"

"No," he said in defiance.

"Then what about that chunk of brain there, on the gear shaft? It has a swatch of hair stuck to it."

"Oh that's gross," he said.

"Chadwick?"

"Yes mum?"

"The gun." She held out her hand. "You've just lost your privileges."

Sitting out on the porch waiting for either the ribeyes to find their plates or the South Texas sun to set, Jerry and The Boys each puffed on a Padron Maduro cigar. The boys—Jerry's co-investors on just about everything, including this NHL Houston Hammerhead fiasco—loved coming out here, and this was the reason. Away from the wives and the prying eyes, they could conduct their business and drink their whiskey without as much as a whisper of protest. The quiet was as good as the moment of silence at a ballgame.

All good things do come to an end though, and so Charles broke the respite with a question.

"So, where's Tracy, this week?"

A damned fine question, too.

Jerry peered through the smoke at Charles, who sat back with his stogie at arms length, almost dragging it across the damned flagstone. There was one single reason the boys wanted to know where Tracy was and when he'd return. They had the same beef with him as Jerry.

The goddamned Kunkle contract.

Jerry took a long puff, waited, and said, "He's working on our little issue."

Charles said, "Sure he's not off workin' your help instead?" He laughed.

Blake stayed quiet as a night prayer, and Earl as stiff as a virgin bride. They may each have a dog in the fight, but they knew better than to hit below the belt, so to speak.

But Charles continued, "Come on, Jerry, we all know the boy's got a reputation. That said, I don't give a toad's anus what he does with his private life." He paused for a few seconds, and continued, "As long as it doesn't affect our investments."

Jerry said, "He's made his mistakes, but no worse than any of the other boys." He turned to Blake who knew damned well that his own son had married the town hussy. It was rumored that half the football team had her during senior year. And that was before prom.

Of course, Jerry was cleaning up after Trace, as usual. Toilet paper. Hell, Jerry should've given the boy a drawing of a shop-vac.

Then Charles said, "Jerry, let's be honest here. And I realize this may feel personal, but…" he trailed off, took a good slug of whiskey, then said, "but we're as good as family here. And I got to say…sometimes, well, that boy acts like he's two bricks shy of a full load."

Everyone stayed silent for a patch and Jerry nodded, took a long smoke and exhaled. Then he finished his own whiskey. Turning his head enough to cut his eyes to Charles, he said, "And I said he's taking care of it."

"And if he doesn't?" Charles forced a nervous laugh. "We all know why we're here. This is not an end of season party. We are in one deep pile of hog shit, boys."

"How long can we make it?" Blake asked

Charles said, "If we pay the contract?" Then looked to Earl. "Well?"

Pursing his lips, Earl said, "If we trade the top three players… and with Jerry's generous offer of little Tracy's trust fund? We'll still burn out before December."

"See there? We won't even make it to the All-Star break. Which is ironic, considering we would be the highest paying team in the league. A goddamned expansion team, Jerry." Charles stuffed his cigar into the glass.

Blake said, "Well maybe that display will help, you know, with season tickets sales and all."

"You talking about them sharks?" Charles laughed. "Another Tracy-brained goat fuck. Who ever heard of something so stupid as a fish tank in a hockey rink?"

Blake continued the thought and Jerry wished he would shut his mouth. Blake said, "They are hammerheads. It's unique."

"And what happens when a drunk cowboy gets the idea that he's gonna' go for a swim in the tank? Talk about liability." Charles shook his head and, holding his ashy glass, looked around for the help. He clearly needed another drink.

Jerry said, "That's a sunken cost, so forget it." He immediately regretted using the word sunken.

Earl said, "If sales rise fifty-five percent, it'll be a wash."

"Fifty-five percent," Charles said, "Look. At the end of the day, we are in the business of making money. And this little hockey venture has done nothing but drain cash from us. Worse than my third wife. I mean, what were we thinking anyway? A bunch of Texans in a Yankee sport."

Both Blake and Earl glanced at Jerry on that last line, and Jerry braced for the finish.

Charles cleared his throat, then said, "We have a quorum here, I say we settle this right here, right now."

"A vote?" Blake asked.

"Damned straight." Charles sat up and said, "I hereby suggest that if this contract business isn't resolved by week's end, then we file."

"Bankruptcy," Earl said, almost, matter of fact. They must've had themselves a whisper before today.

"No re-org. Just flush it." Charles slammed his glass down on the ceramic table, so hard that should have broken.

Jerry shook his head and looked away. If they filed, Jerry stood to lose the most out of all of them. He'd dumped over a quarter of a billion of his own money into the team, buying the expansion card and all. But as much as he hated to admit it, Charles was right. At this rate, he'd be out another fifty million before the summer oaks had even shed their leaves.

He glanced back and they were all looking at him, like three deputies gearing up to arrest the sheriff.

Charles said, "Do I have a second?" and looked at Earl then Blake.

Earl raised his brow to Jerry. "He's right, you know."

Jerry smoked his cigar and stared him down.

Staring back at him, Earl said, "I second."

"All in favor?" Charles held up his hand, stabbing the thick air with a stubby finger.

"Aye," Earl said.

Charles and Earl both turned to Blake, who raised his brow to Jerry and said, "I'm sorry," then, "aye."

Charles said, "Jerry, we don't need your vote, but we'd sure like to have it. It's the right thing."

"The right thing." Jerry screwed up his mouth and said, "Would have been to wait for all five members of the board to be here for the vote."

Then, standing, he said, "I vote no." Stubbing out his cigar and walking away, he said, "Enjoy the afternoon boys. You can show yourselves out."

As he walked away, he thought that if that idiot boy Tracy didn't fix the whole Kunkle business, Jerry may kill him too.

It had taken Finn a mere two phone calls to track down Tracy Cashmore. One to the FAA, Finn claiming he was with the Southwest Aviation Insurance Group needing manifest information on the jet owned by Jerry Cashmore—this confirmed Finn's suspicion that Tracy had in fact come out to the Bahamas. The second call was to the fanciest joint on the island, The Parrot Bay Resort. And with about as much surprise as finding sucking lice on a monkey, he confirmed the Cashmores had checked in the previous evening.

Then a cab ride and the beginnings of a rainstorm later, and Finn entered the resort wondering if Tracy was poisoned more by arrogance or idiocy.

Maybe a perfect balance of both.

Almost hard to believe. Tracy came to an island known for its offshore banking facilities, then picked the most expensive hotel without any attempt to hide his name? The only other explanation would be world-class ignorance.

Could a Cashmore legacy be that naive?

Tracy must have known that Patrick and Lew were still alive. That's how these things worked. Simplified, you hire a hitman—or hitmen in this instance—first pay a percentage of the agreed-amount for the job up-front, then receive confirmation that the job has been completed, and pay the remainder. So, at this point, Tracy would know that Finn and Kunkle were still alive, the job wasn't finished.

And that would also explain Tracy's little trip to the Bahamas.

He needed to regroup with his little project of *Kill the Finn*.

Shielding his face from the bulbous raindrops, Finn hurried into the lobby. His new rubber flip-flops squeaked on the checkered marble floor as he stepped inside, causing both front desk clerks to look at him.

Finn brushed the water off his Rooney jersey and gave them a wave. Don't mind me, just another dumb tourist.

Turning back around, he almost ran right into a woman. With two children, two nannies, and more attendants than Victoria Beckham, he knew who she was in an instant. Of course she didn't recognize Finn—she'd only met him twice and both times he'd worn a suit—so she walked right past him and up to the double glass doors leading outside. Wearing sunglasses the size of ski goggles, an ultra-mini white sequined skirt, and grapefruit-colored, high-heeled rubber over-the-knee rain boots, she puckered her lips when she noticed the rain. A perfect product of Texas-sized entitlement.

Faith Cashmore.

The kids were bickering behind her, and their nannies rolled pink-and-blue-checkered Burberry luggage. Four hotel bellboys plus the concierge walked in tow, two pushing an over-loaded luggage cart, two hauling bags labeled *Parrot Bay Gift Shop*, and a sole, short, puffy white man behind them all, talking on a cell phone with a slight accent. Was it Australian or New Zealand? Finn could never tell the difference.

In any case, it sounded as though he were confirming flight details.

Finn eased into a dark leather chair, its back to the entrance of the hotel, and pretended to play with his phone as he listened.

The boy said, "Mom, I need a new battery for my iPad. I forgot to plug mine in and Courtney May won't let me use hers."

Courtney May responded, "You can't just buy one, you have to recharge it, you moron."

The conversation turned ugly from there, as the kids used some soft but extensive expletives to describe each other. The most colorful of them were *blubberbutt* and *buttface*.

Faith restored control by instructing the nannies to go back to the gift shop to see if they had any iPads they could buy. Quickly, she said, they didn't have all day to shop.

She should write a book on effective parenting, this one.

The concierge said, "The pilot is ready, ma'am," then he paused, and said, "but expects the weather will be holding you up for a bit."

Faith said, "Well I'd rather leave now. I want to be gone before Mr. Cashmore returns."

"We are doing all we can on such a short notice."

"Well, can't we like…you know…move to the front of the plane line? We should have priority takeoff or something."

The concierge said, "Mrs. Cashmore, there are many people who are traveling today. And I can tell you that there is no such service."

"Then bribe them. You know? With pesos or whatever."

He gave her a look then said, "That is not possible, I assure you, even with American dollars."

"Can't you just bend the policy a bit?" She licked her lips, as if she'd always gotten whatever it is she wanted with a hint of sexual advance.

But it was met with silence.

A few moments later, the silence was broken with the sound of a zipper, some crumpling and then, "Okay, how about this? I want to get back home as soon as possible. Before that bastard—er, my husband returns from fishing." Then she muttered, "Or whatever it is he's doing."

Tracy put out a contract on Finn and then he went...fishing?

From the corner of his eye, Finn made out the concierge stuffing a wad of bills in his pocket. If they were twenties, it could be a couple hundred bucks.

Peering harder, Finn made out the corner of one of the bills still untucked.

It was a hundred.

Finn cursed her for overpaying and skewing the information market for him.

Faith's phone rang, a muffled rendition of Lady Gaga's *Like a G6*, and she retrieved it from deep inside her yellow suede purse. How many colors could one woman wear, anyway?

"Kimberly?" Faith said.

She waited, then responded, "I'm certain of it." It almost sounded like she was going to cry. And then she sniffled. "It's been going on for months."

She waited again and dug into her purse. Walking right in front of Finn, she dabbed her eyes underneath the glasses with the corner of a tissue. She paced as she spoke.

"Because that Hermes Birkin purse is Melissa's life. She would never, ever take it off unless..." then she whispered, "unless it was for..." and spelled it out as if her kids were still standing there, "S...E...X."

Finn wondered who Melissa was, though he'd wager it was one of Faith's friends.

Faith said, "I confronted her with two text messages and a phone call. She admitted everything." She whispered, "Even oral... S...E...X."

Detective Finn, at it again.

A few moments later she continued, "The worst part, the pilot of my own airplane had to discover that purse, one that everyone knows I've always wanted and Tracy wouldn't buy for me. I mean, my own pilot had to see another woman's Birkin in my husband's car. How humiliating."

Pause.

"I wasn't even going to let him drive that one home, but I thought, why not? Tracy could just buy a new one if the pilot crashed it."

A pause, then, "No, I don't think teal is that hard to find. It's a Bentley, not like a black onyx Chanel watch or something."

Pause.

"I know. I like the white one too."

Pause.

"Maybe I can get one of each with the divorce money." And, "Chanel really does make the best watches. Rolexes aren't even close to as nice as them. Or even work as good. I mean, you have to wind those every day."

Before they could finish the deep and thought-provoking conversation about the merits of designer watch fabrication, the concierge walked back into the lobby and said, "Mrs. Cashmore, the car is ready and your luggage is loaded."

"Kimberly, I have to go. But I will call you as soon as I land in Houston. Gather the girls, everyone but Melissa of course, and you all come over to my house. I'll have the Houston Country Club cater dinner on the Cashmore's tab. We'll weather this storm together."

Pause.

"Yes, it is raining here, but I meant this personal storm."

Pause.

"You're my BBF." Then, "What? Oh, I thought it was *Best Blonde Friend*."

Pause.

"Okay, BFF then." And she hung up.

Finn imagined Kimberly hanging up and then calling all of her closest friends for a rally of *bless her hearts* and desperate search for all the graphic details. Shaking his head, he watched Faith and her entourage file outside. The kids rolled into the back of a faded-black Town Car with Faith, and the two nannies got into a dented taxi behind them. A few moments later, the short caravan drove away.

They should rename themselves the Classmores.

Timing it so that the concierge would enter the lobby when he stood, Finn approached him.

Towering over the man, Finn said, "I was wondering if you could help me."

The concierge glanced at the jersey and frowned. "With?"

Maybe the guy was a Liverpool fan. Finn said, "I'm supposed to meet someone here to go fishing, but I'm late and think that he left without me."

"Is this someone a guest of the hotel?"

"His name is Tracy Cashmore."

The concierge stiffened.

Finn reached for his wallet and said, "Look, I sell life insurance and he's my biggest client. I have a card here." Finn made a show of digging around in his wet wallet while displaying the fold of twenties inside.

The concierge waited.

"Maybe the card is stuck between these." Finn handed him a few twenties. "You know where he went?"

Peering around then taking the money, the concierge stuffed it in his pocket. "I do."

Finn waited.

Bastard.

Then he gave him two more twenties. "Where?"

The concierge smiled like he was having a grand time will all of this. "He went to see the shark lady."

"The shark lady."

"Obsessed they say, and a bit crazy too—you know, like a recluse. But...if you want shark fishing out here, you need to see the shark lady."

Sharks.

The picture began to come into focus for Finn as he thought about the new arena in Houston and the talk of a big fish tank inside. Ludicrous. Perhaps they ought to be focused on assembling a quality team, not ticket-sales gimmicks.

"Okay." Finn raised his brow as he put his wallet away. "Where is this shark lady?"

The concierge frowned and glanced at Finn's back pocket.

Finn leaned forward and whispered, "If you want more money, you'll have to take it from me."

The concierge cleared his throat and said, "And if you want..." his voice trailed off as Finn placed a palm on the guy's shoulder. And squeezed.

The concierge's nostrils flared, and he looked like a fat stingray as he said, "The end of the island, a street called *No Man's Lane*."

"No Man's?"

He nodded, "Named it herself. Manny, that is."

"Her name is Manny."

"I'll hail a taxi for you. Mr. Cashmore has been there all day." He rushed off.

A few minutes later, Finn sat in the back of a taxi that smelled like a combination of McDonald's and stale rum, headed to Manny's on *No Man's*, when he had an idea. He pulled out his phone, dialed the number from memory, and waited for the older woman named Ginny to pick up. A woman with an ax to grind in this little situation. After four rings, she answered with her telltale smoker's rasp, "National Hockey League, Rizzoli here."

"Ginny, it's Patrick Finn."

The cabbie turned up the volume of the music and the tinny speakers buzzed each time a deep electric drum was beat. Made it hard to hear on the crappy little cell phone, so Finn plugged his open ear with a finger.

"Finn....Finn..." she hesitated, then said, "Patrick, how the heck are you?"

"Great, listen—"

"You miss a filing or something? Season's over."

"No, I just—"

"I can help you, don't mind. I always liked you."

"It's not that."

"What is it?"

"Ginny, I'm out of the..." and he hesitated, then decided to tell her less, "I'm out of state and need a copy of a contract, one of my players."

"That's going to be over in the commish's office."

"I know, I was wondering if you could help me. I really need a copy of this."

"Can't your secretary send it?"

"That's the thing, she's here. With me."

Finn winced.

After a while, she said, "Ooooh. I get it. Okay. It's gonna' take me a bit though."

Finn said, "I understand, it's a favor."

"Nah, anything for a fellow Irishman."

Rizzoli? Irish?

"Then fax it to this number, okay?" And Finn gave her his home number.

"That's a Boston number, *617 area code*, isn't it?"

"It'll get forwarded to me."

"Okay, whatever you say. Like I said, give me a few hours."

"Thanks Ginny, I owe you." And he hung up.

Staring out the window at the darkening sky and imminent rain, Finn had the feeling he was on the right trail here. If he was, the contract Ginny faxed would look a bit different from the one he had in his home office. And if that was the case, then all the questions would be answered but one.

Should Finn just kill that little bastard Tracy, or should he make him suffer first?

"You can't be serious," Nikki said, watching Lew peel a tomato then feed it to one of the dogs. Having changed into long, red board-shorts with a green t-shirt and green plastic flip-flops, he looked like a brain-damaged elf.

Lew shrugged. "They're picky. And it's all we have left."

"Let me get this straight. They'll eat the tomato, but not the skin."

"I think it gets caught in their teeth or something." Lew dropped the skinned tomato into a dog bowl with a plop.

The two dogs nudged into each other, their snouts battling for position. One of them bit the other, causing a yelp, a fury of barking, and then one of them whimpering into the corner of the kitchen.

Nikki almost felt sorry for the dog, and she contemplated hopping down from the counter and consoling the pooch, but then it lifted its leg and a fire hose spray of bright yellow pee splattered the door and then puddled in front of Nikki, filling the kitchen with a stench, like wet, mildewed sweat socks.

"Oops," Lew said. "Where else can he go, eh?" He looked around, emphasizing that they were still stuck on a yacht.

"Lew, you ever consider giving the dogs up? You know, to someone who doesn't live on a boat?"

"Like, give them away?"

"Not like."

"That's abandonment, dude."

"It's not—"

"Who would take care of them? Who would understand their

emotional needs?"

"I'm sure you could—"

"I wouldn't do it. Never. They need me, eh?" He stood with his arms wide, a Christmas colored *Oompa Loompa*.

Keeping her face straight, she said, "Need is a strong word, but..." and she let her voice trail off as she watched Lew wander out of the kitchen.

Then, returning with a pink-striped towel the size of a quilt, he slopped up the dog pee. Nikki decided to dig for insight on more important matters and changed the subject. "So Lew, you have any clue who might put out a hit on you?"

"Who? Glovesave stop." Lew pushed the dog back again and said, "Hold on." He then left, gripping both dogs by their collars. She heard a door slam, some scratching and a few barks, and he returned, sans pooches.

Nikki stood with her arms crossed, unsure how to respond to either his last comment or the dog circus. She said, "The fat guy with a gun?"

"Oh that." Lew looked up at the ceiling and squinted. Then he said, "You think that hurt? You know, the faucet in his..." he made a face.

Avoiding the graphic imagery that question elicited, she said, "You mean Benny."

"Yeah, if that's even his name." Lew tied the straps of the blue bag closed, sending a waft of pee smell into the air.

Nikki coughed. "You think Colleen's lying about that?"

"Sure, or maybe your friends. Those Beran guys."

"We can trust The Berans." She pushed from the counter and, hopping over the damp spot, leaned into the hallway for fresh air. She said, "But then who were the Brits?"

"Maybe they were partners with the guy Benny. Like they steal from the rich and stuff, eh?"

Nikki raised her brow, torn because Lew was right about one thing. They had no hard evidence of anything they'd been told.

And a lot of their information had come from a fucking CIA agent. One who Patrick had dated for almost a year and had left.

Because of trust issues.

She was about to ask Lew about the last owners of the yacht when a sound startled her. Like a buzzing or loud humming.

Like a boat.

Lew heard it too, standing up straight and turning an ear to the hallway. "Think they're back already?"

"Who?" Nikki made a face.

"Patrick and Colleen, dude."

"That boat sounds way bigger than the one they left in, Lew."

"Maybe they traded up."

She ignored him and hurried out into the hallway, through the bachelor lounge and up the stairs. Reaching the wheelhouse, she peered through the rain-splattered windows and made out the blue-green vessel headed toward them.

"Think they have food?" Lew said, almost causing Nikki to jump. "That was our last tomato."

"Let's hope they have gas."

"That might be good, too. If they see us."

"Lew, they're speeding toward us like they're on a mission."

He nodded. "They must know we're starving."

Glancing back at him, she said, "Or maybe they're not friendly."

"Like pirates?"

She tilted her head. "I don't think they have pirates out here."

"Dude, haven't you seen the movies? Pirates of the Caribbean? They're so many pirates out here that they made three sequels!"

And before she could correct him, they'd made an original and *two* sequels, a loud bang sounded from below deck. Then a rustling and a double thud followed by barking. Lew yelled, "Kicksave!" and by the time Nikki had turned around to see, the dogs had bounded the stairs and entered the wheelhouse.

"I said, no!"

Both dogs ignored Lew as they skidded past him and, falling

over each other, they then burst through the glass door onto the deck. Lew gave a futile chase, lunging for their collars and falling between them on the rain-slicked deck.

The dogs kept going.

Barking and bounding, they accelerated toward the railing and didn't slow.

Lew scrambled to his knees, already drenched from the storm, and yelled again.

Then Kicksave leapt up to the top of the railing, with Glovesave climbing up his back and biting Kicksave's neck. Kicksave yelped and hopped up. Glovesave held tight and his weight and momentum took Kicksave up and over the railing with him. And before Lew could yell one last time, both dogs disappeared into the water below.

Lew yelled and ran to the edge of the railing and made a move to jump in after them, but by then, the dark blue and white boat had reached them. Throttling loud and circling alongside the yacht, the boat neared as it slowed.

The half-peeled stencil lettering read RBDF. *Royal Bahamian Defense Force.*

A tall man with arms long and thin like black bamboo and hands the size of dinner platters reached forward in a ready stance. Holding a pistol pointed at Lew's chest, he shook his head as he said, "Stop right there, doc." Then he waved the gun in Nikki's direction.

"That goes for the punk rocker, too."

CHAPTER SEVENTEEN

RAINING NOW, JUST BLOODY WONDERFUL VANESSA THOUGHT, the sky had darkened to an island pewter and threatened to turn black. Chadwick, showing his lack of inclement weather driving experience, jerked the taxi to avoid mere puddles for God's sake. The last swerve caused Vanessa to fall over the middle glovebox and her face planted in Chaddy's crotch.

Hello *Sir James.*

That cheered her up a bit, but Chadwick jumped and his zipper almost chipped her tooth.

Straightening back up and brushing herself off, Vanessa pointed to the curb. "Pull over!"

Chadwick scrunched up his face. "Why?"

"Because you couldn't steer a train on a railroad. You've no business operating a moving vehicle in the rain."

"I'm being cautious. You should be wary of slippery spots. That's what my mum taught me."

"I bet she did." Vanessa rolled her eyes trying to recall who had made the first move, Oedipus or his mother. "The bank is one block up, let's get on with it."

"I am." Chadwick accelerated again and almost hit a street vendor. The man yelled and jumped aside.

The taxi's bumper tapped his cart and it rolled to the curb.

Vanessa covered her eyes. "Tell me when we arrive."

Less than a minute later, the van stopped. Chadwick said, "We have—"

"Yes, I see," Vanessa said, peering through the rain toward the bank. Two policemen stood at the front door and beyond this, she couldn't make out anyone through the gold-tinted windows. By design, for sure, banks such as this one would present a strong sense of discretion for its customers.

Chadwick said, "What to do now?" His face sagged like a wet sack of grain.

"We wait." Wishing she could ignore every single part of this man's body except for the hog with a helmet, Vanessa stared at a yellowed roll of packing tape on the floorboard and thought about that.

Wouldn't it be lovely? If women could merely focus all of their energy and time and effort into the penis. Forget the dimwitted, testosterone-soaked brain knocking around inside their skulls. You could take a pill and never hear a single moronic syllable that the man utters. It would automatically trigger answers to all their stupid questions without you even hearing your own ridiculous words in response. Then, at the end of every day, a muted version of *Hide the Moby Dick* would play out in the bedroom. Even Captain Ahab would have his fun.

Disturbing her utopian vision, Chadwick said, "How do we even know they're at this bank?"

Vanessa turned her head toward Chadwick and narrowed her eyes. "We've reviewed this, like…a hundred times!"

"I don't remember."

"Well, I won't make you worry about forgetting again then." She turned away. "Do you see their car anywhere?"

"What do they drive?"

"An SUV, Chaddy. They'll be driving a black Lexus today, for the one hundred and first time."

"Like that one?" He pointed out the window at a tall black vehicle, parked in what appeared to be a special spot at the edge of the far side of the building.

"Exactly like that one." Vanessa squinted to read the tags, but couldn't make out any of the letters in the rain.

Chadwick cut the engine and grabbed the door handle.

"Wait." Vanessa took hold of his arm. "What're you doing?"

"Going to get Mickel."

"Chadwick. You can't very well march inside of an international bank and drag out one of their prized customers."

He took his hand off the door. "Other ideas?"

Staring at the golden windows, she said, "I'm thinking." She peered past Chadwick at the hideous turquoise building across the street. Her terrible luck-streak extended, it was a station of the Royal Bahama Police.

Chadwick said, "Do you think this is a tropical storm? I've never been in one before."

"And you still haven't. This is a storm that just happens to be in the tropics, nothing more."

"It's a tropical storm then."

"No, it's not. The label tropical storm implies something bigger."

"This is big." He nodded so hard his jowls jiggered.

She squeezed her eyes closed and pinched her nose. It was a wonder the man could find the floor in the morning. She glanced at the tape on the floor. "Mention the storm again and I'll tape your pie hole shut."

Then he said, "Hey Vanny, I have an idea."

And Vanessa tilted her head to him. "Oh this should be ripe."

"But I'll need to borrow the gun."

Standing in the Parrot Bay lobby, the only spot in the entire hotel that he could receive a consistent phone signal on the stupid island,

Trace listened to Faith on the other end of the line. When she finished her little tirade, Trace said he was sorry and that it was all a misunderstanding. He never ever screwed Melissa in their bed. Not even once. I mean, what kind of guy did she think he was, anyway? Trace had insisted they do it on Faith's vanity chair instead.

And Faith hung up.

That bitch Melissa had sold him out on everything.

Trace kept talking so nobody in the lobby would see that she'd hung up on him. After realizing that nobody was listening anyway, he hung up too.

What the hell did he care if Faith and the kids left early? It would become a little vacation for him then, no fat off his bacon. Trace glanced around and caught the eye of the only white guy in a hotel uniform. He must have been the GM or something.

The short, fatty man looked away.

With oily olive skin and dark hair, the guy actually looked more Middle Eastern than white.

Trace snapped his fingers, but Ali Baba didn't respond. He snapped them again and said, "Hey, I need help here. Aren't you the manager or concierge or whatever?"

Ali Baba gave him a look of annoyance.

Trace sighed. He wasn't about to walk all the way across the lobby to talk to him. Ali Baba should have hurried over as soon as Trace had caught his eye. All good concierges do that. The guy would need to be taught.

In fact the whole hotel could use a good review on hospitality. Five stars my ass.

Ali Baba raised his chin and approached Trace.

"Yes, Mr. Cashmore?"

"You remember my name." Kudos, Ali Baba got something right. "I need help and it is very important. Do you understand?"

"I understand what very means, yes."

Trace eyed him. What a jerk.

"I'm going to the casino tonight. You know, Grand Lucayan?"

"Good for you sir." He shrugged his shoulders, adjusting his jacket.

"I'm not finished." Trace held out his hands palms up.

"Go on."

"So..." Trace smoothed his hair back. "Like I said, the casino. But I don't like going alone."

"I can only imagine."

Trace was about to ask what the hell that meant, but decided to put the guy on the defensive instead. "And since you and the rest of the staff helped jet my wife out of here, I figured you could help me."

"How is it that we can help? You." He looked at his fingernails, an annoying diversion.

Trace ignored that and said, "Alone, get it? I like to be with someone."

"Right." He let his hands fall away and looked up again. "Would you like a female or...male companion, sir?"

Trace's face tightened into a knot. "What, do I look like some sort of backdoor bouncer to you?"

"Well—"

"A girl. Not underage, of course, but if she's close, that's okay."

"Of course." Ali Baba raised his brow. "And we can even be discreet."

"Discreet? What the hell does that matter?"

"Well sir..." Ali Baba looked around.

Trace whispered, "And make sure she's not fat. I don't even care what nationality she is."

And before the guy could respond, Trace's phone triple-dinged with a text message. Slipping it from his shorts, he flipped it open and checked the sender.

Faith.

She had sent one line, four words. Four tedious and very expensive words.

I want a divorce.

"You know what?" Trace snapped the phone closed and turned to the concierge.

"Make it twins."

The rain had begun to pound the cab so hard that it leaked from under the door and onto the floorboards beneath Finn. Lifting his feet, he straddled the growing puddle with the doorframe and hump. His ass was starting to get wet somehow too.

"Here it is, mon." The driver turned onto a gravel drive and up to a purple house.

Thanking him, Finn showed him the puddle.

"That's no problem." The driver said, peering over the seat. "You should see the trunk."

That explained his soaked shorts.

Finn paid the man and exited the taxi, then walked to the door. Shielding his head from the rain by standing under a short palm tree, he leaned forward and knocked. No other cars in the drive, he assumed Trace had already left. Unless the privileged son actually took a taxi out there.

But he saw no movement in the house and heard no voices.

Nice house, too. And she had her own pond way out in the front yard.

He knocked again. He had no idea what this shark lady named Manny could be like, but if the Massachusetts fishing harbor women were any indication, she'd have fewer teeth than a flounder.

Boy was he wrong.

When she opened the door, Finn stood paralyzed for a full five seconds. Quite a long time, he realized, standing before someone who's ready to greet you.

"Lost?" She asked.

"I'm looking…" and son of bitch if he didn't let his gaze drop to her bare feet and then run all the way up her long tan legs and across her substantial, but tight, chest. He cleared his throat and continued, "for a woman named Manny?"

"And what a look you got." She raised her brow.

"I just didn't expect—"

"Used to it," she said. "You want in?"

Was that typical island etiquette? Finn was used to waiting outside, especially at a single lady's home. "Sure."

The entry, if you could call it that, was more like an arched foyer, complete with cobblestone and what appeared to be real stucco walls, and smelled like lavender and vanilla. He supposed the scent was coming from the candles flickering in the next room.

She laughed and gave him a good looking over, one that lasted maybe a second or two longer than his own. Then she said, "You are unprepared, my friend."

She walked around the corner and returned a minute later with a huge Turkish bath sheet. "Try this."

"Thanks," he said, then wiped his face and hands and held one out. "Patrick Finn."

"Manny." He noted that her hands were strong but still feminine with long fingers and natural nails. He tried to shake without squeezing too tight.

He stood staring at her high cheekbones for a moment and was about to explain what he was doing there, when she said, "You got a badge?"

"Should I?"

"You're not from Customs?"

"I'm not."

"What a screwy day," she said, surprising him yet again.

"But I am here to see the sharks." Finn tilted his head.

"No you're not."

She sighed loudly and turned away. Then, walking down the

hall, she said, "My money says that you're looking for that ass-hat named Tracy Cashmore."

Impressed with her quick deduction, especially the ass-hat part, Finn called out, "So you know him."

Ten minutes later, she had given him some dry clothes that actually fit, a pair of flowered shorts and XXL faded linen shirt— *island wear from an ex-ex*, she'd said, whatever that meant. Sitting now, on the back porch, and drinking a mug of hot coffee, the best he'd had all week, he was careful not to clink the cup against the pistol in the shorts.

Meanwhile, Manny peppered him with questions.

He supposed she must get lonely all the way out here by herself and let her fire away without much protest. So, in less than twenty minutes, she'd figured out that he was an only child, from the east coast, had been an athlete himself, and—from the look of the inch-wide and six-inch long scar on his knee—was knocked out of commission before his time.

And he'd figured out that she was far wealthier than she'd let on to her fellow islanders. He said, "My turn for questions?"

"Fire away, Mr. Hockey."

"Why the Bahamas?"

"That's not the most interesting one." She smiled and sipped her coffee.

He shrugged at her and she continued, "Bahamas are cheap, well, relatively speaking, they're not Bora Bora or Fiji." Setting her cup down, she said, "The interesting question is, why sharks?"

"And?"

"Because men are easy."

"Easy."

"Sharks are a challenge." And to emphasize the point, she raised her leg and extended it in front of her, all the way to the railing. Pointing her toes, she watched Finn take it all in. Folding it again and resting her foot flat on the deck she said, "See?"

"Good point."

"Anyway, I like long periods of solitude. To choose who I'm with and when."

"Doing charters."

She nodded. "And the bonefishing out here is intense."

"Never been." He finished the coffee and set the mug on the floor.

"I can take you out if you like. I'll give you a last-minute rate."

Raising his brow, he looked out to the rain.

She waved a hand. "This'll blow over in..." then she tilted her head out and looked up, in each direction of the horizon, and said, "twenty minutes. Tops."

Finn gave her an incredulous look, and she nodded back. Once.

He said, "Tell you what, I'd rather see those sharks."

"No can do, Mr. Finn."

"I'll pay."

She laughed, solidifying his suspicion that she didn't need money, and said, "They're already gone."

"Gone, as in, you freed them?"

"Hell no." She lifted her chin. "As in, they're in containers and headed to the airport."

And Finn had his answer about Trace returning to Manny's.

She said, "So you came to find Tracy...and while you're here, you want to see the sharks. Why?"

Finn hesitated a moment and said, "Tracy Cashmore owes me a lot of money and I'm interested in finding either him or what he's most interested in. The sharks seem to be the winner these days."

Manny shook her head slowly. "Why is it that richest people are always the stingiest? Especially the ones from the lucky sperm club?"

"A question for the ages."

"Sorry I couldn't be of more help, Mr. Finn."

Finn stood. "Thanks for the coffee...and towel. I can get my clothes." But before he turned away, Manny reached out and touched his arm. Instant electricity of unmistakable body chemistry pulsed through him. Finn saw she felt it too, or rather, heard it in her voice as she said, "He's coming back, you know. If you want to wait."

Finn half-turned to her and searched her eyes. He'd known her for a grand total of about twenty minutes and so he'd have to go on gut feeling with this one. And he felt like he could trust her.

At least more than he could trust Colleen. Though, that was not saying too much.

"When?" He asked.

Without breaking the gaze into his eyes, she said, "A few hours."

"Why?"

Squinting a bit, she said, "He still has to get those sharks out of customs."

Finn nodded. "So...he needs to pay you, maybe a bit more than he figured?"

She leaned back. "You're pretty smart for an old hockey player."

"And you're pretty...for a fishing guide."

"Not much competition there."

"For me either."

He turned his attention to the rain that had begun to let up.

Manny said, "See?" Then she held a hand out over the railing. "The sun will be out in minutes."

Finn stared at her from behind, wondering what in hell had possessed this woman to come all the way out here to live. Alone. Manny seemed able to handle herself fine, though.

"Tide's out, time's right." She turned, adjusted her tiny shorts and said, "And you seem nice enough, I can tell by your eyes."

"For what?"

She leaned forward and puckering her lips ever so slightly, she asked, "How'd you like to see my little honey hole?"

And what could Finn say to that?

No need for handcuffs, they weren't officially being charged with a crime, the tall Bahamian policeman named Duane had said. Then he'd added with a wink, *yet*.

Nikki had then asked why he'd pointed the gun at their chests, to which he replied, "We've received many reports of smugglers trolling these waters recently. We were being cautious."

"Smugglers?" she'd asked, while Lew stood there with the look of a confused mutt.

"Guns," Duane had said, which explained him waving six men onto the deck, and their proceeding to take a full hour to search the boat. After which, he'd then told them they'd remain in custody until the boat could be fully searched. Glancing at his watch, he'd said, "Probably overnight."

Now, sitting in some sort of holding room at the bottom of the decrepit Coast Guard boat, complete with a hard plastic bench and single-posted steel table, Nikki tried to determine the smell from the hall. Could be burnt nylon or maybe wet rubber, indicating a possible problem with the engine room.

Breathing through her nose, she sat next to Lew on the bench and comforted him. "They're strong dogs, they'll make it ashore," she said.

Lew shook his head. "It's animal cruelty. We need to go back for them."

Duane, who sat with his pistol under folded hands in his lap simply said, "There's no way we can search for runaway dogs in this ocean while we tug that big yacht of yours ashore, doc."

"They're good dogs," Lew said.

Nikki rolled her eyes. Lew, wake up. We're in custody of the Bahamian police here and will probably be thrown into a Bahamian jail for the night. She reached forward and picked up a lone paperclip from the metal table. Playing with it, unfolding and reshaping it, she tried to calm herself.

Duane said, "I'm sure they were. I mean are."

Well said, Duane, well said. Nikki was nearing her end with all this bullshit. She was ready to be back in Boston and in her apartment, feet up with an ice-cold Bud light watching the B's take down Vancouver. No chance of seeing a game or finding American beer any time soon. She'd had that Bahamian beer, what was it called, Kabil or something? Kalik, that was it—that stuff tasted like lizard piss.

Peering over at Duane, Nikki decided she couldn't blame him. The police probably had all kinds of drug and gun smuggling problems in this place. And Duane actually seemed nice enough. Or honest at least.

But then he said, "Your hair looks like an over-ripe mango."

And she wanted to stab his eyeballs out with the paperclip. "Yes. I know."

"Did you do this on purpose, doc?" He asked and waved the gun barrel toward her.

Tilting her head she said, "What the fuck do you think?" And what the fuck is it with you calling everyone doc anyway? Was the guy a Bugs Bunny fan or was it like a nervous tic?

Lew slid about two feet away from her.

Duane raised his eyebrows higher than any man should be able to and shrugged. "I think you lost a bet."

She thrust out her jaw. "A bet."

"A big one, doc."

Lew slid a bit further down the bench and looked away.

"There was no bet."

"Then you're sports fan, yes? What are they called, from the Florida University, you know...gators?"

Keeping her fury in check—all she needed was to give the guy a reason to arrest her—she said, "Football."

Duane squinted his eyes and said, "Wait, wait. I know. You are a music fan. Or fanatic, as they say. Right?"

"A what?"

"Yes, this is it. Isn't it?" He said wagging a finger at her.

She stared at the finger, wanting to snap it right off his bony hand. "It's what?"

"You would have been a child then." He held his chin. "What was her name? She made the music videos, we still play them here, in the bars."

Nikki crossed her arms, wondering who the hell he thought she was idolizing. Who she could possibly be trying to look like. "When?"

And Duane looked deep in thought for a moment, his fingers now tapping his wormy lips. Then he snapped them and said, "Cyndi Lauper!"

She exhaled loudly. Focusing on keeping her emotions under control.

But then he said, "She-bop!"

And Nikki lost it.

CHAPTER EIGHTEEN

WHY DID I AGREE TO THIS? VANESSA thought, as she watched Chadwick roll the vendor's cart up to the Lexus. At least she'd been intelligent enough to refuse his request for the gun. Wedged between a bank and a police station, it would be the last place she'd trust old dunderhead with a firearm. The scheme itself was bad enough.

But—she peered outside—with the rain letting up, it might just work.

A thump from the rear of the taxi reminded her that the vendor himself was now a passenger, though not by choice. She called behind her, "Quiet down, you'll be out soon enough."

Another thump.

She ignored it. Chadwick waved at her from across the lot. Ready.

Navigating the taxi through the crowded parking lot, she pulled directly behind the Lexus and stopped. Then she rolled down the window. "You'd better hope this works."

Chadwick, rain dripping from his nose, held up a giant fried conch. "These are more flammable than starter fuel." He squeezed the fritter and grease dripped down his hand, proving the point.

"Disgusting." Vanessa made a face.

Then Chadwick bit into it. "Quite tasty actually."

Watching him chew away, she said, "Can we please get on with it?"

"Right." He swallowed hard and tossed the bitten conch onto the roof of the Lexus. Then he lifted the pushcart's lid and pushed a button.

Nothing happened.

Vanessa rolled her eyes and he pressed it again, saying, "One minute, it's a touch damp is all."

"It's your brain that's damp."

"You'll see, I have it rigged to blow sky-high. They'll have to send three fire trucks."

"You mean the entire fleet."

"Right." He clicked and clicked and clicked.

Still nothing.

Looking boringly confused, he lifted the lid and lowered it. Lifted and lowered. Clicked and clicked, and lifted and lowered, until Vanessa said, "Chadwick, did you turn the gas?"

He stood up straight as if he had to ponder this and then looked back at her. "Brilliant idea."

Vanessa rolled her window up.

Chadwick fiddled with a knob at the back of the cart and then one on top of a tank. Then he closed the lid and waited. About a minute later he pressed the button again.

And the fire lit.

Not an explosion, like he'd predicted, more of a roast she'd say. Still, with flames ducking out each side, it was rather impressive.

But Chadwick just stood there, staring, as if mesmerized by the bluish wisps.

The thumping behind her resumed.

"Oh do shut up." Vanessa rolled her window back down. She said to Chadwick, "Tip it."

"What?"

"You need to tip it over now."

"Right!" He said, as if it had all been her stunted idea and not his own. He stepped back and then kicked the cart so hard that it not only toppled onto the front of the Lexus, the grease hopped out of the bin and splattered all the way across the hood. A moment later, the entire SUV appeared to be on fire. Or at least the front half of it.

The lingering rain did little to disturb it, just adding smoke to the flames.

"Get in!" She said.

Chadwick ran around the side of the taxi and jumped into the passenger seat.

Vanessa drove out of the lot, then all the way around the back of the bank to a spot on the other side, where they could see the action at the entrance.

As she stopped the taxi, the vendor thumped and thumped again, then kicked the seats with a muffled cry. He was making such a racket that Vanessa couldn't even think. For god's sake, it had been less than five minutes that he'd been muzzled. You'd think it had been all night, the way he was acting. She was about to climb back there and knock him on the skull when the thumping stopped.

Finally.

Chadwick said, "Do you think he's all right?"

"You probably taped him too tight. Poor thing has to breathe through his nose."

"He has big nostrils," Chadwick said.

Eying him, Vanessa said, "You didn't break them did you?"

"Nothing of the sort!"

"Then he's fine." She checked the rear-view mirror but couldn't see him tucked behind the back seat. "Probably scared out of his wits is all."

"Nothing to be scared of," Chadwick said.

She said, "We should switch now."

Chadwick nodded *yes*, and they both got out then ran around the front of the taxi. Chadwick bumped into Vanessa and she fell into the bumper. "Idiot," she muttered as she scurried around and got in the passenger side.

And before she could close her door, both guards exited the bank lobby and bounded to the front of the Lexus. Then one of them ran across the street to the police station, talking into his phone or walkie-talkie—she couldn't tell from there—while the other ran back into the bank.

"It's working," Chadwick The Arsonist announced from the driver's seat.

"We'll see," Vanessa said.

And then both Mickel and Tabia raced across the grass and to the Lexus. Flames from the hood reached higher than Tabia's head. Mickel, appearing injured in some way, hobbled while carrying a large metal case. He held a hand before his face and looked around the conch cart.

"Now!" Vanessa said, hitting Chadwick in the arm.

"Ouch!" He leaned away and jerked the car into gear, then sped them back to the spot behind the Lexus.

As the taxi rolled to a stop, Vanessa pushed open her door and hurried out, gun in hand but held low to keep from view of either the bank or the police station.

"You!" Mickel said.

"Get in," Vanessa said, looking from Mickel to Tabia.

Tabia said, "What are you going to shoot us here?" Then she made a big show of looking around at the bank and police station.

Vanessa turned to Mickel. "What do you think?"

"Shit," he said. Then, taking one glance at the briefcase in his hand, he nodded. "Tabia, meet Vanessa."

"Oh," Tabia said.

"Pleasure." Vanessa smiled.

Mickel shook his head as he leaned over to open the backseat door.

But it was locked.

Exhaling and raising her brow, Vanessa tapped the driver's side window with the barrel of the pistol.

Chadwick lowered it. "Yes, mum?"

"Would you be so kind as to unlock the doors, please, Chaddy? We're in a bit of a hurry here."

"Right."

The doors clicked and Mickel ducked low so as to not bump his head as he got in slowly. Tabia slid next to him.

Vanessa hurried to the other side and, keeping the gun pointed at Mickel through the seat-break, she said, "Now. Let's see that safe house, shall we?"

Mickel leaned over to Tabia and whispered in her ear, as Vanessa and Chadwick bickered about the backstreet route to the safe house.

"Don't worry, these two couldn't kill a chicken if they were farmers."

Tabia still looked worried, so he patted her knee.

"Just don't tell them where the rest of it is."

After calling for a taxi, Colleen Coffey had stood at the entrance of Boney's shop for over thirty minutes, but the cab had never showed. She'd then urged Boney to call for confirmation that a taxi had in fact been sent. The company said that it had, but they were having trouble getting in contact with the driver.

It happens, mon, especially in storms like this...but don't worry, mon, they will send another, Boney had said.

Then she'd stopped to buy a pre-paid mobile phone. A transaction that should have taken four minutes, but had been dragged out by an overloud, self-proclaimed corn-fed Oklahoma couple—evidenced by man's the head-to-toe red Oklahoma

University ensemble and the couple's matching white OU plastic visors—who had stepped to the kiosk mere seconds before Colleen.

What color should we git?

Do we need ten minutes? Twenty?

Maybe we should purchase thirty, so we can call more than once.

Are they color-coded, or can we git any color we like with a thirty minute plan?

Can we call Oh-HI-O with one of these?

Because at the end of the day, we're gonna' wanna' be able to use every last one of them there minutes, you know what I mean, fella?

And a big, fat laugh to go along with an obnoxious slap on the back of the unfortunate phone vendor.

Twenty minutes more of that and a dozen fantasies of killing the couple—including one where she tied them to the anchor of Kunkle's yacht then dragged them along the coral-lined ocean floor —and Colleen had a chance to buy her phone.

And so, it had taken her over two full hours to get to the bank.

Sitting in the back of her taxi, across the street from the police station and a block from the bank, she'd watched the entire scene unfold.

Mickel and Tabia. Vanessa and Chadwick.

Vanessa brandishing a gun.

Then there was the accidental burning of the Lexus—or so it appeared, she knew better—and the commotion that distracted everyone, including the two guards posted at the bank's entrance, the bank manager and his assistant, the entire visible police force from right across the street.

Colleen, meanwhile, sat silent, her worst suspicions confirmed.

She exited the cab to quickly find a car to steal; she needed to follow the unscheduled departure of her team members.

Choosing what she figured to be the bank manager's car, she slipped into and then cracked open the dash of a white Porsche Carrera Cabriolet. Though it wasn't the most inconspicuous of vehicles to choose, it would be the most reliable and no doubt the fastest.

Shifting into third and keeping a safe distance, now, Colleen followed the taxi that contained the crew.

Wriggling in her seat, she adjusted the waist of the long multi-colored skirt to ride above the elastic band of the athletic biking shorts. She'd opted for skin-tight biking shorts over regular panties, thinking they'd provide good cover in the event of a physical altercation. After all, she felt it was bad etiquette to give an opponent a pussy-shot while kicking them in the head. Normally, she wouldn't be concerned with such details, as the moment she'd pull out her pistol the disagreement would end.

But somehow, in the time between reaching shore and buying the new clothes, she'd lost her SIG.

She'd also lost Patrick Finn.

The coincidence was not lost on her.

Now she looked and felt like a rich hippy from La Jolla. Driving the Porsche exaggerated the image. Worth it, though, the car handled like a dream through the narrow side streets of the island.

No surprise to Colleen, the taxi-van continued out of Freeport and straight back to the safe house.

This, however, presented problems.

Stopping the car a good seventy yards away, but with a line of sight to the side of the house where the taxi-van had parked, Colleen dialed the phone and waited.

Well-trained—by Colleen, of course—Relay answered the secure number after a single ring.

"It's me," Colleen said, "I want updates."

"Is the line you're on—"

"Now!" She held her breath for a minute to control her emotion. Mutiny brought out the worst in her. Double mutiny pushed her to the edge.

"The money has been deposited by the client."

"Which. Client."

"I don't know what you're—"

Turning away from the windshield, she raised her voice, "I'm going to make this very clear, are you listening?"

"I am."

"I know about the second order, and so I know there were two more deposits."

Silence echoed from the other end of the line.

"I also know there were two major withdrawals."

No response.

"Think about your answer. Make it a good one," she said.

"It was Mickel's idea. He told me...I didn't—"

"Stanley." And that stopped him cold. Nobody used real names in Network communications. Ever.

It was a cardinal rule.

You could say it was *The Cardinal Rule.*

She heard an audible gulp on the other end of the line.

And she didn't let up.

"I am going to make this even more clear for you."

He sighed.

She continued, "If you don't help me fix this, right now, you will disappear. In fact, I will make it as if you never even existed. You will become shark food, then shark shit, then shrimp food, and then shrimp shit. You will become that long thin turd that everyone seems to be mistaken when they call it a vein, stuck to the inside of fat little Mexican's finger as he 'de-veins' the sorry little shrimp before tossing it in a skillet and then stuffing it into a taco for me. To eat."

No response.

"Do you understand me, Stanley?"

"Yes, ma'am."

"Meet me at the drop in twenty minutes."

"Yes ma'am."

"And Stanley." She paused as she watched the absurdity of the scene before her. She found it laughable that these two had ever been hired by anyone, no less MI6. Benny had far-overestimated their intelligence.

"Yes?" Stanley asked.

Colleen put the Porsche in gear, but then sat stoic as she watched the insanity across the street. These two were dangerous, no denying that.

Shaking her head back to reality, she said, "Bring me a gun."

With perfect direction from Mickel and not a single word from Tabia, Chadwick drove them into the driveway of the safe house. Vanessa then told Chadwick to squeeze the taxi past an enormous trash truck—or recycling vehicle, as Mickel had corrected her—and then to turn off the engine.

"Wait here," she said, then went to the rear of the taxi and opened the hatch. Squeezed behind the back seats, the vendor lay facing away and still.

Very still.

She rolled him over and he fell out of the taxi, thumping to the ground.

"What was that?" Tabia asked.

"Never you mind," Vanessa called forward and continued, "Chaddy. Can you lend a hand?"

"Sure thing, mum." He got out and lumbered to the back of the taxi. Staring down at the body, he said, "Is he okay?"

"Does he look okay?"

"I didn't kill him. I swear it."

Vanessa leaned all the way down and inspected the thick layer of packing tape wrapped around the poor man's head. She knew she should have done this part herself. Chaddy had made a mess of it.

"What do you see?" He asked.

"Well, I see conch vomit on the tape."

"Oh."

She looked up at Chadwick. "Did you feed him conch?"

"Well he wouldn't shut it. Blabbing on and on about how he'd spent his whole life's savings on that stupid cart, and the like. I even warned him."

"You warned him."

"I did." He gave a single nod.

She peered closer. "And how many did you feed him?"

"Just three."

"Three! They were gigantic!"

"Tasty too, you should have had one."

She leaned over the body, tilted her head. "Chaddy, it's oozing from the man's nostrils."

"Rubles."

She put her hands on her hips. "Is that all you can say when you've killed someone? Rubles?"

"It was an accident."

"You're the accident." She leaned around to see Mickel and Tabia sitting close together and looking back.

Vanessa said, "I want you to stand here and look at what you've done. Learn from it. We can't very well go around killing every single person in our path."

"It hasn't been that many."

"It's been three just this morning."

"Oh," he said. Then with the intelligence of a trout, he continued, "Will I get credit for them? You know, for Century Club?"

Vanessa stared at him. "They were not killings that have been requested, paid for."

"So? They're still dead."

Vanessa watched Mickel and Tabia. Whispering now, they were up to something. She said, "Chadwick?"

"Mum."

"Keep it up and you will be too."

Vanessa marched to the side of the taxi. "Out. The both of you."

Mickel and Tabia slid out, hands high.

Waving the pistol toward the case on the back seat, she said, "Open it."

Mickel said, "We're willing to split it." Then stood straight up, as if he were in the position to negotiate. Too bad. Vanessa was done with negotiating for today.

"Are you then?" Vanessa asked.

"We are," Tabia said. Her dress was all wrinkled from the commotion, and a smear of soot extended across her tiny chest. Vanessa wouldn't be scared of this mouse if she were holding a bazooka.

Vanessa waved the pistol at the briefcase.

Tabia sighed and opened it.

Stacks and stacks of euro bills lined the case to the edges. They must have drained the master account.

Vanessa said, "And I'm willing to take this off your hands." Pointing the gun at Mickel, up and down his huge frame, she said, "As well as the rest of it."

Mickel gave her a ridiculous look of innocence.

Vanessa said, "You've either gained fifty pounds and a limp since last month, or you've stashed the rest of it on your person."

Tabia looked away.

Vanessa said, "Thought so. Off with it."

And as Mickel unbuttoned his shirt, she stood in perfect ready stance. It was quite unlikely that he could have or would have carried a weapon into the bank, so she wasn't worried about that. She was worried about the sheer size of him. She'd fought men of his bulk in training, and she knew that one solid blow and he could knock her out cold.

He was a specimen.

She glanced back at Chadwick, who hovered over the vendor's body like a child staring at a broken egg. Despite the situation, she couldn't help but make the comparison. I mean really, if Chadwick hung a billy-club in his trousers, Mickel must be sporting a tree trunk.

She glanced at Tabia. How could this little thing take all of him?

Then Vanessa's thoughts returned to the moment, as she saw the stacks of cash that Mickel was removing from every single pocket and hidey-hole. When he'd removed the stacks from his groin area, there still appeared to be one left. To be sure...

Vanessa leaned low and reached over. Squeezed.

Oh my.

"Hey!" Tabia yelled.

Mickel grunted, then smirked.

Chadwick, who had returned from his little *time-out*, said, "Have we found it all?"

"Oh yes," Vanessa grinned.

Tabia said, "You wish, you Brit-bitch."

"Not what I'm looking for today, afraid." Vanessa winked at Tabia then said, "As for the money, that only looks like, what, six or seven million translated to US dollars? Where's the rest of it?"

"That's all we took," Tabia said.

Vanessa turned to her. "For each lie, he receives a kick." Then she flicked her foot up, hard and fast, and delivering a blow to Mickel.

Doubling over with an *oof*, Mickel held his groin with both hands.

Poor not-so-little Mickey.

Knowing it took a moment for the ball-ache to hit, she watched Mickel.

Then he moaned and fell to his knees, eyes wide and angry.

"What'd you do that for?" Chadwick asked.

"Stop it!" Tabia yelled.

Vanessa turned to Tabia and raised her brow. Then she took a full step back and pointed the pistol at Mickel's groin. "The next kick comes from this." And she waved the pistol.

Mickel squinted and groaned. "Under the back deck. In a blue bag."

"And?" Vanessa asked.

"And what?" Tabia said to Vanessa.

Vanessa sighed, then aimed carefully and pulled the trigger.

A boom echoed between the houses and Mickel jumped. "I felt that!" He yelled. She'd placed the shot right between his legs.

"Good," Vanessa said. "Next time, you'll be in so much pain, you won't."

"Vanny! What's the hurry?" Chadwick said.

"The hurry is we need the rest of the loot, so we can finish this job and get out of the business for good." Then she stared at Mickel. "Which is what I reckon these two were headed off to do."

"It is? We are?" Chadwick said, "Brilliant, Vanny!"

"Our job was finished," Mickel said, his voice scratchy and higher than normal now.

"The rest of it. Where?" Vanessa asked again and pointed the pistol right at his groin this time.

"Upstairs!" Tabia yelled.

Vanessa grinned. Yes, that Tabia knew a good stick when she found it. She'd do anything to keep Vanessa from shooting it off. She turned to Chadwick. "Do you think you can handle them?"

"I do." He nodded and pointed at the pistol. "With that of course."

Vanessa made a face. "Most certainly not."

"Well I'm not very well standing here with that beast, ready to break my neck." He pointed at Mickel.

Vanessa looked around. She could ferry them all inside the house, but that would be a risk. Too many doors to open, too many possibilities for confusion. No, she'd need to keep them contained, in one spot, and under the thumb of imminent threat. Or at least locked up somehow.

Glancing around at the landscape, she searched for something to tie them or fix them to, and her gaze met the recycling vehicle. Waving the gun toward Mickel, she said, "The two of you get into that truck. The back of it."

"With the recycling?" Tabia said with a grimace.

"Yes, I need you locked up."

Chadwick said, "Good one!" and clapped.

"Shut up and get the body," she said.

"Right, mum." Chadwick lumbered over, then grabbed the shoulders of the conch-man and dragged him in the muddy gravel to the back of the recycling truck.

Mickel groaned as he stood and said, "You are going to regret this day."

"I already do," she said. "On with it."

Mickel hung onto Tabia as they hobbled to the back of the truck. Climbing inside and wading through the bottles and boxes, Tabia said, "It's hot and stinky in here. And sticky too." Turning back around, she said, "Wait, what are you doing with him?"

"He's in with you," Chadwick said, heaving the conch-man's legs up first. Vanessa held them with a deep frown, while Chadwick hefted the rest of the small man up and dumped him inside.

"Oh God," Tabia said, falling into Mickel.

"Shut up," Vanessa said.

"Vanny." Chadwick tilted his head. "How're we going to keep them inside?"

"Find the lever to lower the door." Vanessa waved him to the truck's cab.

"Right." Chadwick hurried off.

When he was inside the cab, Vanessa said, "Have you found it?"

"I think so," Chadwick yelled.

"Don't go crushing them, now," Vanessa yelled back and caught a look of horror on Tabia's face.

"Try not to," he called back.

Then the engine of the truck fired, spit once and rumbled to life. A moment later, Chadwick called, "Here goes then." And the door at the back of the truck began to lower.

A fucking miracle, Vanessa thought, he didn't kill them.

And she watched Mickel and Tabia disappear into the darkness.

Walking to the front of the vehicle, she said, "Stay here, I'll be right back."

"Going nowhere," he said, crossing his arms.

Shaking her head, Vanessa returned to the taxi and took the briefcase to the stairs. Underneath, she found the plastic duffel. Damp from the rain, the zipper stuck a bit, but she worked it open. Sure enough, more stacks of bills were inside, all euros.

Quite clever.

Returning to the taxi, she took the bundles of money and cradled them like kindling back to the duffel, then stuffed them inside along with the briefcase euros. Then she pushed the whole lot back under the porch and headed inside the safe house.

She didn't make it up three steps before she heard a loud thump and a muffled scream. Then the scream turned into bloody murder.

Hurrying back outside, she caught a glimpse of Chadwick, nearly standing in the truck's cab and fiddling with something frantically. The look on his face looked like downright panic. The groaning of gears and crunching sound was so loud that Vanessa didn't realize that there was a banging and yelling on top of the scream.

Running to the cab, she shouted, "Chadwick! What on bloody earth are you doing?"

"I'm stopping it! I'm stopping it!"

Bounding up into the cab and pulling him back, she scanned the controls. "Which one? Which one is it?"

"The blue handle. That blue one!" He pointed at a tall lever with blue rubber grip.

Reaching for it, Vanessa tried to heave it in either direction, but it wouldn't budge.

Gripping it with both hands, she leaned all of her weight onto it.

"I tried that," Chadwick said from behind her.

"Shut up." She swatted him.

Then she flicked the small metal switch to the side of the lever.

"That too."

Glancing back at him, she wanted to rip out the lever and shove it all the way down the bloody fool's throat.

Then, with a finality that meant the cycle had completed, the crunching stopped.

The motor whined to a halt.

And silence hovered between them removing all doubt of the fate of the captives. The yelling and screaming had long stopped.

"No!" She said, "No! No! No!" She slapped at Chadwick's shoulder, as if she were scolding a dog. One that had peed on the carpet for the umpteenth time.

Untrainable.

Hopping back down and hurrying to the rear of the truck, she noticed a trickle of blood seeping from the gate.

Chadwick yelled, "Everyone alright in there?"

Vanessa turned to him and stared.

And then he must have noticed the blood because he said, "Rubles."

"Rubles?" Vanessa said, "*Rubles*?"

"Sorry."

"We needed them, you parrot-brained fool! What were you doing?"

Shoulders slumped now, Chadwick said, "They were complaining about the heat in there. I was worried someone would hear them."

"And so you crushed them?"

"No! I was moving it to the shade is all."

Covering her eyes with a hand, she said, "You've done it again."

"Another mistake. Could happen to anyone."

Then Chadwick leaned over to the truck, inspected the blood on the bumper, and as if to remove any doubt, any at all, of the simplicity with which his pulp-brain operated, he said,

"Do you think we've ruined the recyclables?"

CHAPTER NINETEEN

FINN WATCHED FROM BELOW AS MANNY POLED the skiff through the gin-clear shallow water of the Bahamas flats. Tan, wiry and yet not-overly athletic, she deserved to be on a calendar, not a fishing boat. Still, she seemed happy enough with her place here, barefoot with a ball cap pulled low.

Finn wished he had a hat now, as the sun had emerged, heating the fresh rain on the skiff's white deck into a wet smoke.

"Just a bit further," Manny said, seeming to notice his state. "Sure you don't want a cold beer? A whole cooler of lights—all American—below deck, there." She pointed to a trap door in the floor.

"Do I look like I drink light beer?" Finn patted his gut with both hands.

"You look like you have a big frame, not fat."

"Still not what it used to be." He held up the bottle of water she'd given him earlier. "This'll do."

"Your choice," she said.

After a few seconds, Finn said, "So it's my turn for the questions."

Pushing the long white pole with both hands, her biceps flexed and then her triceps. The skiff glided about six or seven feet with each stroke. She said, "Please don't rib me about being a hermit."

Finn shook his head. "Actually I'm interested in your house."

"What about it?"

"Quite a pad. Makes me wonder if you caught a shark that ate a chest full of Krugerrand gold coins." He uncapped the water and took a swig to cut the heat.

"Or I got a great deal on it."

Finn nodded. If she was shy about talking money—like most people were—Finn could respect that. Though getting her to talk may help him determine if she figured into this sordid hit-man picture.

"And the boats. Three pretty nice rigs…for a shark fisher-gal."

"Is that what I am?" She feigned offense and then flipped her ponytail.

"It's all you've shown me."

She stopped stoking, and gripping the pole with both hands, peered down at Finn. "Do you want to see…" she pouted her lips and leaned over a bit, then continued, "more?"

Finn raised a brow. How to answer that?

"Most boys do." Smiling to herself, Manny resumed poling.

Distracting, Finn admitted, while considering another angle.

Before he could come up with a tack, though, Manny said, "I like you."

"Why?"

She shrugged. "You know what you want, but you're smart enough and gentlemanly enough to let me come around to it."

Ol' Manny here was about as sharp as her sharks' teeth.

"And?"

She laughed. "How'd you know there was more?"

"Hunch."

She stopped poling and climbed down the ladder, then leaned against the base of it. The boat stilled as she said, "I see it in your eyes."

"What's that?" Finn asked.

She leaned forward the tiniest bit and said, "You're gonna' knock Trace Cashmore's head in the sand." She raised her brow and crossed her arms as she leaned back.

Finn eyed her. "And you'd like that."

"I'd pay money to see it." She clapped. "Hell I'd even paint my face and wear a Patrick Finn jersey."

Finn asked, "Why's that?"

"Because that little bastard threatened to shut down my business, take my house, and have me deported back to the States." She pointed behind her. "The house that—you're right—took me three years to permit and another four to build."

"Why would he do that?" Finn took a subtle step toward her and raised his chin an inch.

"That..." she reached to the other side of the stairs and unhooked a large pair of binoculars, and continued, "is what I'm about to show you."

Then, without another word, she took Finn's hand and led him up the ladder. Encouraging him to lean close to her, she scanned the water and stopped. She held the binoculars out to him and pointed ahead. "There. Two o'clock."

Taking the binoculars, Finn scanned the area Manny was pointing at. Not sure what he was looking for, he surveyed the surface slowly but saw nothing.

Manny said, "It's not obvious, at first."

And right as she said that, Finn noticed the dark blue circle at the floor of the ocean, about a hundred yards away. Roaming the waters around the dark circle, sleek grayish figures disappeared into the blue and re-emerged. Finn glanced at Manny, who was smiling, and he said, "Is that a blue hole?"

"It's called The Cathedral."

"Because, what...it's so deep?" Finn asked. Though it looked like nothing more than a dark hole in the bottom of the flats. No way to tell from there.

She nodded. "Maybe, but it seems more fitting that you need to pray if it gets you in its clutches."

Craning his neck over her shoulder, he said, "So, I suppose that means we're as close as we can get?"

Checking her watch, she said, "For now."

Finn understood. "When's the next tide?"

"About ten minutes..." she pointed and said, "Looks like those sharks are coming out already. That's a sure sign the water is coming in." Then, removing her ball cap and shaking her hair free, she turned to him.

Finn stood there, two steps below her—making them the same height—and she held his gaze.

Feeling a bit dizzy from the sudden rush of endorphins, Finn cleared his throat. Her lips looked soft and he imagined they would taste salty from the ocean air. He willed himself to not lean forward.

"So now you've seen where I catch them," she said, still holding his gaze.

A small wave tipped the boat and Finn's weight shifted against her leg.

She leaned into him. Her legs felt strong.

Keeping focus, he said, "And, what do you do with them, once they're...caught?"

"I take very good care of them." She reached up and traced Finn's jawbone without touching his skin. Then, leaning back and tapping the binoculars in his hand, she said, "How many do you see?"

Finn eyed her for a second and raised the binoculars. The skiff had drifted a bit closer, and he could make out a swarm of hammerheads circling and exiting the blue hole. No other types of fish, only hammerheads.

"A couple dozen, maybe?" He said.

She gave a *hmm* sound.

"Why do they come here?" Finn asked.

"I asked myself the same question."

"So?"

She smiled. "So, I went down there."

Lowering the binoculars, Finn asked, "How far?"

She gave him a wry grin. "All the way."

"With a scuba tank, I assume?"

"Nah." She patted her chest. "I've got good lungs."

I'll say, Finn thought. "What did you see?"

"A lot of beautiful nothing." She shrugged and turned away. "The sharks are here and keep coming back. And so will I."

"Okay," Finn said, "but that still doesn't explain how the Cashmores could have you deported." He pointed the binoculars toward the Cathedral. "Unless you're poaching illegally."

"Nothing illegal in catching sharks. But selling them to be exported?" She scrunched her nose and continued, "That's a bit of a gray area."

"How gray?"

"Maybe graphite-ish?"

Right.

Finn peered out to the blue hole. All but one shark had fled the area. The lone straggler swept his tail fin back and forth hard, but barely moved against the incoming current. Finn descended the ladder. "Then what's your work-around?"

"I'm a pretty white girl on a Bahamian island." She descended the ladder and pulled her ball cap on, threading a makeshift ponytail through the back of the hat, then continued, face to face with Finn again, "I get to bend the rules with, you know, a little manipulation. Nothing real of course, just a hint."

"I get it."

"Do you?"

"Sure. Women have been doing that for centuries. Can't say I blame them. It's only fair."

She eyed him then turned away, rocking the boat a bit as she stepped toward the bow. Unhooking a metal tube from the lip of the boat, she unscrewed the cap and pulled out a cloth sheath. Then she drew four sections of what appeared to be a fly rod from the sheath and assembled them to make one long one.

"What are you—"

"Bet you never caught a shark before," she said.

"Can't say I have." Finn leaned back against the ladder.

"On a fly, no less." She peered back at him. "Can you cast one of these?" She held up the rod.

Finn crossed his arms and shrugged. "I've been out for stripers, but..."

She rocked her head left and right and said, "Not too different." Then she reached under the lip of the boat and unhooked a large, round, flat shiny nickel reel with bright yellow fly line spooled inside. "But sharks tend to run a bit harder at first. You'll see."

"Manny."

She ignored him while threading the line through the rod's eyeholes.

"Manny," he said again.

"Yes, Patrick."

"We don't have time for this."

She turned back to him. Pointing the rod toward the blue hole, she said, "In about three minutes, that hammerhead is going to be sucked into the Cathedral and killed."

"Killed." Finn laughed. "As in drowned?"

She lowered her eyes in exasperation. "As in battered against the cave walls, knocked unconscious, and pumped out as a floater tomorrow morning."

"You serious?"

"Dead."

"So it's a shark. The world could use fewer of them."

"And it could use fewer infomercials and lawyers, but we don't let them die in emergency rooms, do we?"

Almost following the logic, Finn said, "What's the last infomercial you saw?"

She winced. "The Potty Putter."

"The what?"

"It's a mini golf green, you know...use your imagination."

"You're shitting me."

She laughed. "Anyway, I have a satellite dish."

He looked back toward the shore.

"And fax, high-speed Internet, even a cell phone booster."

"I thought you said you like seclusion."

"I said solitude, not seclusion." She walked to the center of the bow and pulled open a door from the floor. Retrieving a small metal box, she closed it again. Then she took a long, thickly woven metal leader and a bright pink fluffy fly from the box and began to tie them onto the clear end of the fly line. Biting the extra line off, she tightened the knot and held out the rod to Finn. "Here."

"Me?"

"I'll direct you."

Shaking his head, Finn took the rod and slipped past her to the front of the bow.

Manny smiled, wiggling her ass obnoxiously in triumph and ascending the ladder. Poling them forward a few strokes, she said, "Strip out about seventy yards of that line and get ready."

"All right." Finn yanked the line from the reel and let it fall around his feet.

"I'd tidy up a bit though." She nodded to the pile of line. "Don't want to be tangled in that when he runs."

"Right." Finn kicked the line free of his feet and stepped back.

"Get the line up in the air, about forty yards of it."

Finn imagined a hundred feet of line up in the air and started stroking the rod back and forth in the best rhythm he could muster.

"Slower," she said, "that line needs to jump when I tell you."

"Right." Finn flicked his wrist and arm back and forth in a slower beat. The line furling and unfurling behind him and then in front of him. Twenty yards of it, then thirty, then forty.

"Good," she said. "Now get ready, that shark is right outside the hole, he doesn't know he's being pulled backwards by the current. He thinks he's just swimming."

If the creature is so stupid, it doesn't deserve to live, Finn thought.

Manny said, "It's not that he's stupid, it's that he's unaware. There's a difference there too."

Ignorance, right.

"And it's not ignorance," she said. "That can only come with denial of teaching or experience."

Good point.

"Move it to three o'clock," Manny said, holding the boat steady with the pole.

Finn shifted his feet and shoulders to turn toward his right a bit. Swinging the line above him, he concentrated on hitting the spot directly to the right of the boat. Three o'clock.

"Faster now," she said.

Finn picked up the speed.

"Longer. You need more line, ten yards." Manny stood tall on the platform above him, staring to the right.

Finn let a few more feet strip out into the air and floated the line back and forth, the pink puff extending all the way out behind him and then all the way forward.

"Perfect." She tilted her head. "But he's moving, getting pulled back. Move to two o'clock! Hurry!"

Finn angled a bit to the left, pointing at two o'clock from the boat's bow.

"On the count of three, ready? One."

Finn tightened his forearm and waited for the line to extend and then back again.

"Two!" She turned to him. "We need to get his attention. Make the fly hit hard!"

Finn gritted his teeth as the line bent the long rod tip over his head. "Hard?"

"Hard!" She pointed high in the air. "Now!"

And he let the line unfurl all the way behind him and then forward again in one, long, smooth motion. The pink fly drifted fifty yards back and then fifty forward, a long bright yellow line streaming behind it and hovering over the surface just before the fly plopped into the water.

Unable to see anything below the surface, Finn trusted that Manny had placed him in the right spot. He expected her to tell him to strip the line in order to move the fly or something, but before he could even react, the surface exploded before him. The hammerhead flew from the water and swung its thick head, right before crashing back to the surface, the pink fly hooked into the corner of its mouth.

"He's on!" Manny yelled and clapped.

Great, Finn thought. Now what?

The rod bowed, hard.

Holding the tip high, he watched the pile of line at his feet disappear in mere seconds. Then the reel began to spin, whining as the line stripped into the water.

Manny hurried down the ladder. "Shit!" She yelled.

Finn turned his head to see her ripping off her hat and leaning over the side of the skiff.

Then she rolled back over and dumped a hat full of water on the reel and his hands. "Forgot that part, sorry."

Finn held the rod and watched the line spool off in long rips.

A hundred yards.

Two hundred.

Two-fifty.

"Get ready," she said, standing right behind him now, so close that he could feel her breath as she spoke.

And the line stopped spooling.

"Reel!" She yelled, reaching around him with both hands and directing him.

He reeled.

"Good. Faster!" She made a reeling motion herself. "Go!"

He reeled faster, glancing back.

"Yes!"

No resistance at all now, the shark felt like dead weight at the end of the line.

"Oh shit," she said. "Here it comes."

"Here what—"

And the rod jerked forward as the line began stripping from the reel again, spraying their faces with saltwater as it screamed off.

"Whoa!" Manny said, grabbing the back of Finn's shirt.

He steadied his arms as the rod bent.

"Get ready," she said, "Here it comes again."

And the line stopped.

She squeezed his shirt. "Now!"

And Finn reeled.

"Faster," she said. "Sharks go hard and fast. But watch out if he turns."

"If he what?"

And just as he said it, the shark swiveled in the water and raced toward them.

Right at the boat.

"Faster. Reel faster!" She yelled. "He'll go right under us!"

Finn reeled the line as fast as he could. The shark kept coming, so fast that a wake swelled behind it.

"He's a biggie!" Manny said. "Hurry!"

He reeled faster.

The shark swung its wide-brimmed hammerhead back and forth as it barreled toward them.

"Shit!" Manny yelled.

The shark, now twenty feet away, sped up.

Manny backed away.

Finn reeled.

The shark sped. Ten feet.

Five.

Manny ran halfway up the ladder.

And right as the shark was about to dive under the boat, Finn's reeling caught up to him. The rod bent, Finn pulled, and the shark popped out of the water.

And it slammed onto the deck of the boat.

"Uh oh!" Finn yelled.

"Get it off, get it off!" Manny screamed.

The shark swung back and forth, chomping its jaws at Finn's legs.

"Mother—"

"Get away from it!" Manny screamed.

It chomped at Finn again, cornering him to the tip of the skiff.

"Shit!"

The shark opened its jaws.

Manny screamed.

And Finn reared back his fist, coiled his strength, and he clobbered it. Right between the eyes.

Stunned, the shark stopped moving.

Finn nudged its bulbous belly with the bottom of his foot, rolling it back into the water.

And the shark spun once, then sauntered off.

Manny, out of breath, hopped off the ladder. "Did you just punch a shark? In the nose?"

"Sorry." Finn said, shaking his hand by his side. "I know you love them."

"No." She walked closer to him. "That was hot."

Out of breath, hand still vibrating, Finn looked at her with suspicion. "For real?"

Walking even closer, she stopped in front of him and looked up into his eyes.

"Smoking," she said.

And then she reached her arm around his neck, pulling him down and herself up, and she kissed him.

And Finn kissed her back.

She pushed away from him, took hold of the bottom of her shirt, and said, "How would like a peek at those lungs?"

Trace had taken one look at the chicks through his peephole and knew they weren't twins. At least the younger one wore a miniskirt, unstylish as it was with the checkered pattern. And she had an ass to show off with it.

When they'd entered the room, he noticed that younger one also had much hipper tattoos, you know, like the angel wings on her shoulder blades. The older one had some sort of ankle tattoo, so eighties, and she wore brown leather gladiator shoes.

The older introduced them as Grace and Maura, the *Tickler Twins*.

He swigged his drink—and closed the door.

"So, Maura," he said, turning the lock, "You're of age, right?" He didn't care, but he didn't want to spend the night in jail for some stupid technicality. Big eyes, small tits, sticky legs, totally fuckable. But he'd have to let grandma watch or something. No way he could do her.

She didn't respond, so Trace took that as a yes. He leaned over and whispered in her ear, "Ever duked a billionaire before?"

She giggled.

Then Grace came up behind him and started tickling his neck and upper back. That felt pretty good. Maybe he'd let her do that while the other one sucked him off.

"Ready to get this party started?" Grace asked.

"Sure," Trace said, his eyes fluttering closed.

Maura began to knead his groin.

As if they'd read his mind, Grace continued to tickle Trace's neck, while Maura knelt down before him. Unzipping his fly, she took out his almost-woody and tickled him with her long nails.

Tickle Twins it was.

And just as Trace was beginning to enjoy the service enough to give the concierge a pass for the swindle, he opened his eyes and looked down at Maura.

She winked and then gave him a big, wide, open-mouth, smile.

Trace stumbled backwards, dropping his drink. It plunked on her head. With more teeth than an alligator gar, none of them pointing down, she looked like that ugly girl character from Looney Tunes.

"Ouch!" She yelled and rubbed her head.

"Hey!" Grace pushed him off her, sending them both to the hotel room floor.

Trace landed with a thud, almost hitting his head on the desk leg, and Grace toppled over Maura, sending them to the floor right where Faith had been passed out that morning. Grace's legs flopped open and Maura's face planted between the pasty thighs.

Money shot.

Trace started laughing and couldn't stop. He kept laughing and laughing as he watched the two chicks, mom and daughter, whatever, gather their fake purses and storm out of the room. Trace fell backwards and kept laughing until his stomach hurt. Then he laughed some more. And then he realized that his entertainment for the evening had left.

Shit.

Propping himself up on both elbows, he sulked for a minute.

Ugly bitches anyway, he thought.

He walked back over to the mini-bar and poured the fourth, and last, bottle of shitty vodka into the last clean glass in the room. No ice left, he swigged it down in a single, hot gulp.

More.

Rummaging through the remaining bottles, he found two bottles of shitty gin. Pouring them both into the glass, he slugged those too. Then he grabbed the keycard from the desk, stepped into his loafers—wrong feet at first, fixed that—and headed out of the room toward the casino. The party would have to be there tonight.

Stumbling to the elevator, he pressed the button, and an eternity later, the elevator arrived, empty, thank God. He stepped inside, careful not to trip on the lip of the floor, and in his overcompensation, he fell into the mirrored elevator wall.

A gin burp surfaced and he blew it to the other side of the elevator and waved his hand at the smell, hoping no honeys got on before he reached the ground floor.

Reaching bottom without incident, Trace straightened his shirt and walked out of the elevator, chin high. He didn't see the concierge anywhere. The casino was all the way across the street, like over a hundred feet away. No way he could walk that far in this heat. He'd have to get the hotel to ferry him over there. Walking up to the front desk, Trace snapped his fingers at two clerks chatting away about some stupid reality show or something.

They turned to him, full-on attitude.

"I need a ride," Trace said, burping again, but swallowing it this time.

"Certainly, Mr. Cashmore. And where will you be going this evening?"

"The casino." He pointed, but his arm flailed a bit wider than he meant it to.

"In Nassau?" She raised her eyebrows really high.

"No." He pointed again. "That one."

She stared at him until her front-desk partner took over. "Of course, Mr. Cashmore. A ride can be arranged. Please." Pointing to the couches across the lobby, she said, "have a seat and we will alert the driver."

"I'll stand." Trace wobbled to the front door and waited, arms crossed.

Four whole goddamned minutes later the driver finally pulled into the circle and opened the rear door.

"Took you so long?" Trace asked.

But the sour-faced driver ignored him. He sped out of the driveway so hard that Trace hit his head on the seat-belt clip. Then he stopped short and Trace smacked his face on the seatback in front of him.

Asshole.

Trace didn't wait for him to open the door, he flung it open himself.

The car sped off.

Trace stood in front of the casino entrance in disbelief. A Radisson? The casino was in a three star hotel?

Sulking to the door, Trace hoped they had good vodka in the dump. Or gin, whatever.

Nobody even greeted him as he entered.

I mean really. How did they expect to keep the high rollers with service like that?

And the place was dead.

Maybe a hundred people in the whole joint, most of them employees. Though, it was four o'clock. Or maybe five—hard to tell with the Rolex. But some sort of Reggae-looking band was setting up on a small stage in the restaurant at the center of the casino.

Trace hoped they didn't suck.

Pulling out his wallet, he wandered to the blackjack area where three dealers were working the front three tables, all set as ten-dollar minimums. All three were guys. Walking past those, he noticed that a single dealer was working a twenty-five dollar table. Of course, it was the only chick blackjack dealer in the whole place. The casino knew how to push guys to the high-dollar tables. Didn't matter to Trace though, ten, twenty-five minimum, what did he care? Could be a thousand minimum and make no difference to him.

Plus, as far as he could tell, there was no high-roller room on the whole floor.

What a dump.

Trace approached the table, empty of other patrons. Too steep, he supposed. The dealer raised her head and looked right at Trace. With long, thick black hair and a tiny nose, she smiled.

"Welcome to Treasure Bay," she said in a throaty voice.

Unfortunately, the hot ones always aced him out, and she was way hot.

Trace gave her a chin-thrust and said *hey*, casual as a carrot, then sat down on the bamboo-style chair and tossed a few hundred-dollar bills her way. One fluttered from the fan above and sailed past her to the floor.

Oops.

She turned and looked at it and then at Trace.

Trace rolled his eyes, remembering some stupid rule about dealers only being allowed to touch money that's been placed on the table. He groaned and pushed back, knocking the stool to the floor.

He shrugged at the manager and then stumbled around the table to pick up the C-note.

Bending to the floor on the other side, Trace turned his head and saw the dealer was wearing pink lace panties.

Nice.

Then he was hit with an idea reeking of Edison-brilliance. He'd tip this chick before she ever dealt him a card. In fact…

Trace crawled a step toward her on his knees and, crumpling the *hundo* in his palm, he reached up and stuffed the bill in the hot little dealer's crotch.

Money.

Or—as he was tackled by two monsters from behind—maybe not.

Glovesave cantered across the hot white sand, a bit tired from the long swim and trying to keep up with Kicksave. Sniffing the sand and snorting it back out, Glovesave stopped at a wrapper. Some sort of candy?

Nothing left.

That's okay. What they really needed was water. The ocean had plenty, but it was salty and only made him want more. He needed a bowl of the good stuff, like from the toilet.

Glovesave stopped and shook all over, spraying saltwater in every direction. Then he bounded up to Kicksave and kept going.

Kicksave caught back up, bit Glovesave in the ass, and took off.

Hey you rascal! That hurt!

Glovesave bounded across the sand and chased him.

Kicksave darted left and up the beach toward a house.

Glovesave jumped over a sprout of grass and tackled him, biting Kicksave's ass.

See how you like it.

They rolled and rolled down the hill and to the edge of a path, barking and biting each other. Then Kicksave rolled on top of him, growled, and stopped.

They both looked to the side, under the porch.

Hey, a shoe!

Two, actually!

And there's a person in them.

Leaping up, they both ran to the shoes and sniffed.

Gamey.

But hey look, Glovesave kept walking.

Half a taco.

Yummy.

CHAPTER TWENTY

MANNY POLED THE SKIFF FROM THE REAR, while Finn stood up on the platform, holding his phone straight up in the air, staring at the screen. He needed to check up on Lew and Nikki and maybe scan his messages.

The blue green water extended to infinity in the distance, glittering with the remnants of the afternoon sun, and the ocean sounded calm there on the flats—the birds having all but disappeared in search for mangroves to roost in for the night.

"A little closer," he said.

She stopped poling. "Should be getting one by now."

The antenna icon on his phone blinked once, then showed a bar. A moment later, it showed two. "Perfect."

Manny hopped out of the skiff and into the waist-deep water, widened her feet, and leaned onto the lip with both elbows, holding it still. "Go ahead."

Finn dialed Lew's cell number and it went straight to voicemail. Finn asked him to call back and hung up. Then he tried Nikki's cell.

Same thing.

Either both phones were turned off or they had run out of battery. Possible, if the phones were scanning for a signal non-stop, but Nikki was pretty savvy. She'd have switched hers off. In any case, neither number gave him an out-of-service-area message.

Strange.

Finn dialed the number to the voicemail of the phone that got water-fried on his little swim to shore from the raft. After pressing his code, he listened. He had seven messages. The first five were GMs, each of them were wanting to discuss the Kunkle business and get details on his contract. The next one was from his mom. She wanted to discuss plans for Thanksgiving.

Mom, it's June.

Skip.

The last message was from a number he didn't recognize. A 242 area code.

Bahamas.

He pressed Play and listened.

Nikki's voice, "Patrick? You should be ashore by now, and if, uhm, you get this, could you please…" her voice trailed off and he could hear her asking for a number, then she resumed, "call this number." She recited the number and ended with, "I'm going to need you to post bail."

Good ol' Nikki.

He dialed the number and a female voice answered, "First Bahamas Royal Police, Sergeant Nix."

"This is Patrick Finn, I'm calling for a Nikki O'Callahan." He glanced at Manny, who had her head tucked into her arms, resting. He said, "I'm her attorney."

Manny raised her head and then her eyebrows.

He shrugged.

Sergeant Nix, said, "Hold on." Finn waited for a bit and when she returned, she said, "Their bail hearing isn't until tomorrow."

"What's the charge?"

"Let me look here…says, Assault of a Police Officer."

Nikki, looks like you're in the pokey for the night. At least you'll be safe there. Hopefully.

Then it hit him and Finn said, "Wait. Did you say they?"

"Her accomplice, a Mr. Lewmond Kunkle. It'll be a joint hearing."

Great Nikki, now Lew's tabloid fodder.

"Mr. Finn, are you also Mr. Kunkle's attorney, then?"

"Yes," Finn said. "Can I speak with them?"

"Not on the phone. But visiting hours go for…" her voice faded and returned, "another thirty minutes."

"Then what time is the hearing?"

"Hasn't been set yet. Call tomorrow, open at nine."

"Thanks." He hung up.

Manny said, "That didn't sound good."

Finn shook his head and descended the ladder. "Long story."

"Yeah?" She stood still at the side of the skiff. "How about a swim?"

Then Finn realized she was naked again.

"May help calm your mind," she said.

Why not?

Finn stepped back out of the shorts and set them down without clattering the gun, then slipped into the water beside Manny. It was warm, but still refreshing.

After about a minute of this, Manny asked, "How come you're not married?"

"Why?"

"Well. You're good looking, large enough to make women feel safe, and intelligent. All attractive qualities in a husband." She glanced down, and continued, "And brave. I mean look at you all naked and exposed to the elements."

Finn gave her a sidelong glance. "Are you an element?"

She laughed. "Like cadmium."

Searching back to the grid of letters and numbers representing all the things that made up this world, Finn raised a brow. "So, you're what, shiny and metallic?"

"White metallic, strong…" she made a muscle with her bicep with a mock mean face and then leaned back and looked up. "Malleable though, like all metals…and conductive of energy."

"You give people what they need."

"To a fault."

Finn turned his head to her. "So, what? I needed this?"

"Truthfully?" She winked. "I did."

Finn smiled, then said, "Wait, isn't cadmium toxic?"

"Highly."

He wondered what exactly she was telling him, but before he could ask, she said, "So just consider this relationship for what it is."

"And what's that?"

"Over before it started."

Noted.

"Besides..." Manny stretched a long leg out of the water and letting it shimmer in the glow from the horizon. "You have work to do."

"About that," Finn said, "Tracy isn't coming back, is he?"

Manny cleared her throat and said, "Not here, no. But I'll see him again."

"And you'll lead me to him."

She smiled. "He can't get off this island without me."

"So let me see if I have this straight then." Finn nodded out to the water. "You caught sharks for Tracy. He wants them for his new arena in Houston, where the Hammerheads play...his NHL team."

She gave him a look of suspicion.

Finn continued, "You've arranged for those sharks to be transported off this island, and he needs you to pass customs, so you need to be with him when he boards the boat or whatever."

"Plane."

"You can send sharks on a plane?"

"Special tanks. Ever seen Discovery Channel?"

"No."

"Well, it can be done. But...I was less than forthright about the customs part."

"How much less?"

"Let's just say he needs me to drug the fish, you know, so they don't thrash themselves to death when the plane takes off. They apparently don't like pressurized cabins."

"How do you drug them?"

"Easy as putting the right amount of *MS 222* into the water. It's automatically administered through the gills."

"Like a tranquilizer."

"Sort of. Makes 'em sluggish, that's about all."

Finn took a deep breath. "And so what time is Nurse Manny arriving at the airport?"

"Nine am."

Finn nodded and looked out to the calm waters, wondering if Colleen had made any progress on the hitmen. He knew she wouldn't go directly for Tracy at first, because she'd want information about this so-called network for her own advancement. If she happened to save some lives along the way, well, great. She was as narcissistic as they came, and Finn had to watch out for her.

But he had a plan to take down the one that mattered. Because Finn could eliminate every hitman sent to kill him and there'd only be more. It wouldn't stop unless Finn took down the source of the threat.

Tracy Cashmore.

In the meantime, by staying put, he could avoid Colleen and any noise she rustled up.

Moving behind him and putting her arms around his ribs, Manny said, "So what does this guy owe you?"

He leaned back into her, enjoying the feel of her warm hands.

Finn said, "It's not what he owes me."

He could feel her head pull away as she said, "You're after him for someone else?"

"Not exactly."

"Are you really a lawyer?"

He said, "Yes, but not his."

"Fascinating." She reached down and began to stroke him.

This made it difficult to concentrate. Again.

Finn let his eyes close as he said, "Tracy is the General Manager of an NHL team called the Hammerheads. He's also part owner."

"So?" She continued as she breathed warm air on his neck.

"So." Finn exhaled. "I'm a sports agent. And I represent a player Tracy is trying to…screw…out of a lot of money."

"Now it makes sense," she whispered, "How much…money?"

Finn hesitated, then said, "Twelve million dollars."

"Whoa." She gripped him a bit tighter. "And how much of that is yours?"

Finn opened his eyes. Glancing back, he said, "I get the standard four percent."

Without hesitation, she said, "Four-hundred and eighty thousand? For one contract?"

It was all Finn could do to nod to her.

"Wow." She picked up the pace a bit. Then, leaning forward and licking his earlobe as she brought him closer to climax, she said, "Now tell me this."

Anything, Finn thought.

"What are you really doing in the Bahamas?"

The drop, located in the courtyard of the Freeport International School, was surrounded by thickets of trees and provided excellent coverage from the street and houses on all sides, but the air smelled stale without circulation.

Edging between the trees, Colleen replayed the scene she'd just witnessed. Vanessa and Chadwick had taken the money. Then they'd stuffed Mickel and Tabia in the back of a recycling truck.

And then they'd crushed them.

Shaking it off and concentrating on the task at hand, Colleen found Stanley and his tight pile of curly red hair standing in the courtyard's center.

She skipped the greeting and nodded at his backpack.

He drew a weapon from inside the pack and handed it to her. With a thick black rubber grip and dark green industrial-plastic housing, the gun looked like a futuristic pistol of sorts.

"A Taser." Colleen turned the device in her hands.

"Two, actually." He handed her another Taser gun and shrugged. "It's all we have left."

Shaking her head, Colleen asked, "And where's the rest of it? We had an arsenal stocked away."

"Between Benny, Vanessa, and James—well, and you—all the SIGs are out. And then Mickel took the AKs and the launcher. This is all we have left, I swear."

"The launcher. As in a grenade launcher?"

"Actually, its an *XM25 Counter Defilade Target Engagement System*. Or CDTE for short." Stanley smiled, all smug.

"What the hell is a CDTE?"

"I just told—"

"In English, you little snot."

His smile faded. "It uses a laser to determine target distance."

"And?"

"And… the grenade is automatically programmed at launch to explode right before impact."

She stared at him. "And why, Stanley, would we need one of these?"

He blinked twice, then managed, "I suppose…maybe we could use it for a large project? Or perhaps multiple targets?"

She let out a big sigh. These children did not understand precision killing. "How did we get it?"

"Mickel."

Of course. Fucking former army intelligence, a CIA-wannabe.

She held up the Taser. "And this too? That's why it's green?"

He nodded.

"Does it work?"

"I don't know, I just…" he glanced from Colleen to the gun and back to Colleen.

"Let's see, shall we?" She raised the gun and inspected it. Then she flipped a small switch above the handle down, exposing a red triangle.

"Wait." Stanley's eyes widened. "What are you—"

But before he could finish, she pulled the trigger.

Two small metal darts blasted from the gun and struck Stanley in the chest. His arms spasmed to his sides and he fell over like a plank of wood, his head hitting the ground. The electricity pulsed into him for a five full seconds.

"Ow," he muttered feebly.

Colleen walked over and stared down at him. "How many more shots do I have?"

Stanley groaned but she couldn't understand him.

"Blink the answer."

He blinked twice.

She held up the other gun. "And three here too?"

He gave the world's shortest nod.

"Good." Colleen popped out the spent cartridge and dropped in on his chest, leaving the wires and darts in him. "And Stanley?"

She turned and said over her shoulder, "Don't ever cross me again."

"Where'd you learn to fight like that, dude?" Lew asked Nikki. He was sitting on the pipe extending from concrete wall down to the toilet.

Picking her head up from the jail cell's blue-painted metal bench, she touched a few fingers to the welt over her eye. It wasn't the arrest that upset her so much, it was the three cops teaming up on her like a junior hockey team. The first one had pulled her off of Officer Duane's head.

She'd just gotten a finger hooked into the man's eye-socket too.

Then the second one held her legs and they swung her right into the metal table, face first.

Two minutes and a raging brawl later—though it was hard to call it a brawl, what with Lew doing no more than standing and staring the whole time—they'd cuffed her hands behind her back and her legs together.

Then they'd stuffed her own sock in her mouth.

Bastards.

"Older brothers." She shrugged.

Lew nodded, brows high. "You're crazy a chick."

"I'm a chick who stands up for herself."

"I wouldn't fight you." He tapped the toilet with a flip-flop.

She had to admit, with a spotless concrete floor and newly painted walls, the cell was cleaner than a nun's ass. The moment the plastic zip ties had closed on her wrists and feet, she'd envisioned the basement cell on Devil's Island in Papillon. Complete with shit-stained walls and tin pots to both piss into and eat out of.

The only disturbing part of the whole imprisoned on an island thing was the relentless and maddening rattle of air vents right outside the cell. Unable to see more than a few feet down the hall either way, though, she chose to just keep quiet and not make a fuss on that simple point.

Lew didn't seem affected a bit about the whole ordeal, and was humming now.

"Is that Dancing Queen?"

"Gotta love ABBA," he said.

She stared at him.

"Lew."

"Yep?"

"How often do the shots hit your head?"

"The melon?" He looked pensive for a full minute, then said, "At least once a game by a puck, and..." he tilted his head and continued, "then once or twice by a body or stick or something."

"So, maybe...what...two, three hundred times in a year?"

"Sounds fair." No comment beyond that, he said "Anyway, maybe it's better this way, you know, for Kicksave and Glovesave."

Nikki said, "Better?"

"They seemed so confused," he said.

"They're dogs, Lew. I think their emotions stop at hunger," she said. And before she could elaborate on that, a loud clang sounded from the hall. Then the shouting began.

"You don't know who you're screwing with!"

A few moments.

"I'll have your badge, pal!"

And then, *"Yours too!"*

And before he even spelled it out for them, *C-A-S-H-M-O-R-E*, she knew who the slurring rage belonged to.

"Cashmere?" Someone, presumably a guard asked, "Sounds luxurious, mon."

"Cash...More, you moron. I said Cash. More. *Get it?*"

"Got it, mon. Here you go."

They rounded the corner and stood before the cell.

And there he was, the dipshit incarnate. Tracy—*Trace to my Friends*—Cashmore.

Nikki had met him at an over-ceremonious tour of the new arena in Houston for the Hammerheads. She, along with about forty other lucky souls, got to hear all about how the Hammerheads were going to drive themselves right into bankruptcy.

I mean, who the hell heard of putting a shark tank inside an ice rink, anyway?

Under the ice, no less.

He stumbled to the front of her cell. Shirt torn from collar to chest. Tangled hair in his face.

One loafer.

Then she realized, with the sudden epiphany of a monkey who's just discovered his own penis, exactly what Finn had hunched. That this *shitbum* was the one behind the hitmen. Why else would he be on this island with them? *Today*, no less.

The policeman unlocked the cell and nudged Trace inside.

Lew stood up fast. "Mr. Cashmore?"

Nikki eased over to Lew and put the back of a hand on his chest, lowered her head, and glared at the overgrown wasted sperm before her.

Trace stared at them with a look that settled somewhere between indifference and oblivion.

Then he burped.

"Fuck are you?" He said, a bit too loud.

And before Lew answered, Trace pushed past both of them and went straight to the toilet. Burping again, he said, "Uh oh."

Then he fell to his knees, placed both forearms on the toilet seat, and stared into the steel bowl for a moment before dropping his head.

Right into the water.

CHAPTER TWENTY-ONE

HAVING PARKED A FULL TWO BLOCKS AWAY to be sure they couldn't hear the rumble of the Porsche, Colleen tiptoed behind the taxi van and across the gravel drive of the safe house—while holding the Taser ready. The recycling truck was gone, no surprise. She stopped before the edge of the porch and looked up at the back of the house. No lights were on, and she couldn't hear anything over the sound of the surf.

She studied the deck.

Wooden, with stilts and warped at the edges, it may creak when she ascended the stairs.

Only one way to find out.

She took a single step and the board creaked so loudly that two crabs scurried across the deck and flipped themselves onto the sandy grass.

Colleen creaked back off and listened.

Nothing.

Confident that Vanessa and Chadwick were still inside, Colleen didn't see a better way of getting the whole situation under control. She needed to rein them in, maybe knock them off herself, take back the money, and resolve the Cashmore business once and for all.

Then she could either re-establish The Network from scratch or disappear herself.

Fading back into the shadow of a thick palm tree, Colleen thought about the Brits, Vanessa and Chadwick. Bumbling and foolish, they happened to be dangerous. Lethal, in fact. They had killed dozens of people for the network, and Colleen had just witnessed them crushing two of their own colleagues to death.

These two would have to go. For good.

She would stun them each with the Taser, then tie them up and drop them into the water. They could float into oblivion or drown. Maybe be eaten by sharks, even better.

Peering around the other side of the tree, she searched the side of the house. One window stood propped open, the thin gauze of a white sheer drapery flittering in and out like a ghost.

Flicking the safety off the Taser, she took a single step out from behind the tree when she felt a thud on the back of her head.

And before she even hit the ground, the world fell black.

"You hit her hard enough," Chadwick said, hovering over Colleen's body as Vanessa finished taping her limbs together. To be safe, she wound a few extra wraps around each spot.

"But I didn't kill her, did I?" Vanessa stood up.

Chadwick pouted as he moved to the other side of the kitchen. "You could have."

"How?"

"Well, you could've missed the back of her head and sent her nose into her brain, for one."

"Oh that's only in the movies. Doesn't happen in real life."

"All right then, you could've broken her neck."

"And she would've been paralyzed, not killed."

"Same difference."

Vanessa stared at Chadwick, and unwilling to proceed with this discussion, she looked past him. "Let's have a look at the Tasers."

She pointed at the devices on the countertop.

He handed one to her. One of the cartridges in the front of this one seemed to be missing. Or perhaps it had been used.

"Do you suppose she was coming to Tase us?" Chadwick inspected the other gun.

"Well I don't think she was sneaking into the yard, holding two of these," she held up the gun, and continued, "with the intention of having crumpets and tea."

"How do they work?" Chadwick fiddled with the safety switch.

"No idea," Vanessa said.

Colleen moaned, her eyes fluttered open.

"Look who's waking." Vanessa walked over to Colleen. "Have a nice nappy nap, did we?"

Colleen said in a throaty voice, "Screw you."

Vanessa tilted her head. "Now, now. I'm not the one who was stalking around with these, am I?" She held up the Taser.

"Where's the money?" Colleen asked.

And before Vanessa could feign ignorance, Chadwick said, "Which lot?"

Vanessa walked over and slapped his head. "Do shut it."

Colleen said, "You need me."

Vanessa looked down at her. "Do I?"

"Or you would've killed me already." Colleen smiled. "You would've shot me earlier, out on the raft."

"Yes, well, I don't miss often, do I? Though, that stint with the bird pissed me off enough. I should shoot you now for that."

Colleen smiled but didn't respond.

Chadwick flicked the buttons on the gun and blue electric pules flashed from the flat muzzle.

"Careful with that!" Vanessa stepped away from him. Then she said to Colleen, "But I'm teaching old Chaddy here that we musn't kill every person who crosses us, or crosses our paths for that matter."

"I've learned my lesson, mum. Honest." He pointed the gun at

Colleen and then at the ceiling.

"Shut up," Vanessa said.

"I've frozen your passports," Colleen said.

"You did what?" Vanessa snapped her gaze to Colleen.

"All of them. Every single alias."

"Bullocks," Chadwick said.

"So we're stuck here. On this rathole of an island?"

"Like I said, you need me." Colleen smiled.

"I think I've got it, mum!" And before Vanessa could turn to him, she heard a pop, like the sound of a balloon and felt a smack in her back.

First, a flash of burning throughout her whole body—no—her entire being.

Then, every single muscle snapped into contraction, so hard that it felt as though they were literally being ripped off the bone.

She lost the ability to control anything, dropping her own Taser, and then falling to the ground, like a book toppling over, and smacked the linoleum floor with the side of her face. Five full seconds of incapacitation.

And then she came to.

Blinking and stuttering and sucking in her breath, she said, "You Tased me!"

Chadwick looked dumbfounded.

"You fucking Tased me!" Scrambling to her knees and checking her faculties, she searched around her. "You stupid, cow-brained, minimal excuse for a living creature! You fucking—"

"Sorry." Chadwick approached her. "Don't move."

Colleen glanced from Vanessa to Chadwick, mouth agape.

"What're you—?" and before Vanessa could react, Chadwick pulled one dart from her back and then the other. They felt like fishhooks being torn from the skin.

"Ouch!" Vanessa said.

"Idiots," Colleen said, shaking her head.

Chadwick said, "I'm sorry, I didn't mean to—"

"Give me that!" Vanessa said, shaking as she stood.

Chadwick reached forward with the gun in a slow, hesitant fashion. "I said I was sorry."

Vanessa snatched the Taser. Then she flicked off the safety, pointed it at Chadwick, and shot him in the face.

His arms clutched his chest and he fell to the ground in one long plank, like a surfboard, muttering, "*Ow!*" while shaking all over.

"You two are a circus act!" Colleen said.

"Oh, you." Vanessa turned.

Chadwick groaned. His eyes flickered open.

"You're like Dumb and Dumber," Colleen said, "Worse! You two are like Beavis and Butthead."

"Do shut up!" Vanessa dropped the gun, grabbed the other, and shot Colleen's chest.

She yelled and fell over.

Chadwick sat up. "You Tased her tit!"

Vanessa, red with rage, held the button and watched Colleen thrash and spasm on the floor. Drooling and eyes wide, she jerked so hard that her head hit the cabinets.

"Stop pressing, Vanny, you'll kill her!"

But Vanessa kept pressing the trigger, blue electric bolts flashing from the muzzle and down the wires.

"Vanny!" Chadwick wobbled over and smacked the gun from her hand, sending it toppling to the floor.

Colleen lay still.

Breathing hard, Vanessa watched Chadwick lumber across the kitchen and stare down at Colleen. Then he felt for her pulse.

Shaking his head, he turned to Vanessa, and with two darts stuck in his face, their wires extending to the gun on the floor, he said, "I think you've killed her."

CHAPTER TWENTY-TWO

HER OWN PRIVATE OCEAN PARKING SPOT, MANNY had called it. Then she'd poled them to a place that had a long, flat yellow-green rock and, hidden underneath, some sort of hook or bolt to secure the skiff. Off in the distance, and with the sun setting in a blood-orange glow, Finn could make out the silhouette of Manny's house on the cliff. Manny, using two huge beach towels—one of them NASCAR themed with Jeff Gordon's face superimposed over a car—formed a makeshift pallet, and they slept naked under the stars, out in the quiet flats.

Exhausted to the point of incapacitation, Finn slept better than he had in months. Manny lay with her head tucked into the crook of his shoulder, one leg thrown over his midsection, and with the second towel thrown over them, they hadn't moved from that position all night.

He woke at the first sign of dawn, a glittering of sun over the horizon, and estimated it to be about five-thirty am.

Over three hours to get to the airport. He'd take care of Tracy and then retrieve Nikki and Lew.

Manny breathed hard and long, still deep in sleep.

Finn thought about Colleen and her role in all this the last couple of days. Would she still have showed up if Finn hadn't called her? He suspected the answer to that would be *yes*. And was she using Finn or protecting him? Or was she keeping him in the dark best she could, Finn being neither important nor unimportant to her?

That would fit Colleen.

Finn had deflected most the questions about him being out here, but with her relentless pursuit of his marriage status, he ended up confessing his serious relationship with Colleen. Of course, he glossed over the real issues of trust—sleeping with a CIA agent tended to make one wary of that—and just said that somewhere during their relationship he'd realized he liked to be alone too much to give up that freedom.

Manny could understand that.

As for Colleen, though, Finn figured she had to know who was involved in this scheme.

And how arrogant and ignorant were the Cashmores anyway? Reneging on a contract was one thing, but trying to kill your way out of one?

He glanced at his shorts, still balled into his shirt on the other side of the skiff.

Gun secured.

Finn felt better than he had since stepping off that plane two days ago. Rested and armed, both with intelligence and a pistol for backup, he considered his chances of coming out on top of Tracy and gang to be pretty damned good.

The question was, had that British couple survived the boat crash?

Likely not, unless they were somehow rescued.

At least Lew and Nikki were tucked away safely. Even if it was in a Bahamas jail cell.

Manny stirred, with a small throaty hum and then covered her eyes with a hand. She whispered, "You're the first person I've shared this with."

"What, your NASCAR towel?"

She laughed then peered down the towel. "Looks more like a NASCAR tent to me."

Finn followed her gaze to Jeff's nose which appeared to have grown a bit. Well, well. Apparently the Finn shuttle was refueled and ready to launch again.

Manny climbed on Finn and, without even requesting permission from the control room, she played cache the missile.

This time, they tried enough positions as to make Vatsya blush, and ended with a contortion that had Manny's ankles tucked behind Finn's head...while she was on top.

If he could only remember how they got there.

Almost falling back to sleep afterwards, but feeling even better than he had upon waking, Finn slowly turned to Manny. She looked quite content too, flat on her back with her eyes closed.

She must have sensed his gaze, as she reached over and felt for his leg, then let her hand rest on his thigh.

"Remember," she said, "Cadmium."

He patted her hand. "About that."

She blinked her eyes open and turned to him.

He said, "You ready to tell me?"

"Tell you what?"

Finn shrugged and raised his chin. "The house, the boats."

Manny stared at Finn for a moment, squinted, and then got up.

Maybe he'd pushed too far on the whole money thing. He'd have to let it go.

She walked across the skiff, bent at the door in the decking, opened it, and drew out a bottle of beer from the cooler below.

"Manny, it's a bit early for—"

"Just take it." She handed him the beer and sat down, cross-legged, before him.

"Manny, I told you—"

"Take off the label."

Finn raised a brow. "The label."

"Go ahead." She nodded toward the bottle. "Try."

Finn said, "Beer bottle labels don't come off. Well without steaming them, I suppose."

"It takes hot water and baking soda, actually."

Finn said, "And you know this because...?"

She said, "It's by design. Beer bottles are used in all kinds of environments. Anything from a bar in Anchorage, to a backyard cooler in Tampa, to a soccer stadium in Brazil."

"Okay, so they're supposed to stay on regardless—cold temperatures, wet conditions, and humid environments." Finn peeled a tiny corner of the label back.

"Not supposed to. They do."

"Right. So..." he fixed the corner back into place.

"So, beer makers paid a massive amount of money to engineer and develop the optimum mix of adhesive substance that would stick to the glass, and the paper—without ruining the label—and without being affected by, as you said, water, cold, heat, humidity, you name it."

"Is this leading back to the table of elements?"

She tapped the bottle. "They became obsessed over it. Years and years of changing the recipe, changing the paper, even changing the shipping methods. All to keep the damned labels from coming off."

"And this is important because?"

"That glue?" She reached over and took the bottle, peeled back the label showing the paper stuck to the glue underneath, and said, "This glue. Was invented by my grandfather."

"He was a brilliant scientist."

"Mad too. Sniffed too much of it, if you ask me."

"And he made a fair amount of money from it."

"He made a fortune."

Finn knew better than to ask her to define fortune. Though, he suspected that it was enough that she could compete with a Tracy Cashmore.

But then she said, "And he lost it all."

Finn eyed her. "How?"

"He bought a hockey team in Hartford."

Finn sat up. "The Whalers? Your grandfather owned the Whalers?"

"Lost over a hundred million dollars."

"And you..."

"Watched it happen."

Finn looked at the boat and then toward the house, barely visible in the distance.

She winked. "We were First Bahamian Trust's very first customer."

Offshore banking. Ah yes, the secret playground of America's wealthy. He couldn't say he blamed her for it, though. He imagined a team of banks looking to liquidate Manny's family assets and leave them with nothing. Now you have it—*oh, look at that*—now Uncle Sam and his cronies do.

She continued, "So on my eighteenth birthday, the night before the bankruptcy ruling, good old granddad gave me an envelope. Told me to open it when I was twenty-one. Then he disappeared forever."

"He set up an account for you."

"And he left me the bank details."

"You've been here ever since?"

"Ever since."

Finn was about to respond to that, but his attention was diverted by the buzz of a water vehicle.

Looking back to the shore, just West of Manny's house he saw it, well, actually them—two Jet Skis—cruising along the shoreline, spitting a stream of water out the back of each one. From this distance he couldn't tell who was on them, but it seemed strange that they would be out here so far from any hotel or resort, on the north side of the island, no less.

He turned to Manny, who had followed his gaze to the Jet Skis. "Ever see tourists out this far?"

She shook her head slowly.

The Jet Skis pulled up to Manny's dock, and Finn said, "Looks like it's time to get dressed."

Vanessa used Relay and his extensive network of island eyes to find precisely where Finn had ended up. Now she would drop this Finn character, finish the job, and get the hell off this dingy excuse for an island and find true paradise. Like Christmas Island or Maldives. Far, far away from the reach of Colleen Coffey.

Not that she was too much of a threat now. After all, they'd left her on the kitchen floor, taped to high heaven. God knows what the police would think when they found her. But by then, Vanessa would be well on her way.

For now, though, buzzing along the shoreline on the Jet Skis they'd "borrowed" from Mickel, money tucked safely in the compartment under her seat, she and Chadwick were looking for this Manny the Shark Lady's place.

Vanessa glanced back.

Poor Chaddy was still cross about the dart marks on his cheeks.

He was so mad, that she had no choice but to agree to let him take Mickel's grenade launching device from the Planning Room cupboard. The damned thing looked like a mini-bazooka. Not a chance they'd be able to hide it if stopped by the coastal police. In that case, he agreed to drop it in the water, no questions.

She hoped he didn't get any Chaddy-like ideas in the meantime.

Slowing the Jet Ski down, she held up a hand for Chadwick to follow.

Chadwick yelled, "*What do you see?*"

She waved it toward the water, signaling for him to shut up.

But he didn't. "*What? What is it, mum?*"

She turned and scowled as she put a finger to her lips. "*Shhh!*"

He made an *oh* face and shut it as he slowed his Jet Ski with hers.

She shook her head. The man couldn't sneak up on a cadaver.

Pulling up to the dock, she took inventory. Two boats, one a larger vessel for deep-sea fishing or the like and another smaller boat of the cruising or leisure variety. A third set of moorings had a rope tied to them, but no boat.

"Go check the house," she said, knowing full well that there wouldn't be anyone inside.

Chadwick shrugged and shut off the engine to his Jet Ski. Then, placing the mini-bazooka on the dock, he climbed off of the Jet Ski and onto the dock himself.

She whispered loud, "Don't go blasting anything you don't have to, do you hear?"

He made an okay circle with his finger and thumb, then crept up the long walkway to the house, holding the bazooka like a battering ram.

Watching him, Vanessa wondered how on earth the man had ever been hired by anyone, no less British Intelligence. She wondered what it said about the country. And then the man walked up the path, and clomping across the back deck, he strode straight to the door, peered inside, and rang the bloody doorbell.

What the hell was he going to say? Hello, I'm selling encyclopedias, and then *blam*!

Blow them to bits?

Thank God nobody was home.

Although that now meant they'd have to go find them.

Peering out onto the water, she couldn't make out much in the glare of the sun near the horizon. Though she thought she could make out some sort of vessel, something small and white, floating off in the distance.

Something worth a closer look.

"Take us for a spin," he said to Manny but kept his eyes on the Jet Skis and the man who had walked up to the door and back down to the docks.

"Spin?"

"If these two are who I think they are, they aren't selling girl scout cookies."

"Oh I haven't had those in years. Why'd you have to remind me?" She slid into the water and unhooked the skiff from the rock.

"Tell you what, get this skiff moving and I'll send you some."

Climbing back aboard, she said, "Really? Samoas? I love Samoas."

"I think they're called Carmel DeLites now."

"What? Why?"

Finn shrugged. "PC."

"Oh for hell. Really? What about Tagalongs?" She sat down.

Finn scrunched his face, thinking, then said, "I think those are Peanut Butter Patties now."

"Do-Si-Dos?"

"Peanut Butter Sandwiches."

"See why I moved? Next thing you know, they're going to say that Florida State can't be the Seminoles."

"It went to court."

"You can't be serious."

"No worries, suit was voted down. They kept the name. But the Washington Redskins are on the hot-seat." He kept his gaze out at the docks. "And the way you're sitting now?"

She looked down. "What, Indian style?"

Finn shook his head. "Criss-cross, applesauce."

"Oh for fuck's sake."

The Jet Skis buzzed out from the dock and started toward them. Hopping up and climbing to the back of the skiff, she started the motor, then asked, "So, Patrick, are you going to tell me who that is?"

Finn reached down and felt the SIG in the shorts pocket as

Manny steered them toward the open water.

"Let's just say they work with Tracy Cashmore. For him, actually." Finn glanced at Manny and then behind himself. "Can you get us to that island there?"

"It's actually just a tangle of mangroves, but sure."

"OK. Get to the mangroves and sneak inside them."

"What, are you going to have a boat fight? Afraid I might get launched?"

"Trust me, okay?"

"If you're really worried, then I'll go hide in the cooler for a bit."

"No. This could become..." no way to soften this now, he said, "violent."

"I know violence," she said, rolling her eyes.

Finn pulled the stainless steel SIG from his pocket.

"Whoa!" Manny jerked the motor and Finn fell over. The gun flopped onto the deck.

"Can you keep steady, please?"

"Sorry, I just..." she glanced back and then to Finn. "I thought you were being hyperbolic, exaggerating."

The Jet Skis were catching up fast.

"Tell you what," Finn said, "You take cover, and I'll take care of them. Deal?"

"And if something happens to you?"

"I have experience with this sort of thing." Finn squinted to see better. The man was carrying something like a mini-bazooka. He was pretty sure Manny had yet to see this detail. He glanced behind them at the approaching mangrove island, then said, "we're almost there."

She slowed the skiff, and as they reached the trees, she said, "Let me help you."

"No," Finn said.

She shifted the motor into idle and said, "Yes." She crossed her arms, but they were shaking. Her whole body was shaking. She was staring at the madman with a bazooka.

"Off," he said. "Now."

The Jet Skis were screaming across the water at them.

Manny shook her head the tiniest bit.

Finn pointed the gun at the mangroves. "GO."

"Okay, but." She glanced back, took one more look at the man with the bazooka and dove into the water. Resurfacing at the edge of the trees, she called out, "Patrick, don't go too far, it's almost high tide."

Waiting until Manny had disappeared into the brush, Finn climbed back and steered the skiff to the side of the island, enticing the Jet Skis to follow. *Too far?*

Then the Jet Skis split up.

The woman, who appeared to be giving the man direction with one hand, raced her Jet Ski toward Finn.

Easing the skiff to the far edge of the trees, well away from Manny, Finn lay flat on the bow and got in the ready position, arms forward, gun pointed at the approaching woman.

Seemed she had the same idea, as she raised a pistol and pointed at him, too.

Finn wasn't one to wait.

He took a shot and right as he pulled the trigger, the woman leaned to the right, cutting the Jet Ski far enough to avoid the bullet.

A Jet Ski screamed behind Finn as it rounded the mangroves and barreled down on him.

Finn rolled to look back just as the woman shot at him. A *thunk* sounded in the composite material behind his left foot.

Finn rolled off the skiff and splashed into the water. Shielding his body with the hull, he peered around the side at the woman. She'd cut again and was now headed to the far side of the skiff.

The man popped up high on his Jet Ski behind Finn.

The woman shot again. This time, the bullet shattered the tip of the boat, one foot from Finn's face.

He darted out and shot at her again. He must have struck the handlebar, because the Jet Ski jerked hard to the right and the woman almost fell off.

"No!" the man yelled. Then, raising his weapon, he pointed it at Finn.

Finn dove away from the boat, but with the water as clear as triple distilled vodka, it was hard to hide. He couldn't swim into the mangroves, that would put Manny in danger. So, he thought of a better idea.

Diving under the skiff, he re-emerged, and located the woman.

Not giving her enough time to aim and shoot, he dove back under the skiff again.

Re-emerging on the other side, he found the man with the bazooka.

The man pointed as he turned.

Banking on the time it would take to aim that thing, Finn grabbed the side of the skiff with both hands, and heaved himself onto the deck.

The man swung the bazooka upwards.

The woman yelled, in a British accent, "No Chadwick! Don't!"

Too late, the man pulled the trigger.

Finn dove off the bow again and plugged his ears as he swam as far as he could.

A *boom* shook the water and little scraps of white wood and composite exploded above and around him, as the skiff was annihilated.

Popping to the surface, Finn watched the woman try to steer from the wreckage, but overcompensating, she flung the Jet Ski upward and fell back into the water.

Finn raised his pistol and aimed it to where he thought she would surface.

And then the damnedest thing happened.

The woman emerged, screaming, "You fucking maniac! You almost killed me! I've had it! I have fucking goddamned bloody well *had it!*"

And then she pointed another, larger green and black pistol at the man as he passed her in his Jet Ski.

He yelled, "No!" Thrusting his hand up in a feeble attempt to shield himself.

And she shot him.

The man turned into a helpless spazoid and jerked right off the Jet Ski and into the water. Then he sunk.

Finn waded toward them as he watched in disbelief. The two killers were killing each other.

But then, not.

Because the woman dropped the gun and yelled, "Chaddy. Wait, Chaddy! I'm sorry," as she dove into the water after him.

And Finn realized.

The tide had turned.

It was coming in. Hard.

And the three of them were too close. Way too close to The Cathedral.

A swarm of water swept his feet from him, and Finn went under. Gasping for air, he pushed to the surface and thrust his legs. But it didn't help.

The woman yelled, "Chaddy! Please come back Chaddy!" And she dove under again, recklessly toward the blue hole.

The current surged in power, so strong that Finn couldn't even kick. It had taken his legs and arms and sucked him. Sucked him with all its disastrously godly power toward its hole.

He pushed to the surface and took a deep breath.

"I love you Chaddy! I love you!" The woman bellowed.

Finn pushed. Stunned that the tidal spin could swallow a man of Finn's size, he reached, fighting to stay surfaced as the woman held the man and they swirled above the deep, dark, blue hole.

"I'll die with you, I will," she said. "I'm sorry, James. I'm so sorry."

The Jet Ski swirled around them.

And then it was gone.

Clinging to each other, the Brits swirled above it.

And then they were gone.

Finn kicked as hard as he could. But it was useless. He took one last, deep, long breath.

And then he was gone too.

CHAPTER TWENTY-THREE

COLLEEN LOOKED AROUND THE KITCHEN, TRYING TO place where she was for almost ten seconds before she recalled what had happened last night. Then she felt the soreness in her leg and arm muscles, and the tape wrapped tight on her limbs. Plus, she had a massive headache and her right breast hurt like hell.

Propping herself to a sitting position, she glanced around.

Nothing within reach to cut the tape.

She caterpillared on her ass across the room and into the hallway. The hardwood floors allowed her to move a bit faster down the hall. No lights on, she made her way with the sunlight creeping in from the room at the end of the hall.

The Planning Room.

This was where they hatched their most intricate and delicate operations. Like the time they'd picked off the Oregon Congressman's girlfriend. That one had some serious complications, having to be pulled off in DC.

Talk about a city wired with closed circuit cameras.

Colleen glided her ass over the threshold and peered past the tall square table covered with maps and pens, to find what she needed, yes, a three-foot, metal yardstick.

Gliding into the corner, she kicked the yardstick over, and it clanked to the floor.

No reaction from anywhere else in the house, the two half-wits were long gone.

Kicking the yardstick with her feet as she glided, she stopped at the doorway. Then, she kicked off her tennis shoes and, though it was not easy with socks on, she pinched her toes around the yardstick and lifted it. Then she guided it to the crook of the door and placed it onto the bottom set of hinges.

Spinning herself around, Colleen wiggled backwards until the yardstick was secured under her ass and up onto the hinge. Then she lifted her hands and maneuvered them to the spot where metal met tape.

And she rubbed her hands up and down.

One minute later, her hands were free.

Less than a minute later, her feet were free too.

Drawing her phone from her pocket, she checked the battery. Plenty of power as she'd used it but three times yesterday.

She began to dial Stanley's number, she needed the address of this so-called shark-lady, but the phone began to ring in her hand. She stared at the caller ID, even though she had only given one other person this number yesterday. She knew exactly who it was.

What the hell could he want now? She told him she was working on their issue and she'd have it resolved by morning. Hell, it was barely six am where he was sitting.

Then she noticed he had called three times already today. Maybe that's what woke her up.

She answered.

"This secure?" he asked.

"I told you it's untraceable."

"Good girl, where are you?"

She rolled her eyes. "About a mile away from the spot I was when we spoke yesterday, Mr. Cashmore."

"Then why aren't you taking my calls?"

"My phone...died. I recharged it. All set now."

"I need your help, Ms. Coffey."

No shit, she thought, that's why you hired me. "Look, Mr.

Cashmore...Jerry. I'm working on the—"

"I'm not talking 'bout that, darling. I need you to help my son."

She closed her eyes. The prodigal son needed help.

Shocking.

"How?"

"Seems the po-lice out that way have themselves a bit of a mix up. They've gone and accused my son of rape. Or something near to it."

Colleen sighed to herself. "Who did he...who are they saying that he...raped, Jerry?"

"Some woe-man down there at that there cas-ino. I'm sure it was more of groping-type of behavior."

"Oh, well now that's much more understandable."

"Look, I don't need judgment on the boy, I just need you to go down there and bail his sorry ass out."

"Bail."

"And I need you to bring him and the two cowpokes who also got themselves incarcerated back to me."

"Cowpokes?"

"That Lew Kunkle and his agent's girlfriend, what's her name?"

"Nikki? They were arrested too?"

"Tough country you're in, out there in them Bahamas."

"Mr...Jerry, look, I can get them out of jail here, but...I don't have a way to get everyone off the island and into the states, in my possession, if you understand what I mean."

"Darling, don't you worry your pretty little head about that. It's taken care of. Old Tracy there has a whole DC-8 waiting for him this morning. All his sharks are loaded, and he just has to get on board and bring his ass home. I want you to be sure he does that. Chaperone him."

"A DC-8?"

"We leased it from the United Parcel Systems. Now don't forget that Kunkle and company. We need them too. And if you can somehow locate that Patrick Finn, I'll gladly double our agreed-to contract. But don't kill 'em. Just bring 'em to me."

"Five hundred thousand more?"

"That's correct, darling."

A flood of goosebumps spread across Colleen's neck and back as she stared out the window at the ocean. The surf rolled but was calm and the black birds swooped down to eat little bits on the surface. Colleen felt like one of those birds right then. The bits dangling out there for the taking.

"A million in total then?"

"Just get the job done and it's yours." He hung up.

That'll help, thought Colleen. With that kind of cash, she could locate Vanessa and Chadwick and take back the rest of the money. She slipped the phone in her waistband again and headed upstairs. If she knew Finn, he'd gone into hiding, guessing exactly when to show up and where. Which meant he'd be coming straight to her.

Time to see what kind of weapons Mickel left behind.

Swirled into the darkness, Finn was disoriented and couldn't tell which way was up. So he held onto the waterlogged Jet Ski, thinking that once the swirling stopped, he would be able to let go and watch it sink, then he could kick in the opposite direction. Toward the surface.

But the swirling didn't stop.

Finn held tight as the Jet Ski bounced off a sharp coral wall. The seat popped open, and a large bag floated out. The Jet Ski weighted him in one direction and the bag floated off in another.

Finn realized he must have been under water for almost thirty seconds by then. Most people couldn't make it to a minute.

Watching the bag, Finn concentrated.

It began to float in the opposite direction of the Jet Ski. But it was floating, not swirling.

Willing his mind, and relying on his gut, Finn kicked hard toward the bag.

His muscles began to burn first. Then his lungs.

A flicker of light appeared above him. Far, far above him, the size of a candle flame.

Was that the surface? What else could it be? It was light.

If it was the ocean surface, it looked to be a mile away.

He remembered reading about the blue holes. He remembered how they emptied into either deep black caves far beyond the ocean floor with no exit, or into dark blue pools at the surface inland. He hoped the light was a pool. But if it was, it could be a hundred yards away. His lungs could be full of water by then.

He kicked as hard as he could. All his energy and all his power.

Ten yards.

And then he kicked again. Twenty.

Pins and needles began to prick his fingertips and toes.

Thirty.

He kicked.

The pinpricks spread to his scalp and his calves.

Forty. The light was spreading, the surface growing larger. He was getting closer.

Willing his mind to take control and ignore the body's limits, he kicked again. Harder.

Fifty.

The numbness spread across his forearms and into his armpits.

Sixty.

And then the numbness spread like wildfire, burning his lungs and his chest. A torch inside his veins, commanding him to stop. To give up. To take a breath. A satisfying deep, long breath of air. Perfect, pure oxygen into his lungs and into his heart.

But his mind was playing tricks. The light was growing lighter and larger but then it was getting closer and tighter, as if all this work, all this will was for nothing. The darkness was taking over. The surface was getting farther.

One breath would end it all.

As the blackness spread from his mind to his eyes, closing in like a camera shutter pinching to darkness, Finn refused.

He kicked.

One. Last. Time.

And he surfaced.

Gasping for air, he fought to stay afloat. Kicking up and lying back, his chest heaved and he extended his neck to keep his mouth above water. And then he heard her.

"Patrick!"

A splash sounded and the yelling continued. A woman's voice.

Manny's voice.

"Patrick!"

And he felt her pull him into her, his back to her chest, but he didn't look. He didn't need to. He knew. The Cathedral connected to her pond, her very own blue hole. It all made sense now. He was in Manny's front yard.

And she was dragging him to shore.

He'd somehow survived.

Ten minutes later, laying on the sandy rim of Manny's blue hole, Finn told her what had happened. He told her about the Brit couple disappearing into the darkness. Then the Jet Ski and the coral.

"They're gone," she said. "They went down the wrong hole."

"How do you—"

"I dove in. After you."

Finn stared at her in disbelief.

Finally, Manny leaned over and dragged the big bag he'd hung onto closer to them. Made of some sort of plastic or shiny hard rubber, it looked to be a surfer's bag. Waterproof, watertight, it was quite large.

She unfastened the zipper from a locking hook, and unzipped the bag.

"Well, well," she said.

Finn sat up and looked past her, and almost fell over.

Stacks and stacks and stacks of euros lined the entire bag. Guessing that there were about a hundred bills in each stack and what looked to be over a hundred stacks—all denominated in 500s, smart, since American dollars came in 100s at most—Finn figured they were looking at more than six or seven million euros, or with the exchange rate, about...

Ten million dollars.

Seeing money in the movies is one thing. Seeing a check for a million or more is another. Finn knew from experience, he'd deposited checks this large for clients before, and had even cashed in one for himself that totaled over a hundred thousand once. That was quite a rush.

But to see. To touch. To smell. Ten million dollars...

"Told you this was serious."

"Who's is this?" she said, and then put a hand up. "No. Wait. Don't tell me. I don't want to know."

"Maybe that's better. But we need to get it up to the house."

"I don't want it."

"Just for now, promise. What time is it?" He asked and struggled to stand.

She glanced at her watch. "Eight o'clock. Why?"

"How long to the airport?"

And before she could answer, the rumble of a car sounded from the road. Finn stood up high to see over the brush and made out a green and white taxi bouncing along the dirt road toward them.

"Expecting more visitors?" he asked.

"No," she said and took a step back.

"Duck," he said. He had no weapon and was still feeling sick from his little blue hole dive.

She dropped to a knee, and they watched through the branches of the brush.

The taxi stopped and the back door popped open. Two figures, both much smaller than Finn, even shorter than Manny, got out. Then they began to strut up the driveway, toward the front door. No bags or luggage, but both wearing two long black trench coats and one of them holding up a folder. Without even seeing their faces, he knew who they were.

But he had no idea why they were here or how they had found him.

"You can't be serious." Manny peered at the brothers.

"It's okay, they're friends," he said and then called out to them.

"Patrick, how are ya'?"

The Berans walked up to Finn and Bobby said, "Heck happened to you, bro?"

"Looks like you been dunked in a toilet."

"And who's the broad?"

"Nice, guys. This is Manny. Manny, the Beran brothers, Bobby and Billy."

"Pleasure." The Berans shook her hand and stared at her.

Manny looked at Finn.

Finn snapped his fingers at the twins.

"Right." Bobby handed Finn a folder. "All here, Kunkle's original contract."

Finn flipped it open and found the section he was looking for. Bingo.

"What the hell are you guys doing here?" Finn asked, closing the folder.

"Wait, that's not all. Look at the back."

"What is it?" Manny asked, peering over Finn's shoulder.

Bobby leaned around Finn. "See it?"

Finn flipped to the back where there was a sheet of thinner paper, fax paper.

"Found that on your office floor. Figured you may want to see it, since it is Kunkle's contract and all, see?" He pointed at the page. "Check the date."

Finn nodded. They had brought the fax from the NHL

Commissioner's office, Ginny had sent it over to him. He owed her big-time now. This was all he needed.

Finn snapped the folder closed. "This is perfect guys. But why did you come all the way here?"

The Berans glanced at each other and Billy shrugged. "No B's game last night."

Bobby said, "But we gotta' get on a flight to make it back for tonight."

Billy said, "Yeah, and we want front row, you know, right behind the bench again."

"Vancouver's bench, not Boston's," Bobby said.

"That's what I meant," his brother said.

Manny stared at both of them. "Aren't you guys hot in those coats?"

They looked at each other and shook their heads.

"But they look cool, am I right?" Billy said.

Bobby nodded. "Is he right?"

Finn wondered what kind of poisoning these two could've sustained as kids. Asbestos? He heard there was an old nuclear facility in Quincy. Maybe that was it.

"You got food in here?" Billy leaned close to Finn and whispered, "Hey, she got food?"

"Yeah, we're starvin'. Been up since four am. No breakfast."

"You had a donut," Billy said.

"You had a donut. I had half a donut."

"Shoulda' eaten it all then."

"We were at airport security. You made me throw it away, rememba'?"

"You coulda' stuffed it down your throat."

"Maybe I should've stuffed it down your throat."

"Guys!" Finn held up his hands and the folder. Definitely radiation poisoning. Mental meltdown, the two of them.

Manny stood silent and had moved behind him. He was certain she was shell-shocked from the total social dysfunction displayed before her.

Finn turned to her. "Do you have anything that they can eat in the car?"

"I have barbeque potato chips."

"I love those!"

"Those rock!" They high-fived again.

"Eat 'em by the handful."

"Yeah." Billy gave Manny a double brow raise and said, "Could eat you by the—" but didn't finish the sentence as Finn's hand collided with Billy's head.

Billy yelped and stepped back, both hands up. "Right, I get it."

"Before we go." Finn turned to Manny and held up the papers. "I'm going to need to use your fax."

"Homeland security?" Nikki said to the policewoman as she sat up and nudged Lew awake.

"They've come for you," she said, unlocking the cell. Her badge identified her as Officer Nix. Another, much larger male officer stood behind him.

Trace opened his eyes for the first time since he'd fallen into the toilet. Propped against the wall, his feet were flopped open like a duck's. "About time." He struggled to stand.

"But first, you must put on these." And she held up three pairs of handcuffs.

The other officer helped get the cuffs on each of them, hands in front of their bodies.

Nikki then held Lew back to let Trace exit before them. She wanted to keep him in her sights.

His bare foot slapped the concrete along with his uneven stride.

"Nice shoe," Lew said. "Gucci?"

Trace never answered.

Officer Nix led them down the hallway in the opposite direction they'd come, and Nikki wondered why they weren't heading back to the administrative area. Did this mean they were about to get questioned? Heading to the interrogation room, what?

But Nix led them straight down the hall and to another iron-barred door. She looked up at a camera on the other side of the threshold and the door clicked with a loud *thunk* and then buzzed.

She pushed it open.

Passing another set of doors, both with tiny squares of bulletproof glass, they exited yet another iron-bolted door. But this one had no camera and was solid steel. And the air seemed thicker, warmer in this hall.

As Nix pushed the door open, Trace said, "Hey, wait. What the hell are you...?" and he reached up and pointed outside. Bright sunlight shined into the dim, windowless hallway. "Where's my wallet, honey? And how about my Rolex? I'm not leaving without them."

The officer at the back laughed.

Trace gave him an incredulous look. "That watch cost more than this whole building, pal."

The huge man stopped laughing.

Trace said, "Well at least a whole floor. It's gold."

Nikki shook her head.

Lew said, "Maybe you lost it."

Trace turned to him. "I didn't lose it, they stole it."

"You were wasted dude, how would you—"

"I've got it," Someone said from outside. "And I have your other shoe, too."

Nikki knew the voice. Raspy but strong. And confident as hell.

Colleen Coffey.

Nikki never thought she'd be so happy to see the bitch.

But what was she doing bailing them out?

Lew said, "Colleen!"

Nikki elbowed his ribs. The Bahamas police obviously thought she was Homeland Security, not someone they knew. Lew said ouch, but seemed to understand it was time to be quiet.

"This is United States Homeland Security Agent, Coffey. She will be taking you from here." Officer Nix nudged them forward and outside and into the small back of the building parking lot.

Standing in front of large black SUV, Colleen flashed some sort of badge.

"Department of who?" Trace asked.

Colleen shook her head. "Homeland Security."

Nikki peered up at Trace. He obviously was not in the know. This was good.

Colleen said, "Come with me, please, we have many questions to ask all of you."

"What kind of questions?" Lew asked, as if it sounded fun.

"Where'd you get those?" Trace asked Colleen, nodding toward his watch and shoe.

Colleen said, "Please, we don't have much time."

"Good. I have a flight to catch," Trace said.

"Me too, I'm hungry," Lew said.

And Nikki stayed quiet. Surrounded by imbeciles.

Slamming the steel door behind them, the officers disappeared.

Lew hurried forward. "Colleen, how'd you get us out? How'd you get them to think you're like, Homeland Security or whatever?"

Colleen ignored him and walked forward, opening the back door. She nodded for them to climb inside.

Nikki watched her carefully, wondering what the hell was going on. But with handcuffs on and not much choice in the freedom category, she did as she was told.

"You too," Colleen said to Lew.

He climbed in and sat next to her in the back seat. A skinny young man with a flock of red curls at the top of his head was driving.

"Not you," Colleen said, holding Trace back.

Then Nikki watched as Colleen opened the front door of the vehicle and let Trace in passenger seat. When he was settled, and the door was still opened, she leaned in and un-cuffed him. Then she dropped his shoes and watch in his lap.

"About time," he said, and she slammed the door shut.

Then she walked to the back door and Nikki thought she was going to un-cuff her and Lew too.

But she didn't.

She climbed in, closed the door, then threaded her way to the far back seat.

"Aren't you going to uncuff us?" Lew asked.

"I don't' think so," Nikki said.

The door locks clicked, and she said, "My name is Colleen, Mr. Cashmore, and I've been hired by your father to bring all of you home."

"Oh yeah! Now we're back in business." Trace rubbed his hands together, then held up a high-five to the driver.

The young man just moved a bit further away.

"Home. What does that mean for us?" Nikki nodded to Lew.

"It means..." Trace leaned over and slipped on his shoe and then, making a big show of threading the Rolex back on his wrist and clipping it closed, turned to Lew and—with remarkable lack of shame, any shame whatsoever for the way he was acting just five minutes ago, or his whole life for that matter—said, "We're headed to renegotiate Mr. Kunkle's contract."

"Cool." Lew raised his eyebrows and leaned and said, "Hey, Mr. Cashmore, think we can stop for some tacos on the way?"

CHAPTER TWENTY-FOUR

OLD AS IT WAS, FINN WAS IMPRESSED at how clean Manny had managed to keep her Land Rover out here in the Bahamas. Sitting in the front seat, the Berans in the back and Manny driving, he checked his watch.

"Eight-fifty," he said.

The roadside sped by them as she pressed down on the accelerator. Not much to see out that way, except tall Bahamas pine trees and brown-grass roadside. The sun had burnt off some of the humidity but traded it for sheer temperature, and was pounding the vehicle now. Finn leaned over and flicked the AC higher.

"Going fast as I can," Manny said. "Need to keep it tame on this road, it's the only highway between here and Freeport. Cops love to stop you in the Bahamas for speeding."

"Just..." Finn pointed to the windshield. "You know."

"I a-m," she sang.

"Nice voice," Billy said.

"Yeah, great lungs," Bobby added.

"I'll say," Billy said. "Not to mention—"

Finn turned around and they went back to eating the chips.

"How long?" He asked Manny.

"Maybe forty more minutes."

The Berans chomped away while Finn planned out how this would go down. He expected Trace to be in the airport somewhere, most likely on the plane itself, waiting for Manny to come administer the sedatives to the sharks. They would be all loaded up, and there shouldn't be too much complication. Manny would distract the customs agent and Finn would take possession of Trace.

With the help of Colleen, they would have both Cashmores detail their dealings with this so-called Network of professional killers and then they'd put them away for a while.

Wherever she was.

One thing was for sure, though. The golden-boy son was not going back to the States without answering to Finn.

Picking up the small open-topped wooden box from the floorboard, Finn then turned to Manny. "Just squirt it into the tanks, and the *MS 222* is absorbed through their gills." He examined one of the droppers inside the box.

"Whose gills?" Bobby asked.

"The sharks'," Manny said into the rear-view mirror.

"What sharks," Billy asked.

"The ones she caught for Tracy Cashmore's new arena," Finn said.

"You caught a shark?" Bobby asked.

"That's hot," Billy said.

"Super, fuckin' hot."

Finn glanced back. They returned their attention to the chips.

As Finn placed the box back by his feet, one of the Berans said, "Look at those two dogs."

The other said, "They're huge!"

Finn turned back and glanced out the rear window, in time to see two dogs running around in circles and barking up at the sky. There was no doubt, no doubt in his mind who the dogs were. They were barking at what appeared to be a pair of old tennis shoes caught up on a telephone wire and blowing in the wind.

Sighing at his inability to ignore the stupidity, he said, "Stop the car."

Manny eased off the accelerator. "Why?"

"The dogs," Finn said.

"Serious?"

"Dead. Hurry."

Manny said, "If you're so worried about..." but Finn had exited the car before she could finish.

"Glovesave!" he yelled.

The two dogs tilted their heads at Finn, stood there frozen for an instant, and then bounded toward him.

Opening up the back hatch, he helped them up and into the car.

"What the hell?" The Berans said.

"Yeah, what the?" Manny asked.

Weird. Maybe the dogs had jumped ship and swam to shore.

Finn turned and pet the dogs down to made sure they were okay. A bit smelly, one of them looked to have some sort of hardened queso cheese stuck to his muzzle, but otherwise okay. Their breath, though. Could melt glass.

He shut the hatch and climbed back in front.

"These dogs," Finn said to Manny.

"Yeah..." she said as she put the car back in gear and drove.

"They stink," Billy said.

Finn turned to Manny. "Let's just say that I know their owner."

Her eyes narrowed. "You know them."

"Well." Finn didn't have a good way to explain this part. He still hadn't told her of the yacht. Or of Lew and Nikki being stuck a couple miles out on said yacht before somehow being arrested. Or that the Brits were actually hired killers, though that wouldn't be too hard to explain now. Or that Colleen was CIA.

The dogs were a footnote that would need a whole book of explanation to even make sense.

"And...where's their owner?"

Finn said, "He's supposed to be on a yacht."

"Nice yacht?" Bobby asked.

Finn said, "Yeah, wicked nice."

"That's what I'm talkin' about, baby," Billy said.

Finn said, "But…we kind of ran out of gas before reaching shore."

Manny gave him a sidelong glance. "And?"

"And. The dogs were on that boat. They obviously fell off. Somehow."

"Fell off. And the owner?"

"We'll get to that," Finn said, worried about Nikki and Lew again.

The dogs were circling in the rear compartment, knocking into the backs of the Berans' seats.

"Hey, knock it off," one of them said.

"But first, there's just one thing," Finn said.

"One thing." Manny shook her head. "As in one more thing, or…"

"Well, it's about the dogs," he said.

And the car began to rock back and forth.

Nikki, still sitting in the backseat with Lew, overheard Colleen call the kid Stanley.

"All you have to do is stand guard, got it?" Colleen said to the boy, who had pulled the car into the West End Airport, at the far edge of Grand Bahamas, all the way at the tip of the island. Having passed the only checkpoint—a single booth with a single guard— he drove up to the rear of the huge cargo jet, a DC-8 as Trace had mentioned thirty-seven times or so as they entered the airport. Then, he, Tracy, and Colleen got out.

Stanley nodded his red flock of curls and walked to the front of the jet. Then, crossing his arms, he stood next to the gigantic wheels.

Oh yes, quite formidable, Nikki thought.

Colleen then opened the hatch of the SUV and called for Nikki and Lew to get out.

"Yes ma'am," Nikki said, nudging Lew. Poor Lew hadn't said a word since he'd been snubbed on the taco request.

Following him out, Nikki then saw what Colleen was busy getting from the rear. Though it seemed a tad overkill for the circumstance.

"An AK-47?" Nikki asked.

Colleen didn't answer.

"What's an AK," Lew asked.

"Look back," Nikki said.

"Jesus, dude."

Colleen had it pointed at their backs.

Apparently airport security had all decided to take their midmorning coffee break at the same hour. Either that, or the television monitors were unplugged. Gotta' love spooks and all their nifty little tricks.

"Keep moving." Colleen guided Nikki and Lew to the base of the cargo bay ramp leading up and into the DC-8, then nudged them forward.

"Tell you what," Nikki said to him, "We get out of this alive? I'll buy you a month's worth of quesadillas."

"Why wouldn't we get out of this alive?"

Poor Lew, it was all so confusing.

Then he said, "Besides, quesadillas are a rip-off, dude. Just cheese and tortillas. Don't buy them."

Nikki stumbled as they reached the top, and Colleen leaned forward as if to stabilize her, but seized her cuffed arms instead.

"Stop here," Colleen said.

Behind the bitch, two huge rectangular shipping containers sat with their tops propped open. Too tall to reveal what was inside, but the containers smelled fishy.

A second later, Lew bumped into Nikki from behind. Wanting to hit him back, she refrained from wasting the energy in case she found a window to use it on Colleen. Though it would be hard, seeing how Nikki and Lew's hands were both cuffed and Colleen held a fully automatic rifle in her hands.

Question was, where the hell had Finn disappeared to? Had this bitch done something to him? She found herself sincerely worried about him for the first time. But she knew better than to ask Colleen for answers. Even if she did answer, it'd be with lies.

"What're those, dude?" Lew asked, nodding at the containers.

Nikki couldn't tell if he'd directed the question at her or the bitch.

"Never mind that, just stay put." Colleen walked back down the ramp halfway, AK still in hand. She looked ridiculous holding the thing, like a past-her-prime model in some macho-hippy photo-shoot, tie-dye skirt and all.

Trace walked up the ramp and met her. "Just...I don't know, put them in the cockpit or something."

Nikki leaned over Lew's shoulder to watch.

"And where's the pilot?" Colleen asked.

"Duh. Doing the manifest and all that stuff. They do it before every chartered flight."

"And, duh, how long will he, duh, be duh-doing the paperwork?"

Uh oh, Mr. Trace, don't piss off *Rambette*.

"Are you making fun of me?"

"I'm mocking you. There's a difference."

"Well stop it." Trace sulked off.

"Let's go." Colleen returned to the cargo bay door. "We'll put you in the bathroom for now."

Nudging them forward, she stayed behind them as they walked between the two containers.

The floor was lined with a series of metal notches and nubs, like large hollowed-out metal nipples, and rollers extended up each side all the way to the front. The containers were strapped tight to the walls from both sides.

Nikki worked to not trip on Lew or herself, as Colleen led them through the dark area behind the containers and up to a door.

Feeling a momentary urge to kick Colleen in the face and take the gun, two problems saved Nikki from the impulse: first, the space was too tight to bring even Nikki's short leg to a full kick; and second, there was still the issue of the machinegun.

Lew said, "Can I go first?"

"Go where?" Colleen asked, pushing buttons on the wall until the lights flickered on.

"You know." He leaned forward and put his knees together. "I gotta pee."

Nikki bit her lip, stayed quiet.

Colleen looked at him. "Seriously?"

"No joke."

"Go." She nodded to the door.

"Can you just?" He glanced at his crotch.

"Can I just what?" Colleen said.

Oh brother. Nikki turned away and watched from the corner of her eye.

"It's kinda' hard with the cuffs, dude." He held up his hands.

Colleen sighed and reached over, unzipped his fly. "There."

"And, uh…" Lew whispered, "Can you take it out?"

Colleen glanced at Nikki. "He can't be serious."

Nikki said, "You're problem, not mine, Agent Coffey."

"Oh for God's…" Colleen glanced around and groaned as she helped Lew with his winkle.

Lew laughed, "That tickles."

"Ugh." Colleen stepped back and wiped her hand on her skirt.

Lew stood there.

Colleen leaned forward and propped open the door.

Lew whispered again, as if Nikki couldn't hear, "I don't suppose I could get you to hold it for—"

"Go!" Colleen slammed the door on him.

Nikki turned back to Colleen, who had turned the color of a

radish.

Nikki smiled.

"Fuck you," Colleen said.

Nikki leaned forward and, still smiling, whispered, "And also with you."

Then, for what seemed to be an eternity, the sound of Lew relieving himself echoed through the cargo bay, complete with *ahhs* and a few shudders.

Lew knocked on the door, and Colleen opened it.

"So much better," he said. "Thanks a bunch. Now could you…"

"Figure it out," Colleen said.

Lew turned to Nikki, and she mouthed *not a chance*.

From the rear, Trace clomped up the ramp, yelling, "Is she here yet?"

"Is who here?" Colleen asked, keeping Lew and Nikki covered with the gun, while Lew jumped up and down trying to tuck one-eyed pirate-Lew back into its hull.

"Manny. The shark-chick."

"Who?"

Trace opened his mouth. "She's got to, like, tranquilize these things or they'll eat each other or something."

"Tranquilize what things?" Nikki asked.

"Shut up," both Colleen and Trace said.

Well, at least they're united on that front.

"What're they talking about, dude?" Lew said, struggling with the zipper.

"No idea."

"Well she has fifteen minutes, or else," Trace said.

"Or else what?" Colleen asked, giving him a look of contempt.

Trace stood there, arms crossed for a long time, and finally raised his eyebrows, nodded, and said, "Just…or else."

CHAPTER TWENTY-FIVE

ALMOST NINE NOW, FINN HAD FILLED IN the Berans on Nikki's arrest and the pending hearing for her and Lew. He had to call and find out when bail was going to be set, or if it already had. Manny had shrunk even further away with the latest development, and was probably wondering if she'd shagged an mobster all night.

Glancing over at her, he couldn't catch her eye.

Billy said, "I bet Nikki cold-cocked him!"

"Right in kisser."

"I wouldn't screw with her, tell you that much," Billy said, "Cop or not."

"You gotta' be one sick mother to mess with that crazy broad." Bobby nodded once, cementing his elegant statement.

Manny glanced in the rear-view and then stared back at the road.

Shaking his head, Finn dialed the number to the Freeport Police station. A few rings later, Officer Nix answered again.

And told him about Homeland Security taking custody of all three of them.

Tracy Cashmore included.

"Can you tell me the name of the agent who took custody?"

"That I cannot do."

"Okay, can you tell me if it is *not* a certain agent?"

"Maybe."

Finn said, "Was the agent's name Roy Rogers?"

"Not Roy, no."

Okay. Finn glanced up in the mirror and said, "Then would it happened to have been a tall, black-haired woman, named Agent Coffey?"

"I can't say."

Bingo.

Colleen came through after all. Or did she?

"Okay, thank you very much Officer Nix."

"Nice day." And she hung up.

The Berans said, "So?"

Finn said, "They've already been bailed out, sort of."

"Who?" They asked in unison.

Finn turned around and said, "My ex, Colleen."

"As in Coffey?" Bobby asked.

Finn was sure he hadn't spoken to them of Colleen in a long time, so he was surprised that they remembered her last name. "The one and only."

And they turned to each other, then back to Finn. "Something's not right."

Finn shifted in his seat. "Like what??"

"Like Nikki called us two days ago, asked us to check her out. Said she was working with her and she didn't trust her." Billy shrugged.

"She sounded pissed," Bobby said.

"She always sounds pissed," Billy said.

Of course. Nikki hated Colleen and was digging for dirt to use against her, just in case Finn planned on hooking up with her again.

"And?" Finn asked, half annoyed, half curious.

"Serious shit, brother," Bobby said.

"How. Serious." Finn raised his brows.

"Did you know she got bumped from the Company?" Billy asked.

"Bumped. As in…"

"Fired," Bobby said.

"For what?" Finn turned further to face them both.

"Didn't say, record was sealed."

Finn knew before Bobby finished with, "Means she was bent. You know, crooked."

"Bet she was stealing and lying and the rest of it." Billy nodded. "Never heard of anybody getting kicked out of the CIA. They all lie to each other anyway."

Bobby turned to his brother. "Yeah, but did you see that CIA photo of her? "Speaking of bending."

"Oh yeah. I'd bend her—"

"Guys!" Finn glanced at Manny. She stared straight ahead with both hands on the wheel.

Finn looked at his phone with the long Montenegro sticker across the back. Then he dialed Nikki's number from memory. It rang four times and went to voicemail. Without leaving a message, he dialed again.

This time, after three rings, it was answered by Colleen Coffey.

"Patrick?"

"Colleen."

"West End Airport in fifteen minutes, if you ever want to see Nikki again."

Colleen stood guard of the bathroom, arms folded, her back against the door, and the AK leaned onto her leg. With the two morons, Nikki and Lew, handcuffed and crammed inside, all she had to do now was wait. Tracy was off playing with his fish, and Stanley was down below keeping watch.

Using her disposable phone, she dialed his number.

Stanley answered after a single ring. "Yes?"

"Anything?"

"Nothing yet."

Colleen nodded and said, "The moment you see something."

"I'll call," he said, sounding annoyed, and hung up. Perhaps he was still upset about that little Taser incident.

She shifted her weight to the other leg. From here, she could see out the cargo bay door and all the way down the gray landing strip where it looked like it ran right into the crystalline blue-green water. No clouds, the ocean met the sky, far off in the distance. A slight breeze broke the humidity and kept the air just cool enough.

Too bad there would have to be violence this morning. It would ruin the moment. But that wasn't her fault, she'd given Finn an out. He could have chosen her instead of himself and this all would have worked out perfectly. They would take care of the simple business of killing two people, get paid for the hour's work, and be on their way. They would have over ten million to start with, too.

Sure, Lew and Nikki were mostly innocent, but that's life. Besides, nobody was pure. When you get right down to it, everyone was undeserving of a perfect life. And why should someone with so little intelligence be paid twelve million dollars a year? For what, preventing a little rubber puck from going into a net?

Absurd.

So, as much as Colleen hated dealing with that monumental prick Tracy, she could understand him wanting to save his team, his business, from bankruptcy. He was a survivor, at least.

Could Finn say that?

Though, he was right about one thing. She didn't trust anyone. And after the last few days, with her entire network turning on her like that? Vanessa and Chadwick disappearing with all their money? Then Finn stealing her pistol and turning on her too? He was right.

She would never trust anyone again.

CHAPTER TWENTY-SIX

"YOU HAVE ANY BETTER IDEAS?" FINN LEANED out the window and asked.

The Berans, standing outside, each of them holding the collar of a dog, both shrugged.

"Billy said, not really, but…" he grimaced. "Why do we have to stay with the mutts?"

Manny, now in the passenger seat, fiddled with the box of tranquilizers.

"It's better this way, trust me," Finn said to the Berans, "Just, keep them quiet. Or at least away. I'll be back in twenty minutes."

"You got a plan?"

He thought of Lew and Nikki somehow being held captive by Colleen. "I'll wing it."

"And what about Tracy?" Manny asked.

Finn thought of the fax he sent from Manny's. "He'll get his, soon enough."

"Well don't forget us out here. It's hot already." Bobby thrust his chin up to the sky.

"Hang-tight boys." Finn rolled up the window and drove forward.

About fifty yards later, they pulled through a cheap wire fence, open to the road.

"There," Manny said, pointing at a small adobe-like structure to the right.

Finn followed the road into the small lot of the house and parked next to a picnic table. Pine needles were piled across the house's tall grey rubber-tiled roof, and four blue chairs lay scattered under a sign reading, *Bahamas Customs & Immigration.* Square and faded, the chairs looked like they were made from old fruit crates. The building looked worn, with chipped stucco siding and a stained concrete porch.

"This should be quick, I hope." She got out, carrying the droppers.

Finn kept the car running as he watched her through the faded blue-framed wood and glass door.

A short man in a dark blue uniform talked with Manny in a way that made them look like old friends, patting her shoulder and then laughing at something she said. He nodded at the droppers when she held them up. She said something else, and they both came to the window. The man waved at Finn.

Hesitating for a moment, Finn waved back.

Manny and the man hugged and then he shooed her away.

She slipped back into the car. "No problem, mon."

"That's it?"

"Like I said, they love me here."

"And the waving bit?"

"Told him you were my brother."

"And he didn't want to meet me? See an ID?"

"Why would he want to do that?"

Of course. Manny had fled the States prior to *9/11.* She had no idea what kind of nightmare most airports were these days. Well, passenger airports anyway.

"Never mind." Finn pulled the car out of the lot and drove toward the airstrip. At the far end, an enormous brown jet, a DC-8 from the looks of it, sat idle. The side cargo bay was open, but nobody stood in view.

Out of view of the customs building, Manny said, "This is a

good spot." She pointed to a row of pine trees about thirty yards from the landing strip. "Those run all the way to the end of the strip."

"Got it," Finn said.

"Give me at least ten minutes to administer the tranquilizers and leave, then you can do your thing."

"My thing."

"Whatever that is, I don't want to know." She waved a hand in the air.

Turning to her, he asked, "So this is it?"

"Cadmium," she said. Then, after pausing a long moment and looking pensive, she added, "Look, it's really not you. I think..." she let her voice trail off and then said, "Just go."

Right.

Finn leaned over, kissed Manny on the cheek, and patted her leg. Getting out, he watched Manny drive off and jogged low to the trees. Right as he got there, he heard a bark.

Then another.

"Damn," he said to himself.

Better hurry.

Hey, Glovesave, look. A monkey!
Where?
There, he's running!
That's not a monkey that's a lizard.
Right. Let's get him!
Good idea!

Finn watched from between two tall pines. From the vantage, he could see the entire plane, nose to fin. A young, wiry man stood under the cockpit, leaning against the wheels. With a pile of sweaty red hair, it looked like someone had dumped a bucket of blood orange peels on his head. He also looked bored, with his arms crossed and a cell phone in his hand.

The Lookout.

Finn eased back into the trees, retracing his steps until he was even with the wheels. Lookout's phone rang, a high-pitched submarine pinging noise, and he answered it. Finn couldn't make out what he was saying, but that didn't matter. Point was, Lookout was distracted. That, and the barking sounded to be getting louder. He pictured the Berans struggling with the dogs. It was time to act.

Sorry Manny.

Taking two quick glances left and right, Finn felt confident that nobody within the fuselage could see him all the way to the wheels. And with Lookout staring down, Finn had his chance.

Finn darted out of the woods and, ducking as low as he could, raced across the pavement. Not an easy task to keep quiet at two hundred and fifty pounds, but he succeeded.

Just as Lookout hung up, Finn grabbed the back of his red hair. The poor kid was half Finn's size, if that.

Lookout began to yell, but Finn hooked an arm around his straw neck and squeezed. Twenty seconds later, Lookout slumped into unconsciousness in Finn's arms.

Dragging Lookout back over to the thicket of trees, Finn placed him under a pine and covered his legs with leaves.

Then he checked his watch.

It had been almost thirty minutes since he'd spoken with Colleen, and the barking was getting louder. Had to keep moving, no stopping now. He hoped Manny was being efficient. She was right to want to avoid being in the middle of any of this. Finn was hoping for the best here, but knew quite well it could get ugly.

Finn took a couple of quick glances again and darted out onto the runway. It took him about twenty strides to get back under the plane. This time, he kept going until he reached the cargo bay ramp. Tucking himself under the corner of the ramp, Finn listened.

He could make out Tracy's voice and someone else's.

Tracy was talking about a watch. Did he just say he owned twelve Rolexes?

Whoever was lucky enough to hear about Trace's extensive timepiece collection was not Colleen or Manny. Too bad. He was sure she'd be fascinated by the comparison of the Datejust with the GMT.

Reaching up, Finn took hold of the ramp. He needed to locate Colleen. Then, as he began to pull himself over the ledge, he felt cool metal press against his neck.

"Don't move."

Colleen located. Check.

"Hands on your head, you know the drill."

Finn complied.

"Now turn around."

He did.

Standing on the corner of the cargo ramp, Colleen was wearing the tie-dye skirt and baby blue golf shirt she'd chosen at Boney's yesterday. With one leg propped up on the ramp and the other flat on the ground below, and holding an AK-47. She looked like a Manga cartoon, preppy school dress and all.

"What?" she said.

Looking her over, he stopped his gaze on the AK. "You ever shot one of those?"

"Of course." She shifted her weight and glanced around.

"You're lying." Finn lifted a hand off his head and she swung the gun to aim at his groin. Then she raised her brows.

"Want to find out?"

Dead Serious Manga.

Easing his hand back onto his head, he said, "Relax. I was going to show you where the safety is."

"Aren't you scared?"

"Of course."

"You don't look it."

Finn stared at her. "This network? Is it yours?"

"You'd do yourself a favor by shutting up now."

"Tell you what," he said, mindful of the fully automatic rifle pointed at his testicles. "Bring me to Tracy, I'll cut a deal with him. Then, you can have your money and leave. Disappear, whatever it is you do."

Eying him for good five or six-seconds, she nodded. Then she stepped forward and jammed the barrel of the rifle into his ribs.

Finn doubled over. *Guess not.*

"Get up," she said.

Finn stared at her as he straightened back up, grimacing.

"This operation has been screwed from the start, so now we're going to do things my way. You can't negotiate out of this one, Mr. Big-Time Agent. Got it?"

"Noted."

"Good. Now up the ramp."

Climbing the ramp with Colleen behind him, Finn noticed the strong smell of salt water as they entered the cargo bay. Two huge blue plastic shipping containers sat in the middle of the hold. Both tops were propped open and a metal rolling stairwell was pulled up to the edge of one of them. Trace stood at the top of the stairs, his right hand holding the chain links of Nikki's handcuffs in such a way that she was leaned over the tank. The guy was bigger than Finn remembered. Though dapper as ever, wearing a yellow plastic visor and loafers.

Nikki was staring into the tank below.

"Stop right there," Trace said.

Finn stopped. "Where's Lew?"

"He's locked away," Trace said.

"I'm pooping!" Lew called out in a muffled, echoed voice.

Good ol' Lew.

"Okay, shut up now, everyone." Trace leaned Nikki further

over, and she squealed. Something thrashed in the tank below, splashing water up and over the sides.

Finn guessed that was the prized hammerhead Manny had described. He wondered where she was now.

"You couldn't let things be, could you? Had to be the hero." Trace said to Finn.

Finn said, "We're all trying to live up to your legacy, Trace."

"Then you should have let the contract be!" His voice piped high and he drew out the words, "but no...you insisted on that stupid clause!"

Finn glanced at Colleen behind him. "Can I put my hands down now?"

"Better not," she said.

Fine. "The clause, Tracy, was your idea."

"Trace! My name is Trace!"

Almost dropping Nikki on the outburst, the shark thrashed again, this time so hard that its dorsal fin rose about the lip of the tank. Nikki whimpered.

Easy, Trace.

He continued in a whiny voice, "And I only suggested it because you wouldn't agree to my terms."

Finn couldn't remember what those were, but he recalled something having to do with Lew giving back some of his pay for each goal he let in. It was along the lines of moronic.

"Well now you've had it. My dad wants to talk to you."

Finn said, "Trace, why are you holding Nikki like that? I'm not doing anything threatening."

"She made me mad."

"Sweet little Nikki?"

She glared at Finn.

"Tell her that if she makes fun of me again, saying that I can't tell time, I'll drop her right into this tank."

"I think you just told her yourself, Trace."

"Got it?" He said to Nikki. "Now move." Trace shoved her

away from the tank and back toward the stairwell.

Legs rubbery, Nikki descended the stairs. She passed Finn and said, "That fucking shark is huge."

Colleen nudged Finn from behind. "What did you do with Stanley?"

So that was Lookout's real name.

"You suddenly care?" Finn asked.

"Only if it'll be a problem for me later," Colleen said.

"Relax," Finn said. "He's taking a little nap in the woods."

Colleen said, "Perfect," as the sound of barking began to echo up into the plane.

"What's that?" Trace asked.

Finn swiveled far enough to see past Colleen, where a blur of dogs and trenchcoats appeared and then disappeared under the ramp.

"Sit! Heal! Fuck, just stop!"

And then the dog and a Beran, hard to tell which one, came bounding up the ramp.

"Stop!" Colleen yelled.

But the Beran had his hand jammed under the collar and was being dragged by the enormous beast.

"I said stop!" Colleen stepped back, almost bumping into Finn, and pulsed a few rounds from the AK.

The dog yelped, the Beran yelled, and Colleen fell backwards with the force of the AK's kick, landing on her ass.

The second set of dog and Beran bounded up the ramp and stopped at the first set. The second dog sniffed the first. Then it whimpered.

"Okay, enough! Everyone inside!" Tracy yelled.

"Sorry Patrick," Bobby said. Both he and Billy were covered in pine needles and dust. "These dogs don't listen."

The dogs sat still, one panting, one licking his paw.

"Looks like the bullet went between his toes, lucky bastard," Billy said.

"I said now! I really mean it!" Tracy yelled then looked at Colleen. "The pilots will be here any minute!"

Colleen pointed the AK at the Berans, as she got back up. "You two...four, whatever, go first." She then said to Finn, "You go last."

"You're the boss." Finn said.

"Got that right," Colleen said, as she smacked a large orange button on the wall, closing the huge bay door.

Trace moved the rolling stairwell to the edge of the other tank. Pointing, he said, "Y'all are riding in there."

The dogs, perfectly tame now, ascended the stairs lock and step with each Beran. One of them hobbled a bit though, with a shot foot and all.

Stopping at the top, Bobby said, "Are those sharks?"

Billy yelled, "Nikki! Lew!"

"Glovesave, Kicksave!" Lew's voice echoed from inside the container. "I missed you guys!"

Then Bobby said, "Manny, you invited to this party, too?"

"Lucky me," she said.

Five minutes later, all of them sitting in the three-feet deep water and pitch blackness, sharks swimming slowly in place, Finn asked Nikki, who was sitting right next to him, "You okay?"

"I'm neck deep in sharks, fuck you think?"

Finn held up the disposable cell phone. No signal, but the light worked.

The Berans sat huddled together, the dogs in each of their laps —must have been a nice little bonding session, being dragged through the woods like that—and Lew sat with his chin pointed up to keep it above water.

"These things gonna' get pissed when we take off or what?" Nikki asked, looking at Manny and then the sharks barely moving at the other end of the tank.

Manny said, "They're too drugged to bite for now. The *MS 222* hits their gills right away."

"How long will it last?" Finn asked.

"I dumped both doses in here. They'll be sleepy for days."

"And the big shark?" Finn nodded to the other tank.

"Elvis? Let's hope he makes it to Houston alive," she said.

"He'll make it." Finn glanced around. The Berans looked sleepy all of a sudden. So did Nikki and Lew.

Finn nodded to them as he said to Manny, "MS 222?"

The engines of the airplane fired up and they jolted forward, bouncing along the crappy runway.

Manny said, "It's seeping into our pores. Won't last as long, but will be effective short term, so I'd suggest you sit up straight."

He did, and said, "I'm sorry you're in this mess."

"That's what I get for dealing with crooks."

And before Finn could answer that, he'd fallen asleep.

CHAPTER TWENTY-SEVEN

THE SALTWATER SMELL SUDDENLY BECAME SO STRONG, so noxious, that it jarred Finn awake.

A fat man in a suit stood over him—Jerry Cashmore—waving something in his face. Smelling salts?

"Well, cock-a-doodle-do. He's awake, folks."

Blinking his eyes a few times, Finn cleared his vision. Jerry, backing away now, stopped at the edge of a huge oak desk. Tracy stood to his left, holding a sheath of papers, and Colleen to his right, AK-47 in hand.

She tapped the gun with a fingernail. "Give him a minute to adjust. Manny said the tranquilizer will make him sleepy for a bit."

"We need to hurry, Dad." Trace held up the papers.

"Shut up, boy," Jerry said. "Let the man clear his head. He needs to be able to think."

Finn stretched his neck and tried to lift an arm to rub it, but it was fastened in place. He glanced down. He was strapped to a small metal folding chair with about a mile of duct tape. His feet were taped together and to the chair.

He looked up.

They were all in Jerry's office at the new Hammerhead Arena in Houston. Finn recognized it from their contract negotiations last year. If the blinds were pulled, they'd have a view of both Reliant Stadium and the former Enron Tower, now known as Four Allen

Center.

Nice view, actually. Especially at night. He wondered what time it was, how long he'd been out.

Jerry said, "Sorry about that tape, son. Big as you are, we had to be sure you didn't go berserk or nothing when you awoke."

"Now that I'm awake?" Finn asked.

"Just a wee-bit longer." Jerry said.

"Where's everyone else?"

Colleen stood silent and staring, straight at Finn...well trained by the CIA. Trace though, he glanced away. Right at the bathroom door.

Team members located.

"Don't you worry about them." Jerry leaned more of his weight on the desk and crossed his legs. "Know why you're here?"

"I have a hunch," Finn said.

Jerry nodded. "Well Mr. Finn. We won't waste time doin' a big ol' square dance around the elephant in the room. We'll just go right ahead and address it."

"Let's do it." Finn's purple fingertips were barely visible under the tape. He guessed Master Tracy had done the work.

"My kind of man, gets right to the point. I remember that about you from last year." He pointed a fat finger at Finn. "But also that you're a bit of a negotiator too."

Finn winked at Trace, who grimaced.

"So." Jerry pushed off the desk. "I'll give it to you straight."

Colleen shifted the AK to her other leg. Thing must have been heavy, no strap and all.

Jerry continued, "I started this expansion team with a mind to bring ice hockey to this great city of ours." He swept a hand around the room. "You think Houston deserves hockey, don't you Mr. Finn?"

Finn gave him a serious nod. "I do."

"I thought so. Which was also why I thought we'd be able to work out a deal to be sure that happens."

"Dad." Tracy looked at his watch. "We don't have time for this."

Jerry glared over at Tracy. "I told you to shut up, boy. You've done quite enough already."

Tracy shrunk to the size of a Happy Meal toy.

Colleen shook her head. Finn wondered how much these two bozos were paying her to do this. Hopefully enough to set her up for quite a while, now that she was unemployed and all.

Jerry continued, "The point is, our dear Hammerheads here are out of money. Well, at least they will be if that client of yours insists on taking the entire year's profit and then some."

Finn said, "You mean, if he insists on being paid his contract. The contract you signed."

"That contract is full of fool's gold." Jerry raised one snarled eyebrow, as he walked over to Tracy and snatched the papers from him. "It will force the Hammerheads into bankruptcy. Therefore, the team and its owners…" he pointed to Tracy, himself and then a shelf with a photo of his partners, and continued, "will no longer be obligated to pay it."

Finn stayed quiet as Jerry walked back to the desk.

"Sixty million dollars over five years? Like I said." Jerry then threw the papers in the air. "Fool's gold."

They all sat there silent for a bit, Jerry staring at Finn and Tracy, and Colleen staring at the floor.

Finn felt like he was in the middle of a Glenn Beck chalk talk. Cowboy style.

Jerry folded his arms and leaned back against the desk again. "Ms. Coffey here asked why I don't just renege on the contract. Not pay it. And I explained to her that it's just not the way things work in the NHL. And it's certainly not the way my family operates. It's dishonorable, unethical."

But kidnapping? Killing?

Jerry continued, "And besides, how would we ever be able to sign a player who was actually worth that kind of money if we had the reputation of not paying up?"

"I see your predicament," Finn said.

"I knew you would." Jerry raised his hands, palms up. "So, I'm willing to strike a new deal with you. Something that works for the both of us. You're a businessman. I'm a businessman. Tracy here, well...he's learnin'. And all the rest of this is nonsense." Jerry nodded at Colleen, then said, "Not you darlin', I mean that." He pointed at the AK. "No reason for it. All a big misunderstanding. Isn't that right, Ms. Coffey?"

Colleen looked at Jerry but didn't answer.

"So, to the point." Walking behind his desk, he picked up another stack of papers. This one looked thinner, like it was printed on fax paper.

The ace in the hole. Damn.

Shaking his head, Jerry said, "But then you go and do a stupid thing like this." He held up the papers. "See, I had the vision of a CEO way back when we signed that silly contract that you and my son here negotiated. And so I sent the NHL commissioner's office a record of the contract without that performance clause. I mean, who would dream of an expansion team matching the league's highest paid player's salary and contract? All for what? One lucky season for a rookie goalie? Nonsense. I knew it was going to be trouble. Something told me. Right here." He stabbed his own fat belly with a fat finger.

Jerry the visionary CEO. Thrilled to be in his own presence.

Finn said, "The NHL called."

"Damn straight they did!" He pounded the desk with a fist, knocking over a photo of him standing over a big buck. "This drops in their lap and they want to know why exactly I sent them a fraudulent contract! They're talking about sanctions and suspensions. At the very least, a big ol' fine."

"Your explanation?" Finn asked, trying to figure out some sort of angle to work with here.

"I told them the truth, that it was an administrative error. We accidentally sent over an unamended contract." Jerry shrugged. "Question is, and here it comes, think hard on this one. It's important for you, hear?"

"I do." Finn nodded.

"Good." Jerry held his hands out and said, "Will you confirm that as truth, and thereby save your own life and that of your little sherbet-headed girlfriend?"

What about the others?" Finn asked

"I suppose the twins can be on their way too."

"And Lew?"

"Mr. Finn. You know Mr. Kunkle's career has to end now. And the cleanest way is for him to have a terrible accident. Maybe even a deadly one."

Finn said, "Well I can't agree to those terms."

Jerry stared at him for a long three or four seconds and said, "And if I cut you a personal deal on the side? Some sort of financial incentive?"

Finn pursed his lips, looked up and then said, "No can do."

"I was afraid you'd say that." He let out a big sigh.

And that was that. Finn knew it. Colleen knew it. Even lobster-brained Tracy knew it.

"Boy." Jerry walked over to Finn and, placing a hand on his shoulder, shook his head. "You just dug your own grave."

Then he turned and said, "Unfortunately, you dug your friends' graves too."

At the front of a concentration camp-like death march, Trace led them through the empty arena. Lew walked right behind him, then Nikki, Manny, the Berans, the two dogs, and finally Finn. Colleen brought up the rear with her nifty AK.

"Why does he keep calling us shark food?" Lew asked.

"Because, Lew, that freakazoid hammerhead hasn't eaten in over a week. Ask Manny here." Nikki thumbed the air behind her. "And Captain bug-nuts up there is worried that he'll start eating the smaller ones."

"Watch it, candy corn!" Trace yelled from the front.

"That true?" Finn asked Manny.

"I made the mistake of warning Tracy to be sure to feed them as soon as they landed." Manny glanced back. "Because yes, hammerheads have been known to become cannibals if starving."

The Berans, who had been stripped of their trenchcoats to reveal black jeans and white t-shirts, chimed, "That's fucking great, eaten alive. Mom's going to be pissed."

"A perfect solution, wouldn't you say?" Trace called from the front. "Sharks don't leave a trace behind." Then he laughed. "Get it? Trace. Like me."

Hilarious.

Only half the lights shining in the arena, it made it difficult to see where they where headed at first. But when Trace led them to the stairwell behind the press box, all the way at the back of the second mezzanine, Finn had a pretty solid inclination. This was verified when they all stopped at the door labeled, *Skywalk— DANGER—EMPLOYEES ONLY.*

Opening the door then stepping aside, Trace said, "Check it out. Pretty cool, huh?"

Looking above everyone's head, Finn saw the catwalk had been lowered and now connected to the huge black and blue cube scoreboard hanging from the ceiling and positioned above the center of the ice rink.

Except it being summer and all, there was no ice on the rink.

In a normal NHL arena, the entire floor was smooth concrete embedded with special Freon-filled pipes to freeze water above it, making ice.

But not in Hammerhead Arena.

With Trace's delusional marketing scheme, half the rink had

been dug out of the surface below, creating an enormous pool—or actually in this case, a giant fish tank. In the tank? About twenty prized hammerheads. One of them larger than the rest combined.

Nikki said, "Correct me if I'm wrong, Trace, but isn't hockey played on frozen water?"

"Actually, Lew said, "there's a game called Octopush—"

"No, stupid," Trace said, "The ice will go above the water, you know, on a special Plexiglas surface. One that can get cold enough to make ice above it. Then everyone can see the sharks, like dark silhouettes swimming below. It'll be amazing."

"Why not project digital shadows on the surface? Be a lot cheaper."

"Then how could we have a viewing booth below? You need real sharks for that." Trace left his mouth open on the last word.

"That sounds fiscally responsible," she said.

Finn nodded in agreement, impressed with Nikki's use of the English language. The rest of this he'd heard a few months ago, during a tour of the arena and Jerry's monologue on marketing and brand enhancement, led by none other than the prodigal son.

"What would you know? It's going to be the bomb." Trace curled his lips in an exaggerated smile.

"I agree," Lew said.

Everyone in line looked at him.

"Just saying." Lew scratched his head with both hands.

"You're fuckin' nuts, you know that Chase?" Billy said.

One of the dogs barked in agreement.

"It's Trace, dickweed. As in trés—like a three-pointer." Trace pretended to shoot a basketball.

"That's lovely Trace, but can we get on with this, please?" Colleen called out from the back.

"I'm trying!" He made a face of exhaustion and said, "Everybody walk forward. The skywalk has been lowered into maintenance mode, so we can walk on the top of the scoreboard. And as soon as I get city approval, it'll double as an observation deck." He winked at Nikki.

"Sounds like an insurance agent's wet-dream," Nikki said.

Finn glanced back at Colleen. "You really with these guys?"

"You gave me no choice," she said.

The group wobbled on the skywalk—most of them kept their cuffed hands outstretched for stability.

"Because we broke up?" Finn asked her.

"You could have been headed to paradise with me and millions in the bank. Your loss."

As they approached the scoreboard roof—now observation deck—Finn stopped to read an engraving on a small black metal plate.

The weight limit.

Seeing how they were about forty feet in the air, the deck secured to the ceiling with four simple steel-braided cables, Finn figured honoring this limit would be wise. A quick calculation told him that twelve hundred pounds of people had just boarded the deck. Far exceeding the seven hundred pound limit. And that didn't include the dogs, each of which must have weighed a buck-twenty. They were about double the safety rating.

Maybe Trace hadn't excelled in math.

Or maybe he couldn't read.

All huddled at the center, each person's eyes had gotten a bit wider now that they were standing above the shark tank on one side. Below, all the sharks swam in zigzags, erratic and seemingly random movement. But Finn noticed that it wasn't random at all.

They were all avoiding the monster shark cutting between them.

Elvis.

Manny eyed both Colleen and Trace, like she was devising a plan. Nikki stood tall, or as tall as she could, with her chin up, and Lew peered toward the tank. He appeared to be quite impressed by the whole display, nodding to himself with a mock frown.

Standing together at the far side of the deck, Colleen and Trace whispered to each other.

One of the Berans—hard to tell without seeing them—leaned forward and said, "Hey Finn, I gotta' tell you, I'd rather get shot than be eaten by that fucker." He nodded toward Elvis. "I say we jump 'em. What happens, happens."

Finn, who had been thinking the very same thing up until boarding this deck, said, "No need to get shot."

The other Beran leaned to his other ear. "You got a plan, now? Or are we still winging' it?"

Finn leaned back. "When I nod twice fast, get everyone to that side of the deck." He motioned to the opposite side from Trace and Colleen. "Then start jumping up and down. Hard. Get everyone to do it."

"For real? That's the plan?" The whisper came out loud at the end.

Before Finn could answer, Colleen said, "Next person who talks gets shot."

Finn scrolled through their options, one last time. Limited as they were, he could think of a few actions that could throw the balance of power here. One of which was to separate Colleen and Trace somehow. Separating Colleen from her AK would be a good start, too. Calculating that there were about three and a half steps between him and Colleen, Finn edged further to the front of the group.

Lew smiled up at him.

Three steps now.

He'd have to hit her quick. And if he knocked her hard enough, she would bump into Trace. The gun could be knocked over the edge. Or maybe even Trace.

Not likely though.

Colleen nodded at Trace. Then she raised the AK. She pointed it at Nikki. "You're first."

"Big fuckin' surprise," she said. Brave as always, Nikki took a step forward. But before she could go any further, Finn said, "Wait.

Let me go first. It's only right."

Trace said, in a whiny voice, "I get it. You just don't want to see all your friends die, you're nothing but a big old baby and a coward."

"Please shut up," Colleen said.

"But what if Elvis isn't hungry after eating him?" Trace's voice sounded tinny. "Look how big he is!"

Manny said, "Let me go first, then." She winked at Finn.

"Oh for God's sake. This isn't musical chairs." Colleen pointed the AK at Finn, but said to Nikki, "Let's go Orangina."

Trace grabbed Nikki's arm and pushed her to the railing.

Nikki wrested free. "Let go of me, you throatstain."

"Nice hair," Trace said.

"Ooh. Think of that yourself?"

Trace said, "Climb, bitchy."

Nikki glanced back at Finn, gave him a small smile, and then grabbed the top rail as she climbed up.

Trace stepped behind her and raised a palm to her back.

Finn glanced back at the Berans.

Starting forward, Finn nodded twice. By the time he had taken a second step, the Berans had pulled Manny, Lew and the dogs back to the far edge and they all started jumping.

"Jump around!" Lew sang.

"What the—" Trace turned.

"Hey!" Colleen yelled.

And the distraction gave Finn enough time to leap forward and drive his shoulder into Colleen's chest while yanking Nikki backwards. The AK popped out of Colleen's hands and slammed to the deck.

Colleen fell to the ground and the deck tilted, the scoreboard swaying now.

The dogs began barking. The others kept jumping. The deck swayed fast, back and forth. Back again, tilting hard.

Trace shrieked.

Nikki crawled toward the gun and a loud creak sounded. Then a snap, like a lightning bolt.

One cable gone.

Manny slid to the other side of the deck and almost fell off, hanging onto the bottom rail and dangling off the back.

The gun slid down the deck and stopped a few feet shy of Nikki's hands.

Finn struggled to his feet. Looked up.

The deck swung back past center and over the water. Another loud creak and then another snap.

Two down.

"Jump! Jump!" Lew yelled.

The deck faltered again, this time tilting all the way to the back, the last two cables kitty-corner from each other. Trace scurried toward the catwalk.

Both dogs, barking uncontrollably now, scratched at the deck's surface to keep from falling off.

The gun slid a few feet further.

Nikki grabbed the AK, tried to cradle it with both hands, but the cuffs made it impossible to hold, so she tucked it beneath her armpit and found the trigger.

Another big crack, Trace yelled, "Stop! It's going to fall!"

Colleen pushed at Finn and ran behind Trace.

Nikki swung the AK and pulled the trigger, just as the deck tipped back.

The bullets popped in succession, all the way across the front of the decking and to the ceiling.

Nikki fell to her back, and the gun slid off the deck and plunked into the water.

"A little help, please?" Manny called as she hung from the deck.

One of the Berans took hold of Manny, while the other had both dogs by the paws, keeping them from falling to the concrete.

And then Finn felt an unmistakable warmth spreading from his shoulder.

Blood?

Nikki had shot him.

Finn stood still. Very still. Blood seeping down his arm and into his hand.

Nikki slid into the pack of bodies, now hanging in balance.

They all looked up. Even Colleen.

But not Trace.

He was already on the catwalk, looking back at everyone, as if wondering what would happen if the scoreboard fell. He looked at his feet.

The catwalk would swing free.

Blood dripped from Finn's hand, onto the deck's railing, and into the water below.

"Shit. I'm sorry, Finn," Nikki said.

"Happens." He watched it drip into the water.

A moment later, Elvis thrashed to the surface.

"I'm so fired." Nikki glanced at the concrete below on one side and Elvis on the other.

Lew's face jammed between two pairs of shoes, he said, "Whoever's pressing my bladder, stop it. I'm going to pee."

One dog barked and then the other.

Colleen said, "Nobody move."

"Fuck you think we're going?" Nikki yelled.

Finn turned and stared at Colleen. Then he said, "Don't."

Colleen turned and glared back at him. "Like I said, you had your chance."

Then she bolted forward and jumped onto the catwalk with both feet.

The scoreboard swayed and the catwalk gave, unhooking from the deck and swinging free.

Straight. Down.

Trace, shrieked, "You idiot!" Hanging on with both hands, he jammed his feet on the inside of the railing to keep from falling off.

"Shit!" Colleen yelled as her footing gave—stepping on her own skirt—and she swung downward. Then she reached up and took hold of Trace's pants' cuff.

"Let go!" He screeched again. "You'll kill us both!"

Elvis thrashed below them, Colleen's bare legs dangling straight over the water.

Elvis jumped.

Colleen yelled.

Trace kicked. "Get off! Get off me!"

Swinging her legs, Colleen's grip began to slide. Her hands slipped lower. She swung harder. Her eyes widened, watching the monster below. She swung even harder, one last time, knowing her fate, and as her grip gave, she managed to fling herself away from the ladder. Far enough to miss the water below.

But what she hit was even less forgiving than Elvis.

Solid concrete.

Lew said, "I think she missed."

Finn glanced back at the tangle of bodies behind him, everyone afraid to move. Manny and the dogs hanging off the edge.

Trace scrambled up the catwalk, stepping on the railing posts and using it like a ladder.

"Hang on everyone," Finn yelled.

Then he took three steps back and, staring straight at his target and willing his injured arm to give him one last play, he ran. One step. Two. Three.

Faster.

Four. Higher.

Five!

And he jumped.

Soaring through the open air, Finn slammed into the dangling catwalk and held on with all he had left. With both feet planted onto the posts of the railing and the wind knocked from his lungs, Finn almost fell backwards, but held on and tried not to look down.

But he couldn't help it.

Circling below him now, Elvis, swung his enormous head back

and forth, as he thrashed at the surface. Strong incentive.

Finn began to climb.

And as he climbed the rungs of the makeshift ladder, he heard another creak behind him. And then a fourth pop. Everyone on the deck yelled as the last of the cables gave and the scoreboard dropped into free-fall.

In a strange twist, loyal to the law of physics, the scoreboard flipped all the way around and, just as it slammed to the ground, flung all its dangling occupants up and over, back up to the top— which used to be the bottom—sparing them from Colleen's fate, as she was buried by the scoreboard when it landed.

Right on her head.

Kicksave and Glovesave licked everyone's faces and darted around, then leapt off the side of the scoreboard and ran off, with Lew, holding his own ankle, yelling, "Sit! Stay!"

Nikki and the Berans checked each other for mortal wounds, but looked okay, and Manny was pushing up from her knees.

Miracle.

Finn glanced back up at Trace who had neared the top, where he could pull himself over the ledge to the door.

Finn hauled himself up the catwalk a few feet, causing it to sway.

Trace slipped from the ledge and hugged the railing. "Wait, you maniac!" he yelled from above. "I'll slip off!"

"Don't worry. Elvis will break the fall," Finn said.

The dogs started barking from somewhere in the arena, echoing throughout the space.

Lew called to them.

Trace scrambled for his footing again.

As long as the catwalk held, Finn didn't care. He could hang here all day.

Tightening his face, Trace gave Finn the middle finger and climbed up again.

The catwalk swayed and Finn held tight. He climbed up a few

more feet, gaining on Trace.

Then Trace got smart. He reached over and, pulling a hanging light fixture to himself, unscrewed the bulb. And he threw it.

Right at Finn's head.

Smash.

"How you like that, huh?"

"Let him go, Finn, just hold on." Nikki called from below.

The dogs barked again, but from a different spot this time. It sounded like they were above Finn now.

Trace reached over and grabbed another lamp. Pulling it closer, he unscrewed the bulb.

Finn ducked his head.

Trace threw the bulb.

Smash.

This one hit Finn in the shoulder.

Glass in a bullet wound. Son of a bitch. That hurt.

"Told you," Trace muttered.

Finn's blood dripped down his hand and into the water below.

"Finn, don't be a martyr!" Manny yelled, "We're going to find a rope!"

"Patrick, listen to her, please!" Nikki said.

Elvis thrashed again, sending a wave of water up over the edge and out of the pool.

Then, as Trace reached the top, he put his hand up to the ledge, began to pull himself over, and stopped.

Kicksave and Glovesave stood in the doorway above him, panting and drooling onto Trace's face.

"Yuck," Trace said.

Good dogs.

Trace yelled, "Get these dogs out of here! I can't get up. I can't get up!"

Finn climbed another rung on the catwalk and his shoulder began to burn so badly that it made his vision close in and pushed him to the point of blacking out. He had to stop.

"Tell them to move!" Trace called from above. He had another bulb in his hand.

Stalemate.

Looking past Trace, Finn stared at the enormous Mastiffs standing above, their heads swaying like wrecking balls.

"Good doggies," Trace said. "Sit, doggies. Stay." Then he turned back to Lew. "Call them off!"

"No point," Lew yelled back. "They're stubborn."

Trace stamped his foot against the railing.

Finn said, "Stay there, I'll help you."

"The hell you will!" He looked back up at the dogs.

"I'm serious," Finn said, reaching toward Trace. Really, he'd rather see the dipshit rot in prison than get an easy death cut. Finn glanced at Elvis, pacing the pool below now. Well, not easy.

Trace said, "You just want to push me into the water."

"We can work this out Trace."

"No!" Trace looked back up at the dogs. "Move doggies. Move and I'll give you a cookie."

"Don't!" Finn said, but it was too late.

The dogs had already begun circling and sniffing and...

"What the hell? What are they doing?" Trace said. "Wait! That's gross!"

Lew yelled, "No Glovesave, sit!"

And the catwalk began to shake.

"Stop them!" Trace yelled. "It's blasphemous—"

And it shook harder and faster and Finn hooked his ankles into the makeshift rungs and held on as hard as he could. The skywalk shook and rattled and then swung hard.

"Sit!" Trace yelled. His grip slipped.

He screamed, "Oh my God!" He reached up and grabbed one of the dogs with both hands.

Finn ducked his head into the rails.

And then they fell. All three of them.

Right into the water.

Elvis thrashed and, taking hold of Trace, dragged him deep into the tank.

Paddling to the surface, the dogs looked panicked now, the smaller sharks beginning to circle below them.

"Kicksave! Glovesave! Here! Come here!" Lew yelled, crawling to the side of the scoreboard and putting out a hand. He was over ten feet from the water.

The dogs swam in circles, peering up at Lew and barking. Lew leaned all the way over and slipped, almost falling into the pool.

"Whoa!" Lew yelled. Manny grabbed his leg, steadying him.

"Hold hold hold," she said.

"Lew, don't move!" Finn yelled.

Then he took a long, deep breath and exhaled slowly. Closing his eyes, he took another long, deep breath...pushed from the catwalk and fell into the water below.

Hearing the yells from Nikki and the Berans, then a scream from Manny, Finn plunged into the pool. The red ink of Trace's blood clouded the water, but he found the surface fast, then the dogs. He dragged them to the edge, both of them together.

No time to mess around, fellas.

Finn hoisted them up over the pool's ledge.

A black Gucci loafer popped to the surface. And then another.

More blood, but it wasn't coming from below. It was coming from his shoulder.

The huge, dark shape of Elvis began to rise from the deep, and Finn reached up, both arms, but his shoulder wouldn't hold him.

Damn.

He tried again, water in his ears, his clothes bogging him down, and reached. A searing pain dug all the way into his arm and down his ribs. His hand, slick with water and blood, slipped off the edge.

The shadow grew below him. Larger. Closer.

Then, heart pounding, ears ringing, yells and more sharks coming, Finn felt one hand. And then another. And a third. And then a fourth. On his arms, his shirt, his neck, someone even grabbed his hair.

And they yanked.

Manny, Nikki, and the Berans pulled him—no—dragged all two-hundred and fifty pounds of him, up and out of the water, just as Elvis opened his mouth, snapped it closed—empty—and then ducked back down below.

All five of them lay on the concrete, chests heaving, exhausted and injured, but alive.

A full minute later, Nikki turned to Finn.

"Your ass...is going on a diet."

CHAPTER TWENTY-EIGHT

One Week Later

FINN STARED OUT AT THE SUN RISING over the Atlantic, far off in the east. Wearing nothing but boxers and a t-shirt, he sat on the small deck of a house he'd rented—one of only forty-three residences on the entire island of No Name Key—cupping a warm mug of coffee in his good hand and savoring the silence. He understood Manny's reference to solitude now, it made perfect sense to him.

And he knew it wouldn't last.

A native No Name Deer peeked from behind the porch and then tiptoed across the white sand, about fifteen feet away. Turning its head, it locked eyes with Finn and froze. Neither of them moved for a good ten seconds, then the deer let out a big snort and darted, back into the woods.

Finn's phone vibrated on the kitchen table inside the house.

Glancing back, he debated whether to check it. The press had been so relentless that he'd had to change his mobile number. Twice. He hoped they hadn't tracked him down for a third time. Ignoring the phone, he leaned his head back.

Not ten seconds later, it began to buzz again.

Silence expired, Finn rocked forward, eased out of the chair and walked inside. He recognized the number, also a new one and answered it.

"Persistent as always."

"Some things stay the same," Nikki said.

Finn walked back outside and slumped into the chair, then took a sip of coffee. "How are you?"

"Fine. You?"

"Fine."

They both sat in silence for a few moments. Nikki said, "They found Jerry. Or...his body."

"Suicide?" Finn asked.

"Unless you call taking a nose-dive off the fifteenth floor of a parking garage an accident."

"Maybe he fell," Finn said.

"He was in his car."

Finn nodded. Yep, airtight, that case. "Which car?"

"A custom teal Bentley."

"A touch of class."

More silence and Nikki said, "How's Lew?"

"Haven't talked to him," Finn said. "Well, not for a couple of days, anyway."

"He still in bum-butt-fuck Ontario?"

"As far from water as can be." Finn took another sip. He didn't blame Lew for going into hiding, deep on the mainland. Finn understood when he declared that he could only deal with frozen water for a while. No lakes, ponds, oceans, or even pools.

"The yacht?"

"Auction's tomorrow."

"He'll take a bath on it."

"Maybe not."

"Finn. It's a boat that used to be owned by drug runners, one that someone died on and was then chopped up in. That's got to impact the value."

"It's America. People love that shit."

"Good point."

"How are the Berans?"

"Still pissed they didn't see the B's win."

Finn smiled. Spending four hours with the Houston police and then the CSI Unit that night had caused the Berans to miss the seventh and final game of the Stanley Cup. The Bruins won, but Finn would never live that one down.

"Replay?"

"Yeah, we're headed to Snarky's tonight. They're playing the whole series this week, one game per night, ending with the final on Friday."

"That place is a hole."

"I'm doing it for you, Finn."

"Thanks. I owe you."

"Hey, any word from Manny?"

Finn pictured her leaving that night before the cops and CSI team had arrived. How she'd never even glanced back.

Cadmium.

Then he pictured the bag of euros stuffed under that porch of hers. He was happy to let her have it, after what they'd put her through. He and Nikki had plenty of cash with the new Kunkle contract. "Nah, I don't expect to hear from her for a while."

"Yeah. That's understandable." A moment later, she said, "So when you coming home?"

Finn drained the last of his coffee and set the cup down. "Thinking of staying the rest of the summer, actually."

"What about the draft next week?"

"You go, represent us."

"Us?"

"You wanted to be an agent, right?"

"Yeah, but...think I'm ready for that?"

"No doubt. Besides, you know more about this class than I do. You cover it. Find yourself a few good ones. Start building a book."

"Thanks, boss." She paused then said, "One last one...how's the shoulder?"

Finn glanced at the bandage peeking from under his sleeve. "Getting there."

"Sorry about that."

How exactly do you apologize for shooting someone anyway?

"Could have happened to anyone," he said.

A few moments later, she said, "You know, I feel bad about Colleen."

Finn tightened his brow. "Really?"

"Really."

He said, "Well, I think she was just a confused person, you know? She didn't know what she wanted in life. Kind of a lost soul, so—"

"No, I meant the scoreboard dropping on her head like that."

He snorted. That was about as much sentiment as you'd ever get from Nikki.

He asked, "Your hair back to normal?"

"Sure, if normal is red."

"How red?"

"Fuck off."

Yep, normal again.

"Well, I gotta' go do some shit. But before I go," she said.

"What is it?"

"Call your mother. Four messages now. She still wants to know about Thanksgiving."

"Got it."

"And thanks again."

"Anytime."

They hung up and Finn stared back out to the bright blue ocean. Taking a deep breath of salty air, he leaned his head back against the chair.

Content, relaxed, and happy to be alone for a while.

CHAPTER TWENTY-NINE

"I'M HUNGRY," CHADWICK SAID.

LEANING AGAINST HIS back, legs straddling the useless Jet Ski, and floating somewhere in the middle of the blasted Atlantic Ocean, Vanessa mustered enough energy to nod her head about an inch. "So you've said."

"But I really am, Vanny. I'm starving."

"I just hope it rains again. That water tasted good."

Chadwick said, "I'm dreaming of having a Toe Pointer. I want to go back there. What was that place called?"

"I'm surprised you could ever be hungry again after eating all that."

"You didn't let me finish it, remember?" He glanced back.

"Oh right. My fault." She reached up and patted his neck.

"Ouch! Don't do that, it's sunburnt!"

"Sorry." She sighed. "I want a cigarette."

"How can you think of smoking? It's so hot."

She shrugged to herself.

"So really, how does it look?"

"How does what look?"

"My neck."

She leaned back. "It's the color of a hog's ass."

"You're so mean to me."

"Am not."

"Are so."

"Not."

"Are."

She leaned back down and turned her head, pressing her cheek to his back.

He muttered, "So much for Century Club."

"So much."

The blue-green ocean seemed almost peaceful, calming to Vanessa. She'd stopped hoping for a rescue. She was quite content to die now, holding on to Chadwick. She really did love him. She could die with him. And so she would.

After a while he said, "Vanessa?"

"Yes, Chaddy?"

"Don't call me that."

"Right. Sorry."

He said, "I've been meaning to ask you something."

"Yes?"

"The other night. And then the next morning."

Following him enough to know what he was talking about, she remembered the interludes. The glorious, wonderful meeting of their two souls, joined together in an ecstatic and glorious embrace. A perfect union. Their own private paradise, nothing to be ashamed of or embarrassed by, nothing to get between the two of them. There was not one single thing he could say that would take away from it.

Nothing.

"Yes?" She asked.

"What does it mean, *Vivat Rex*?"

Vanessa leaned back away from Chadwick and stared at his jockey-helmet head. Then, coiling the final reserves of her energy, she reached forward and took two handfuls of his flocked hair.

And she dumped him off the Jet Ski.

ACKNOWLEDGMENTS

To my first readers, TS and DH, you know who you are and what you mean to me. Your input and constructive criticism was essential to the process of creation. To Deb Coonts, for your kind words and encouragement, it's great to have an ally nearby. Thank you all so very much for your time and generosity.

ABOUT THE AUTHOR

Alex Cay is a former athlete, long-time artist, investor, and writer. Author of the Patrick Finn Island Thrillers, Alex was born in Upstate New York but now lives on the West Coast and escapes to the shore every chance he gets. If he's not busy as a husband or a dad, working, or writing, it's a darn good bet that you can find him seaside or on the ocean somewhere.

Connect with Alex online:

www.alexcay.com

https://twitter.com/AlexCayBooks

https://www.facebook.com/AlexCayBooks

If you enjoyed reading *Man Up*, I would appreciate if you would help others enjoy this book, too.

Lend it. This e-book is enabled for lending, so please share.

Recommend it. Please help your friends and family find this book by recommending it to them. Reader groups, social media, discussion boards are also great ways to spread the word.

Review it. Please tell others why you enjoyed this book by reviewing it at Amazon or Goodreads. When you do write a review, please send me an email at alexcaybooks@gmail.com, so I can thank you with a personal email.

ALSO BY ALEX CAY

PATRICK FINN SERIES BOOK 2

ALL TIDE UP!

Finn and Company are back!

In this sequel to MAN UP, sports agent Patrick Finn's newest client extraordinaire is none other than Svetlana Takitov, the rising Russian tennis star and aspiring fashion model. But this one needs loads of attention and a seemingly bottomless bank account, as she intends to become nothing less than a world-famous, socialite diva.

What Finn desperately needs is for Takitov to qualify for the next tournament, a task that becomes all but impossible when a Russian thug is found dead in her condo—death by mango pit—and

Svetlana goes on the run.

Enter Finn.

In a bid to protect his agency's investment, Finn enlists his trusted partner Nikki O'Callahan—along with Svetlana's publicist, and her hair stylist—and tracks the part-time athlete to a paradise island halfway across the globe. Before they have time to grease up for the beach, though, they're all embroiled in a battle between Svetlana and a pair of Russian hitmen. Now with more help than he cares for, it's up to Finn to ward off the killers, save Svetlana, and get the hell out of Paradise.

Available at Amazon.

A PATRICK FINN ISLAND THRILLER SHORT

ICY HOT!

Go for a ride with Vanessa and Chadwick.

In a short story that takes place soon after the end of MAN UP, bumbling British hitmen Vanessa Holmes and Sir James Chadwick are at it again. Just not in the way they ever thought.

Co-conspirator Stanley Cockburn made off with the cash at the end of Vanessa and Chadwick's last assignment, and now they're stranded in Jacksonville, Florida—out of money, out of gas, and all but out of options. So, armed with only an address and a bullet-less SIG, they decide to shake down Stanley's uncle until he gives up his nephew. Only one problem: They have to break into the uncle's pet shop to do it.

With so little to lose and so much to gain, the hapless hitmen take on a literal zoo of hurdles that includes water moccasins, a Komodo dragon, and a hungry school of piranha. It just takes is a handful of bad choices, unlucky timing, and a juvenile bobcat named Boblet for all hell to break loose—forcing the unlikely couple to fight for their lives, once again.

Join Vanessa and Chadwick in this Patrick Finn Island Thriller short - it's a quickie that you don't want to miss.

Available at *Amazon*.